THE
KEEPERS
THE GAMMA SEQUENCE, Book 4
a medical thriller

DAN ALATORRE

THE KEEPERS
THE GAMMA SEQUENCE, Book 4
a medical thriller

OTHER THRILLERS BY DAN ALATORRE

CONTENTS

ACKNOWLEDGMENTS

I have an amazing team of people who help me do what I
do, so thank you to each and every one of them.
You guys ROCK!

Note to Readers

*If you have the time, I would deeply appreciate a review on
Amazon or Goodreads. I learn a great deal from them, and
I'm always grateful for any encouragement. Reviews are a
very big deal and help authors like me to sell a few more
books. Every review matters, even if it's only a few words.*

Thanks,
Dan Alatorre

CHAPTER 1

The nurse raced toward room 431 as screams echoed down the corridor. The elderly patient's heart rate monitor indicated she was coding, filling the dark wing with audible alarms. Throwing open the door, the nurse gasped, putting a hand to her mouth.

The old woman flailed on the bed, kicking and screaming, her restraints ripping into her flesh and splattering the sheets and walls with blood.

"They're killing her!" Spit flew from the patient's mouth. "They're killing her!"

Heaving herself forward, Patrice pushed down on the elderly lady's thin, bony shoulders and forced her to the mattress. *"Calmez-vous, s'il vous plaît. Vous devez être calme."*

"I must go!" The old woman twisted back and forth, her eyes red and raw in the dim light. Veins throbbed on her wrinkly forehead. "Please, let me go! *Laissez-moi partir!* They're killing her!"

1

"No one is killing anyone, *madame*." Patrice held the woman down, staring at the detached sensors. Heart, respiration, temperature, each dangled from their respective machines—sending a chorus of alarms into the little room. She leaned close to the old woman. "You are safe! Look at me! You are safe in hospital."

"No!" She kicked harder. "I must go. They're killing her!"

"No, madame. You are safe. Look with me. This the Pitié-Salpêtrière Hospital, in Paris. See the machines? The bed? It is hospital. You have been here a few days. Do you remember?" The radio on Patrice's hip would alert additional staff, but she was restricted from using it while dealing with this patient—unless it was a life or death emergency. "Madame, please. Look with me. Do you see you are in hospital?"

The elderly patient slowly looked around the ward room. Her muscles relaxed and she sagged into her pillows. Sweat dotted her brow.

Catching her breath, the nurse stood up and grabbed a towel from the side table, wetting it with the water bottle and dabbing the old woman's cheeks. "It is just a dream, yes? A bad dream."

"You don't understand." The elderly lady moaned. *"Vous ne comprenez pas. Je dois partir."*

"Yes, I understand. You are suffering from the fever your injury gave you, and you take off your sensors again. This is very serious, madame. You must not try to move." She glanced at the large gauze bandage over the woman's upper chest. "*Chut*, I fear you have rip your stitches."

"Help me." The woman pushed upward against her restraints. "Please. I must go to her before it's too late."

"You must rest." The nurse shook her head, whispering as she pressed the wet cloth across her patient's forehead. "It is very serious, this injury you have. You almost lose this arm, yes? Maybe you need it one day. Let us fix you. Please be calm, *madame*."

Tears welled in the old woman's eyes. She sank back onto the bed. "She needs me. I—I must go to her."

Patrice put a hand on her hip and wagged a finger. "If you insist on trying these games, I will have to administer *un sédatif*. I know how they scare you, but do you leave me a choice?"

"No." The old woman's eye went wide. "No sedatives. I'll . . . I'll be calm. You're right. It—it was just a bad dream."

Convinced the fight was over, Patrice relaxed and stepped away from the bed. She inspected and cleaned the cuts from the restraints, bandaging the old woman's wrists as she stared at the ceiling. The sensors went back onto the patient's thin upper arm and bony fingers, and the machines were reset.

"*Merci*, Patrice," the old woman said.

The bloodstains would have to wait for now. "I cannot change your sheets until the morning, when the other nurse is here and I can unshackle you from the bed, so no more of this tonight, *oui*?" Patrice slid a few towels under the woman's arms, hiding the mess.

The patient nodded. "I understand."

Picking up the chart, the nurse checked the time and made a few notes. In the upper right-hand corner of the first page was a yellow highlighted area with additional directions. She pursed her lips as she read them, and tucked the chart under her arm.

Her patient lifted her hands, staring at the restraints. "I'm not crazy."

"No, *madame*." Patrice closed her eyes and massaged her forehead. "I think, *peut-être*, it is just the fever—it has imbalanced your levels, and so we will be careful. But we get someone to talk to you anyway, eh? So you can sleep. It is very late, almost two a.m."

The old woman turned her face to the window. "I don't wish to sleep."

"Yes, you have told me this." Patrice sighed. "But if you are to get better, you must rest—do we agree?"

"I . . . will rest." The elderly patient nodded again, waving a frail hand. "Go ahead and bring your intern."

Patrice recoiled. *"Excusez-moi?"*

"The young doctor. The woman. I . . . I won't give you any more trouble. *Fini les ennuis.*"

"Ah . . . then, you rest now, yes?" She headed to the door. "I am just outside, but no more scares tonight. Only rest."

The machines recorded their information, blinking and beeping in the quiet room. The patient, her energy now apparently gone from her frail old bones, clasped her hands to her waist. "Do you wonder why they put me by myself in this wing?"

She looked at Patrice. "All alone. An entire hospital wing for one old woman?"

Patrice shifted on her feet. "I—I don't know this. It is not—"

"The other nurses gossip. They ask you, and you stay quiet. But can you tell me?"

Holding the chart in front of her, the nurse spoke in soft, gentle tones. "I will tell you this. You need to go to slee—*rest*. Get some *rest*." She stepped out of the room and eased the door shut behind her.

In the hallway, Patrice held up the chart, biting her fingernail as she read the highlighted note again.

It is time.

She put a hand to her abdomen and walked toward her station, staring at the phone console the entire way.

At the desk, Patrice glanced back toward room 431—and then to the highlighted note once more—before lowering her fingers to the receiver.

The display on the phone console read 2:18 a.m.

Groaning, she released the phone, sitting down in the desk chair and wiping her hands on the legs of her scrubs. At the end of the corridor, near the elevators, the soda machine's refrigeration unit kicked on. Its low hum was the only sound in the ward.

The console display changed to 2:19 a.m.

You were instructed to do it.

It is time.

Taking a deep breath, Patrice picked up the receiver and dialed the phone number on the note, then waited for the Chief of Medicine of the Pitié-Salpêtrière Hospital to answer the phone.

CHAPTER 2

Dr. René Dechambeau pounded on the rickety door of the intern's *suite de chambre*. In the basement of the old hospital, the large, barrel-chested man clutched a file folder and puffed hard on his *Gauloises* cigarette, peering at his wristwatch. He balled up his thick fingers and knocked again, harder. "Doctor Kittaleye! Wake up, you are needed." Dechambeau stepped back, scowled, and tried again. *"Réveillez-vous, Docteur!"*

The latch clicked on the other side of the door, and a young African-American woman peeked out. *"Docteur Dechambeau?"* Clutching her robe to her chest, Dr. Djimoa Kittaleye adjusted her wire-framed glasses as she opened the door for the Chief of Medicine. *"Que s'est-il passé?"*

Her boss scowled. "What has happened? You are about to earn your pay." He tucked the file folder under his arm and entered the tiny office-apartment suite, exhaling a thick stream of smoke. "Get dressed. We have much to discuss."

"Yes, sir." The slender young woman rubbed her eyes. "What time is it?"

"Time to do your job, *Madame Docteur*." He waved a hand at her. "Now, hurry."

"Yes, of course." Kitt looked around her cold little suite. The desk and filing cabinets took up most of the floor space that the bed didn't occupy. A space heater was pointed at the mattress, working overtime against the drafty, basement accommodations—and failing miserably, based on the frost on the room's tiny window. She pulled a lab coat and a pair of scrubs from the dresser, stepping into the miniscule bathroom as she checked the time on her phone.

What's important enough to get the head of the hospital out of bed at 3 a.m.?

She slipped into her scrubs and pulled her straight, black hair into a ponytail, searching the icy floor for her shoes. One was under the corner of the bed.

The other was under Dechambeau's foot.

"Excusez-moi, s'il vous plait." Kitt bent down and reached for her sneaker.

"Eh?" Dechambeau looked down, grunting as he lifted his foot and stepped away. "Your services are required upstairs, Doctor." He curled his thick fingers around the cigarette, taking a long drag. "I hope I'm not inconveniencing you."

"No, it's just—"

"Très bien." Dechambeau exited the suite, smoke flowing over his shoulder. Kitt hopped on one foot, trailing him as she pulled on her other shoe and

shut the door. He walked quickly, heading for the ancient service elevator at the far end of the narrow, dark hall, and not the staff elevator outside her door. "I make it no secret that I don't care for your specialty, Dr. Kittaleye. Psychology is not medicine, to me. You understand this."

Kitt grabbed the bottom of her scrubs and stuffed it into her pants. "All too plainly, sir."

She pushed aside her ongoing irritation over the way he seemed to purposely mispronounce her name. *Kit-a-LAY-yay*, she had told him—many times, during her brief residency. Others at the hospital called her Kitt, but with the Chief of Medicine it was always butchered into *Kittle-eye*, or *Kit-a-lee*.

"So," he said, "you will understand when I say this matter is of utmost importance and must remain silent to all but you and myself, yes?"

"Yes, sir."

The large man took another puff on his cigarette, exhaling the smoke in a huff. "We've been hosting a guest, *Madame Docteur*. A wing of this fine old institution has always been on reserve for those requiring special services—foreign diplomats, high French government officials, wealthy patricians. Of course, I cannot say who, but the rumors that we've had several members of the French President's family are not far off the mark. *Comprenez-vous?* And it is these . . . special guests of the hospital, shall we call them, that receive the benefit of the special wing. Do I make myself clear?"

No. "Yes."

He waved his hands as he talked, clouds of smoke intermittently wafting over his shoulders. "As the overseer of your grant, it falls to me to ensure that every penny of our budget is used wisely. This is why we provide to you room and board as your intern's *suite de chambre* within our hallowed halls." He stopped at the elevator, turning to face her as he pressed the call button. Behind the old doors, the ancient motor whined as it woke from its idleness.

"Oh, and I appreciate it, sir." She shrugged.

I might ask that you occasionally spring for a light bulb so I can actually see to do my research.

He stubbed out the *Gauloises* in the brass ashtray mounted beneath the call button.

And I'm happy to report I only had to kill two cockroaches last night. But they did manage to eat the cover sheet of my research report first.

Dechambeau shoved the folder under his arm again and fumbled in his pockets for another cigarette. "It is this attitude, *Madame Docteur*, that has put your career in my hands." He withdrew a lighter from his coat and lit the *Gauloises,* taking a hard drag and sending the smoke toward the ceiling. "Research, Doctor Kittalaye, is what a training hospital must provide with its ever-shrinking budget—not the silly, misguided endeavors that saddled you with a grant and me with a headache. Nonetheless, we are both here now, and the challenge before us is grand. That is why—"

"Excuse me, sir," Kitt said. "I'm not yet understanding what it is you're talking about."

Kitt often wondered if the only reason a Doctor of Psychology was residing in a medical hospital instead of a psychiatric hospital was because a certain someone at Pitié-Salpêtrière Hospital had seen the dollar amount of the grant and had overlooked everything else.

Dechambeau pursed his lips, eyeing her. When the *Gauloises* returned to his mouth, his fingers trembling and sweat beaded on his upper lip. "A few days ago, an elderly woman was brought to us at the request of the French government. The details are shrouded in secrecy, but she had suffered a severe injury to the upper chest region—a very damaged pectoralis major, a shattered clavicle, substantial blood loss. Prior to arrival, she was treated by paramedics on a helicopter, and our original attending physician saw on the chart that she had been sedated. He operated at once, to remove . . . well, to address her injury. However, no actual anesthesia had been administered." Dechambeau lowered his cigarette. "The woman underwent a three-hour surgery without pain medication of any kind."

Kitt put her hand to her lip. "Goodness."

"A post-operative review disclosed the error, and the attending physician was immediately disciplined. But during the operation, all members of the surgical staff noted her heart rate was steady, her blood pressure stable—as if she had been under anesthesia the entire time."

"That's . . . remarkable."

"Without knowing what she had been given," Dechambeau said, "they were remiss to administer anything more. The anesthesia was at the ready, but went unused. Of course, as a special guest of the hospital and under such circumstances, we cannot ask too many questions, but the patient had been silent before and after the operation. We assumed trauma or stroke had resulted in neurogenic mutism, but the CT scan and MRI showed no brain injuries. And in what would be her sleep, she has been exhibiting violent seizures that—"

"Excuse me." Kitt looked the Chief of Medicine in the eye. "In 'what would be' her sleep?"

"The patient does not sleep." Dechambeau sighed, exhaling a long stream of smoke. "She has not, to our knowledge, slept since arriving."

"And that was a few days ago."

"But she convulses in the night," he said. "Willfully, it seems, and sometimes during the day. She can put herself into a deep, semi-hypnotic, trancelike state—not unlike what was observed during the errant surgery. And as I say, she had not uttered a word since arriving here, despite being fully awake and apparently in control of her faculties."

"I see." Kitt pushed a strand of her thick, straight black hair from her forehead. "How may I be of service?"

Behind the Chief of Medicine, the ancient elevator motor ground to a stop. The doors opened with a lumbering grunt, revealing the rusty, accordion-style gate. A faint musty odor seeped from the elevator's faded wooden walls.

Dechambeau rubbed his chin. "We have stationed one senior staff member—Patrice Chevalier—to attend to our special guest. It is Mademoiselle Chevalier that awakened me some minutes ago, and for which I now have awakened you."

"Sir?"

"You will conduct a session with this patient, Dr. Kittaleye. Interact with her. You may speak with nurse Chevalier about the woman, but share your findings only with me." He handed her the file folder.

Kitt opened it. The pages inside were almost entirely blacked out.

Dechambeau withdrew a small chrome key from his pocket and shoved open the elevator gate, stepping into the dimly lit compartment and inserting his key into the slot on the tarnished brass panel. As Kitt slipped past him, Dr. Dechambeau pressed the button for the fourth floor. "There are four keys to the special wing," he said. "I have one, the attending nurse has one, her relief has one—and you will retain the fourth key." As the elevator started its slow ascent, he handed Dr. Kittaleye a short key with a rounded tip and a rectangular bow, like that of a vending machine. "Our special guest was scheduled for a follow-up surgery tomorrow—and she would, naturally, be anesthetized for it. But the mere mention of anesthesia, or a sedative of any kind, sends her into convulsions. We are a hospital, a fine training ward, but we are not equipped to handle mental patients. That is the job of Sainte-Anne Hospital."

Kitt nodded. The reason for the presence of a Doctor of Psychology was becoming clear. "Of course. But why—"

"The old woman is a special guest, so we must do as we are asked." Dechambeau's second cigarette was gone. He dropped the smoldering butt to the cold, metal floor and crushed it under his foot. "Conduct an interview, provide to me a preliminary report—and do it quickly."

"Fine, but why in the middle of the night?"

Facing her in the tiny compartment, he swept a hand over his forehead and through his thick, salt-and-pepper hair. "Because an elderly woman who has been shot in the chest and who doesn't sleep or require anesthesia, but who has nearly completely recovered from her injuries after only three days— that is quite an anomaly. When such a patient decides to speak, we need to be there to hear her."

Kitt shifted on her feet. "I don't disagree, but you said she *isn't* speaking, so who knows when that will be?"

The elevator shuddered to a stop on the fourth floor. Dechambeau flipped the metal latch and pushed the creaky gates apart; the doors opened behind them.

The hospital ward was old, its walls tiled halfway up, the way they did in America in the early 1900s. The flooring was a worn and faded linoleum, with cracks and tears; the doors to the rooms were trimmed in a faded dark oak. Nothing from this wing of the hospital appeared to have been touched in the last century except for the desk and computers at the nurses' station near the far end of the corridor. There, a blonde woman in green scrubs sat alone in the sparse illumination of a single round, fluorescent light. Everything else around her was dark and still.

Narrowing his eyes, the Chief of Medicine leaned toward his resident psychologist. "Dr.

Kittaleye, our special guest uttered her first words about an hour ago. Now, go and see what she has to say." He took another cigarette from his pocket, lighting it with shaking fingers, and slid the elevator gate closed. "And *Madame Docteur*, remember— you will discuss your findings with no one but me."

CHAPTER 3

The two women sat at the nurses' station.

"I am glad they called you, Kitt." Patrice handed Dr. Kittaleye the patient's chart. "Did they tell you the situation?"

Kitt raised an eyebrow. "They?"

"He—Dr. Dechambeau."

"A little." Kitt scanned the first page of notes on the chart. "Why don't you fill me in?"

Sighing, Patrice lowered her hands to her lap. "I am afraid I do not know very much, my friend. I have been watching the lady for three days. Aside from the tantrums, I have not much to report."

Kitt leaned back in her chair, peering into the patient's room. "Is she awake?"

"She is always—"

"Right. Silly question." Kitt pushed a strand of hair from her forehead. "She doesn't sleep."

"Not that I have seen. But she puts herself into a trance. I believe it may be—how do you say?

Similar? The same as sleep, for her. And what about you, Kitt? Do you still have the bad dreams?"

"It's just one bad dream. A guy in a black mask. I don't know why, but he's just so . . . ominous. It's unnerving." Kitt got up, looking toward room 431. "Okay, I guess I'll take it from here. Anything else I should know?" She stepped toward the patient's room.

"The restraints are for her protection," Patrice said.

Kitt winced. "Restraints?"

"Oui. I do not think she is dangerous."

"You don't *think* so," Kitt mumbled, glancing toward the patient's door. "Great."

The room was dark, the only light coming from the display screens on the machines attached to the old woman on the bed. Kitt crept toward the patient. Thick leather straps bound her wrists and waist. Other than that, the woman appeared to be peacefully resting, her eyes looking toward the ceiling.

Kitt cleared her throat. "Is it okay for me to come in, ma'am?"

The elderly patient turned her wrinkled head toward the doctor. "Yes, dear. Please." She lifted her shackled arms. "Forgive me for not getting up."

The old woman's accent was slightly British. Kitt took the chair from the corner and pulled it a few inches toward the bed.

"You're an American," the patient said. "I don't think I knew that. But you mustn't fear, Doctor. I won't hurt you." She patted the mattress. "Come.

As Patrice has already mentioned, these horrible restraints are for my protection."

Kitt stood behind the chair.

The old woman has good hearing.

"If . . . if I take those off of you," Kitt said, "will you behave? No tantrums?"

Lifting her old head from the pillows, the woman looked at the thick leather straps. "If you remove these devices from me, I shall tell you everything you wish to know."

Kitt stared at the woman, the respiration monitors gently beeping by her bedside. "Okay."

Stepping to the mattress, the doctor unbuckled the restraint from the woman's right wrist and let it fall to the side of the bed. When she wasn't immediately attacked and mauled, she decided it was okay to remove the other restraints.

"There." Kitt took a step backward. "Is that better?"

The old woman raised her wrists, examining the bandages. "Goodness. I look like I've attempted suicide. And after all I've been through."

"Did you? Attempt suicide?"

"Dear, no. I'm here by mistake. An accident."

Kitt sat, holding the chart on her lap. "Would you like to tell me?"

The old woman clasped her hands to her waist. "As I said, everything you need to know, Doctor."

Nodding, Kitt opened the chart and took out a pen. "How did you come to be here, ma'am?"

"Alexandra—Bergman, to be precise. If you please."

"Thank you, Ms. Bergman. So . . ."

Smiling, the patient cocked her head. "You're young. Where are you from?"

"New York," Kitt said. "I studied at NYU and received a research grant to come to Paris, where—"

"No. You are not from New York. Not originally. Dr. Djimoa Kittaleye. Hmm. Perhaps . . ." She looked Kitt over. "The coloration suggests Kenya, but I believe the dialect is from Uganda. Is that right?"

Kitt put her hand to her arm.

Coloration?

Great. The old girl's a racist.

"You understand," the patient said, "it is the dialect that gives you away, dear. Not your skin color. The Caucasians in South Africa—Johannesburg, Lesotho—most of their accents are the same as anyone else's there." The old woman smiled. "You emigrated as a child, is that right?"

Kitt shifted on her seat.

Rule number one: If a patient catches you in a lie, all trust is lost.

"My parents moved from Uganda when I was eleven," Kitt said. "But I have to admit, no one has mentioned an accent to me since high school."

"Your efforts to erase it have served you well. It's barely there. Certain syllables, that's all."

It was true. A lot of attention was paid to the nightly newscasters on the national broadcasts, who spoke in that clear midwestern U.S. voice. Not the gruff, often whiny, New York dialect, nor the honeyed sweetness of a southern Georgia drawl. A plain, unadorned speech that was hard for young

Djimoa to copy, but that made her assimilation so much easier.

"I've made you uncomfortable," the old woman said. "I'm very sorry. I don't always know what the customs outside of . . . well, what the customs elsewhere are. Forgive me."

Kitt fixed her eyes on the first page of the chart, not reading anything, keeping a non-committal look on her face.

You didn't make me uncomfortable—except see rule number one.

She knows she made me uncomfortable.

So, I have to admit it.

Kitt looked at the patient. "It is slightly awkward to have my accent mentioned, but it's okay. I . . . forget about it, mostly."

"One never forgets where one is from, Doctor. I know I won't. Now, I believe you asked me how I came to be in this hospital, is that right? I should like to tell you some things in that regard. Things that you may consider important."

"Do you remember what happened, Ms. Bergman? Do you know why you're here?"

"There was a car accident."

"Tell me what you can recall."

"Oh, nothing extraordinary. Running late for a business meeting, texting while driving . . . the car in front just stopped suddenly. I don't know why. Anyway, to avoid a crash, it seemed best to swerve, and that put the vehicle directly in the path of an oncoming cement truck. Very big thing, that truck. Oh, and the sound of its brakes—absolutely terrifying, dear. But it was the right decision. I shall never forget the faces of the children in that car."

Kitt wrote quickly while scanning the pages in the chart. Dr. Dechambeau's handwriting was present, as was his signature under his notes. Kitt sat upright. "How did you get the wound to your upper chest and shoulder area?"

"The car accident."

Dr. Dechambeau had said it was a gunshot wound—and his notes repeated that assertion in the pages of the chart.

Kitt looked over the notes, reading parts out loud. "Earlier, you indicated to a nurse—or someone—that your name was Francine DeMond and that you were hospitalized because you had a reaction to an anesthesia they used on you when you went to the dentist for a root canal."

"I suppose I did tell someone that information."

Kitt frowned. She made a note in the file.
Delusional. Possible PTSD.
Evasive.

"You were not in a car accident," Kitt said, "and you didn't go to the dentist and have a reaction. You were shot. Do you remember?"

"I know what happened to me. I'm not delusional—and I don't have PTSD, dear."

"Excuse me?"

"That's what you wrote on my chart."

Kitt glanced at the chart, raising it to hide the notes from her patient. "Someone informed the nurse that you thought you were here for some other reason."

"At the dental appointment, there was a reaction to the anesthesia."

Shaking her head, Dr. Kittaleye closed the file. "I'm sorry, that's not right."

"If I agree I'm delusional, will you allow me to go to my little girl?"

The young psychologist sat back in the chair, looking at the elderly patient.

This is not likely a woman who has a young child.

More delusions, possibly?

Kitt pushed a strand of hair from her eyes. "I've found that these talks are most beneficial when we are honest with each other, ma'am. Is that fair?"

"It is, yes. I'm trying to be helpful. Perhaps when the sun comes up, we could stroll around the grounds and talk."

"No. You're still recovering from your injuries. We can't risk that."

"But my injuries have healed. Dr. Dechambeau said so. He must have told you."

The old woman's face was emotionless, but Kitt sensed she'd wandered into a strange game—or been pushed, as it were, by the Chief of Medicine.

Does she know what Dechambeau said, or is she putting it to me so I'll admit something she doesn't yet know? Something she wants to know?

And by getting that piece of the puzzle, she assembles a bigger and bigger idea of . . . whatever she's after.

Special guest, indeed.

"It may not be a good idea to take you outside," Kitt said. "Paris is still very cold in

February, and . . . well, to be honest, ma'am, I'm not convinced you wouldn't try to run away. They've put you here for a reason."

The old woman sighed, turning away. "Then I should like to get some rest. Will you come and talk with me again?"

"Will you be forthcoming if I do?"

The old woman lifted her bandaged hands and gazed at the doctor. "I told you, I'll reveal everything you need to know, Doctor Kittaleye."

Kitt stood, holding the chart in front of her. "And Ms. Bergman or DeMond or whoever you are, I will look forward to it—but only if we are honest with each other. I can't help you otherwise."

"I understand. Please come see me tomorrow. Get your rest and catch up on the news of the world through your tablet computer. We shall talk after lunch."

"Tablet computer?"

Another guess derived from a logical, generic assumption. Everyone my age uses a tablet. The old woman was good at this game.

She gets people used to this, and they end up telling her things without knowing it.

"All you young folks use them," the patient said. "Nurse Patrice reads hers a lot out there. I can hear the page clicks when she scrolls and the tapping noise when she texts. She hides it in the drawer because Dr. Dechambeau doesn't like the staff to use them at the hospital, but I don't mind." She raised her gaze to look Kitt in the eye. "Two o'clock, say?"

"Two will be fine. You're very interesting, ma'am."

"Thank you, dear."

"But the games need to stop if I'm to help you. Is that fair?"

"Completely, Doctor." She turned her face to the wall. "Two o'clock. We shall speak more then."

* * * * *

In the bowels of Pitié-Salpêtrière Hospital, Kitt typed up her notes on her tablet computer, emailed them to Dr. Dechambeau, and sent a copy to the printer on the first floor. After scurrying up the stairs to retrieve it, she returned to the tiny apartment and shoved the printed copy into the case folder.

Flopping down on the bed, she pulled her tablet off the desk, propped it up on the corner of the mattress, and found an American national news channel. Her heavy eyelids barely staying open, she rolled onto her side and stared at the screen, stuffing one of her thin pillows under her head.

As the first rays of sunshine peeked through her tiny window, her lids grew too tired to keep open, and she drifted off to sleep.

It was the jolt that woke her, like she had been sitting at a desk studying for exams and nodded off—the otoconia in the inner ear's utricle and saccule engage, keeping a person from falling over while asleep. Kitt knew the sensation well, from years of late hours in the NYU library and even more hours writing reports during her internship.

This was not that.

Her eyes opened. She was still lying on her bed, fully alert, the voices from the tablet going on about a chef.

A quick glance at the time told her it was barely after 11 a.m., but the fog of sleep was already gone. Kitt focused on the familiar newscasters, rewinding in her head what they'd just said.

The name.

They said her name.

She sat up, leaning closer to the screen, as an uneasy feeling settling in her stomach.

". . . died tragically in a car wreck in Atlanta. The chef apprenticed in New York's trendy Les Maisons under flamboyant TV personality and celebrity chef Girard Ruger, and she was slated to open her own restaurant in a few days, to grand fanfare." The female host's image was replaced by pictures of a wrecked Mercedes. ". . . sold out for months in anticipation of the grand opening."

The male host appeared, shaking his head. "Such a tragedy."

At the bottom of the screen, a headline scrolled across.

Chef Alexandra Bergman killed in traffic accident.

Kitt bolted upright. She grabbed the tablet with both hands, her heart racing.

". . . according to witnesses at the scene," the female broadcaster said, "she swerved to avoid rear-ending a car full of children and instead hit a cement truck. Bergman was unresponsive at the scene and later died from complications during surgery. She was thirty-three years old."

Kitt tossed the tablet aside and jumped out of bed, grabbing her case file. She flung it open and flipped through the notes.

The old woman's story matched nearly identically to the restauranteur's—but the chef's car wreck happened several hours after the elderly woman told her the story.

She dropped the file, staring at the wall, her mouth hanging open.

What is going on?

Could this be a repeated newscast? Somehow delayed, and the old lady knew ahead of time?

Kitt picked up the tablet, closed the tab with the news, and opened a search engine. Typing "Alexandra Bergman," she barely got the name entered before news stories popped up on the screen.

The estimated time of death was within the last hour.

The patient told me this story almost seven hours before it happened.

Still clutching the tablet, she grabbed the case file and raced out of her apartment, rushing to the old elevator at the end of the hallway.

Seven hours.

What game is this woman playing?

How could she know?

How could she lie about being this chef? Why would she? And why would she pretend to—

Kitt caught herself. As the ancient elevator motor whirred, she opened the file and read over the notes.

". . . here by mistake. An accident."

She didn't say she was in a car accident. She let me assume it.

Kitt flipped another page.

I asked her name. What was her reply?

"Alexandra—Bergman, to be precise. If you please."

So why did she lie?

Or did she?

The notes said the name, but Kitt concentrated on the actual conversation. It had been a bit different.

"How did you come to be here, ma'am?"

"Alexandra—Bergman, to be precise. If you please."

"Thank you, Ms. Bergman. So . . ."

Kitt put a hand to her forehead, groaning. "She never said she was Alexandra Bergman. I called her ma'am and she said a name. I assumed she was correcting me and giving me her name."

So stupid.

But still—not really a game. How could she know Alexandra Bergman would die after giving me that name?

Or is the question, why did she give me that name? She had to think I might find out it wasn't really hers.

Kitt frowned at the elevator, banging on its doors. "Hurry up, you old relic!"

If I thought the stairs would get me to the special wing, I'd take them. But in this old dungeon, who knows?

As the elevator doors opened, she threw back the gate and pulled out her key, sliding it into the slot on the panel. Kitt pressed the button to the fourth floor and pulled the old gate closed.

Bergman. She knew I'd find out. Why would she select a name I'd eventually . . .

A jolt went through her.

She turned the page and ran her finger over the notes, her eyes wildly scanning each word. "Where is it? Where . . ."

Her finger stopped at the other name.

Francine DeMond.

Kitt tucked the file under her arm and tapped her tablet. The search engine opened, but the screen displayed a tiny wheel that spun and spun.

Grimacing, Kitt looked at the ceiling and cursed. "You wretched old building! Get me a signal!"

She tapped her foot, staring at her screen while the elevator lumbered to a stop at the fourth floor. When the doors opened, Kitt pushed back the gate and stepped out—and the website connected.

The name Francine DeMond appeared in the search box.

The results didn't show her at all.

Francine Demild profiles, Facebook.

Frauke Demond profiles, Facebook.

Francine Delgado, Addams Family, Megaman and others.

Rubin & Demond, The Light Ekphrastic.

Then, a row of images—an African-American singer, a man in blue jeans standing in a parking lot, a bus route map, some sort of cartoon—nothing that appeared to be the woman mentioned by the patient.

Kitt rushed toward the nurses' station, taking the file from under her arm and reading over the notes. At the desk, she glanced up. No one was there.

"Patrice? Are you here?" She looked up and down the hallway. The low hum from the soda machine was the only reply. Kitt walked toward the old woman's room, speaking loud enough to be heard throughout the ward. "My patient has some explaining to do, Patrice."

Putting her hand on the door, Kitt pushed it open.

The room was empty.

The bed had been stripped; only the bare mattress remained, resting on the bedframe. The machines were gone, the restraints, the charts, the towels. The trash can had been emptied. It was as if the old woman hadn't been there at all.

Kitt put a hand to her chin. The faint scent of pine and alcohol lingered in the air.

The room's been sterilized.

"Patrice?" Kitt stepped into the hallway. The nurses' station was empty. No reports, no charts . . . the computer had been turned off and the phone was unplugged. The trash can had been emptied there, too. A fresh liner, only partially opened, hung on the rectangular trash can.

Kitt turned and stared at the patient's empty room.

They've moved her and shut down the wing. Why?

One person will know.

Frowning, Kitt gripped her tablet and file, marching toward the elevator.

CHAPTER 4

The receptionist outside of Dr. Dechambeau's office was polite, but firm. *"Il est occupé, Docteur. Si vous voulez bien prendre rendez-vous, s'il vous plaît."*

Kitt frowned. The receptionist spoke perfectly good English when she wanted to. "I don't need an appointment, Gabrielle. I need to speak with René now. *S'il vous plait.*" It was a bold step, but using Dr. Dechambeau's first name—and only his first name—might imply that the Chief of Medicine in fact did want to see Kitt without an appointment. "He woke me at two in the morning and requested my report as soon as possible. I need to give it to him."

Gabrielle chewed her lip, eyeing the large, closed doors of Dr. Dechambeau's suite. At the other desks, one assistant answered the phone; the other typed.

"I will try one time on the intercom." Gabrielle picked up the receiver from the phone console "But that is all. If he becomes angry, rest assured, he will know you are the reason for this interruption."

Kitt nodded. "*Merci*. I just need two minutes."

Dechambeau's voice was audible through the phone pressed to Gabrielle's ear. At the front of the desk, Kitt shifted on her feet. Dechambeau's voice was muffled, but the tone was unmistakably irritated.

"*Oui, Docteur.*" Gabrielle's cheeks turned red. "*Je suis désolé de vous interrompre.*" As she hung up, she glared at Kitt. "The Chief of Medicine requests you make an appointment—and also that you consider making your resignation letter." Narrowing her eyes, she smiled.

Kitt returned the sarcastic look. "Thank you for all your help." Sighing, she walked to the hallway. The tablet glowed in her hands.

The search site had updated. A new story appeared about Francine DeMond. The headline read, "Freak Death Of Student."

Kitt tapped the screen, opening a Canadian website. An image of a woman, roughly in her early thirties, appeared next to the crest of the University of Montreal in Quebec. Kitt quickly scanned the story.

Francine DeMond did go to the dentist for a root canal, and had a reaction to the anesthesia. She was a healthy woman in her thirties who was taking college courses at night at the University of

Montreal. She died a few hours ago. The Canadian CDC is looking into the cause of death.

Kitt leaned against the wall, her jaw hanging open.

What is going on?

The doors to Dr. Dechambeau's suite opened and he walked out, leading a parade of men and women in business suits. Laughing, Dechambeau clapped an old man on the back. *"Et donc, je vous verrai sur le terrain de golf plus tard?"* He bent over and mimicked an exaggeratedly bad golf swing.

"Bien sûr, René!" the elderly gentleman said.

The others laughed and smiled. Dechambeau escorted them to the elevators, shaking the hand of each one as they passed. *"Au revoir. Merci beaucoup d'être venus."*

As the elevator doors closed, he turned toward his office.

Kitt stepped away from the wall. "Sir, may I have a word?"

"Do not think I didn't see you there, Doctor Kittaleye. But I have a busy schedule today."

She mustered her best French, reciting that a man of power and importance is always busy. *"Un homme de pouvoir et d'importance est toujours occupé."*

Dechambeau shook his head, reaching into the pocket of his lab coat. "Do not attempt to flatter me, *Madame Docteur*. It insults us both, and your terrible accent slaughters the French language. Now, what is it that you want?" He withdrew his *Gauloises* cigarettes and lighter.

"You summoned me to see a patient last night, and now you've moved her," Kitt said. "Why?"

"You dare question me in my own hospital?" Dechambeau's voice thundered across the lobby. "And in front of my staff?"

Gabrielle looked up from her desk. The other assistants stopped their work and stared at Kitt.

"No, sir . . . and I apologize for my—my obvious poor choice of words." Kitt looked down, clutching her file and tablet. "I merely wished to continue the task you assigned me, and to do it fully, as I know you would want. But when I went to see the patient today, she was gone."

Dechambeau lit a cigarette. "You sent your report this morning. 'Insanity, Thorazine'—these were your words, yes?"

"Yes, but—"

"Then she is a mental case and belongs at—" Dechambeau glanced at Gabrielle.

"Sainte-Anne Hôpital, monsieur," Gabrielle said.

"Sainte-Anne Hospital." Dechambeau glared at Kitt. *"Pas ici.* Not here." He walked toward his office.

"I know you don't respect my field, sir, but—"

"Perhaps I'm merely challenging you to perfect what you've only studied in books, Doctor."

"Well, sir, I believe this case warrants further review." Kitt trailed after him. "There have been some very irregular coincidences."

"Fine. The staff at Sainte-Anne can address them. I've forwarded your report. Good day, *Madame Docteur*."

Kitt stopped, her shoulders sagging. "Yes, sir."

"And Doctor Kittaleye . . ." Dechambeau took a long puff on his cigarette. "The next time my receptionist tells you to make an appointment, consider who it is you are actually saying no to."

Blowing the smoke in Kitt's face, Dechambeau disappeared into his office and shut the door.

"Yes, sir. Thank you." She turned to the receptionist. "And thank you, Gabrielle."

Because now I know where you've moved my patient.

* * * * *

Dr. Kittaleye sat in her cramped apartment, staring at the hospital-issued computer as the patient information screen loaded.

Technically, this isn't against the rules because I am authorized to update the records. If I happen to see the name used to transfer the patient, or the transfer number, that can't be helped.

The screen finally opened. The elderly woman was transferred at 8:03 a.m., under the French equivalent of Jane Doe, transfer record number 21-10312020.

Dechambeau didn't waste any time getting her out of here.

Kitt made a note of both items.

Now, since I don't have admitting privileges at Sainte-Anne, I can't just show up with a case number or transfer number.

What could I do?

She leaned over and peeked into the mirror, brushing a strand of ebony hair from her brown cheek.

I doubt anyone will think she's my grandmother.

Her gaze drifted to the tiny dresser.

On the other hand, this is France.

* * * * *

Dressed in her long, black winter coat, a scarf, and a stylish knit hat, Kitt hailed a cab. Her ripped skinny jeans and fashionable high heeled boots weren't right for the weather, but they'd be perfect for the admitting desk clerk at *Sainte-Anne Hôpital.*

When a cab finally stopped, Kitt jumped in, invoking her best California girl accent. "Saint Annie Hospital, mon shoor. Por fuh vore."

The cabbie gave her a half smile in the rearview mirror, then rolled his eyes and shook his head. "You are American, eh *mademoiselle*?"

"I am." Kitt flashed a wide grin. She was still young enough to pass as a college student when she dressed the part. "My school has a semester abroad program where you can go to any country, and I picked *Paree.*"

"Yes. The *country* of Paris is so fortunate. Which entrance for the *Sainte-Anne Hôpital* do you wish?"

"Are there more than one?" She stifled a wince. Her overdone California dialect was migrating toward Texas. "Uh, just the main one, I guess. I'm meeting my roommate, and she's already there. She's visiting her grandma."

The cabbie pulled into the thick traffic of downtown Paris, muttering. *"Quelle chance pour la grand-mère."*

Kitt looked out the window, silently translating.

"How lucky for grandmother."

Indeed.

If I play this right, the French will assume I'm an American that doesn't speak French, and they'll let their guard down. Hopefully, enough for me to find my patient's room.

The cab ride to the Sainte-Anne Hospital took about ten minutes. Kitt paid the driver and opened the door, greeted by a frosty gust of winter air. Her long coat whipped her ankles as she rushed to the hospital's *visiteurs* entrance.

The wave of warmth in the lobby was a welcome relief. The massive space was clean and white, a tall, wide, modern-looking area with a long, pristine counter at the far end. It seemed more like an upscale hotel than a psychiatric hospital.

Kitt walked quickly over the large tile floor, her heels echoing off the gleaming walls and high ceiling. As she approached the admitting desk, the clerk lifted her eyes from her computer and looked at the slender, elegant psychologist.

"Hi!" Kitt beamed. She spoke much louder than necessary. "I'm here to meet my roommate—

and she's visiting her granny. Can y'all tell me where they are?"

The petite clerk recoiled. "This is the *Sainte-Anne Hôpital, mademoiselle*. Are you certain this is the facility you are looking for?"

"Yep!" Kitt banged her hand on the counter, leaning over and inspecting the clerk's desk. "Carrie said this is where she'd be. The Saint Annie hospital." She glanced around. "This place is a lot prettier on the inside than the outside. Anyhoo, Ima grab a seat right yonder and wait for my roomie— don't got but about three percent left on my phone battery, and we're goin' out to see some of *Paree* in a bit."

The clerk opened her mouth to speak.

"Say!" Kitt wheeled around and grabbed the counter with both hands. "Would you mind if I plug in and charge up right here?" She pulled her phone out of her pocket. "You got a spare plug? This is an XL. It charges real slow, but I think Carrie said she and her granny were going to be visiting for a few hours, and I don't mind waiting in the lobby. She's my BFF and all." Kitt stepped away from the counter, swinging her hands back and forth and clapping them each time they collided in front of her. "Yep. Give them a few hours to chat, and my phone will be all charged."

"Mademoiselle!" The clerk jumped up from her seat. "Perhaps you would like to visit with your friend and her grandmother upstairs."

"Well, now, that's an idea. 'Course, I don't know her grandma's name."

The clerk typed on her keyboard. "When did she come in?"

"Oh, they brought her over this morning around eight," Kitt said. "Transferred from a hospital on the other side of town. The Petey Saltpepper, or something. And Carrie did give me a transfer number—I have a great head for numbers. I mostly can remember any phone number. Wanna try?" She slapped her arm on the counter and leaned toward the clerk. "I bet I can remember yours. Go ahead. Try."

The clerk leaned away. "*Mademoiselle*, if you have the transfer number, I may be able to locate your friend for you—then you could join them . . . instead of waiting here."

"What a right good idea! Thank you." Kitt rubbed her nose and wiped her hand on the side of her coat, then dug in her pocket until she produced a small piece of paper. She handed it to the clerk, who held it by the corner with fingertips. "Actually," Kitt said, "Carrie might still be fetching lunch—they was gonna eat lunch together in the room. So, is it okay if I just go on up before she gets here?"

"I'm sure we can accommodate such a thing this one time." The clerk stopped typing. "Yes, your friend's grandmother is on unrestricted access. If she will allow it, you may visit with her." A man appeared at the end of the counter, and she gestured to him. "This is Claude. He will escort you to the room."

The clerk looked at Claude and spoke in French. Kitt smiled broadly, listening to their conversation as if she didn't understand a word.

"Take this obnoxious child to the woman in room 1918," the clerk said. "If the patient knows her, she may stay until her friend arrives."

Claude nodded. "And if not?"

"Then take her out." The clerk huffed. "And use any exit but this one."

Kitt kept her big grin plastered to her face.

Claude stepped toward her. "If you will come with me, *mademoiselle*."

"Thank you, mon-shoor." She winked at the clerk. "And thank you, maddamusell."

* * * * *

At room 1918, Claude knocked on the door. "*Madame*, you have a visitor request. Do you know this young lady?"

Kitt stuck her head in the door. "Hi. I'm your granddaughter Carrie's friend. Remember me?"

The old woman smiled from where she lay on the bed. "Of course I remember you, dear." She glanced at Claude. "This will be fine. I was expecting her." Her gaze went to Kitt. "And it's nearly two p.m.—as we agreed earlier."

As Claude left the room, Kitt strolled toward the bed. "Two p.m." She held up her phone, displaying the time. "What a coincidence. It's one of many I've seen today, ma'am."

"Please, call me Helena." The elderly patient waved her hand at a chair that had been positioned near the bed. "And now, Doctor Kittaleye, if you would like to sit with an old woman, I shall tell you the things you have come to hear."

CHAPTER 5

Dr. Kittaleye folded her coat over the back of her chair. "Could you have seen the story on the news, and been confused?"

"How could I be confused?" Helena said. "There was no TV in the ward. I've had no access to a computer or phone."

"Maybe you heard about the chef from Patrice and the other nurses. Same with the college student."

"Are you thinking that is so, or hoping it is?"

Kitt knew the truth. The old woman could not have known about the deaths of two different women, thousands of miles apart, before they happened—even if she had access to phones and tablets and everything else.

"I told you this morning, I'm not crazy." Helena's tone was soft. Patient. "But . . . there are those of us who have abilities that are not easily explained in the traditional sense of things."

Kitt rubbed her eyes with both hands, exhaling sharply. "So, you're a psychic, is that it?"

"Psychic? No, dear. It's difficult to explain. My life has taken quite a unique path, it seems." She adjusted the blankets. "I can tell you how it was explained to me."

"Yes. Let's try that."

"Very well." Helena sighed, her eyes looking at the young doctor but seeming far way. "Did you know that a baby born anywhere in the world will babble all phonemes? Eventually, they will latch onto the ones that are relevant to the language they need, and lose the ability to speak the rest. It begins like that. Then, in time, we learn to . . . *interpret* the things that come. With focus, we can understand it. We see the message in it all—like a dream—and we retain it, we comprehend it."

"I was told you don't dream."

Helena smiled. "It's like a dream, as far as what I conclude from how others describe dreams."

"You understand . . ." Kitt shifted in her seat. "From my viewpoint, it's much more likely you overheard someone or caught part of a radio broadcast—"

"Before it happened?

"Well, that's the part of the trick I can't get my head around—no offense, ma'am."

"Trick. I see." Helena stared at the floor. "I am sympathetic to your skepticism, dear. Let me disperse it now. Did you bring your file with you?"

"The file on you? Yes."

"Would you open it to the fourth page, please?"

Kitt leafed through the file.

"Patient appears lucid," the old woman said. "She is responsive but evasive, possibly suffering from a head injury sustained when the pectoral issue occurred, but the MRI and CT scan displayed no cranial trauma . . ."

As the woman spoke, Kitt stopped turning the pages in the file. Her hands fell to her lap.

"No obvious signs of dementia. Delusional. Possible PTSD. Evasive . . ."

Helena was reciting Kitt's entire session notes—handwritten by her earlier that day—that had never left the file.

". . . the patient's mental state should be considered in light of the reported gunshot wound that resulted in a massive loss of blood, as well as the possibility of a self-reinforcing delusion..."

Kitt read along as Helena said every word on the page, including the scratched-out parts.

"You added, '2 p.m. follow up' at the end." Helena swept her hands out. "And here we are."

"I—I don't understand. How . . . why . . ."

"I need your help." The old woman got up from the bed, clasping her hands in front of her. "There will be an update on the Canadian woman soon. She had no known allergic reaction to the anesthesia, but she marked the box on the form that she did. The hygienist misplaced the form. It went into another patient's file."

Kitt opened a search engine on her tablet and typed the Canadian woman's name in. The story updated at 2:11p.m., the exact time displayed on the tablet's clock. The new information was exactly as Helena said.

Kitt looked at the elderly patient. "How?"

"The same way I knew you left Uganda with your mother and father when you were eleven. I saw it."

"You . . . saw it?"

"The image is clear in my mind. I see it like a movie, but of course that would be how one would describe a dream. You wore your mother's scarf on the plane because you were cold. It was red, yellow, and black—the colors of the Ugandan flag. She called you Pitta, the little bird of your native country. Green wings, with a yellow and black head, and a red underbelly."

Kitt's jaw hung open. "But how?"

Helena's gaze went to the window. "When you look outside at that field of green grass, why don't you see any red cars in it?

Kitt craned her neck to see out the window. "Because there aren't any red cars in that field of grass."

"So, you don't need to see any red. In the same way, I didn't need to engage brain waves on that level until it was necessary. When it came into my field of view, then I saw it."

"But that doesn't—"

"What if people were able to see ultraviolet light or hear ultrasonic transmissions? And what if human genetics had been manipulated to the point where some people could receive thought transmissions from others, or sense a pre-echo in the fabric of time and space the way dogs feel an earthquake before it happens?"

"But it's—the scientists have disowned such studies."

"Have they? Or have they not even seen the latest developments because they were never shared? Some people consider proprietary technology is too easily stolen to share with academics."

"Is what you're saying true? Does it exist, the capabilities—"

"If it did not, how could I have told you the things I've told you?"

"About the deaths of those two women?"

"And your plane flight as a child."

"You . . you see things? Before they happen?"

"Some things. And, sadly, often the most tragic events are the ones I miss. Or maybe my unconscious knows I can't handle them. Maybe that's why you came to me—to help with the things I can't. So, I trust you, Doctor. A young girl who is very important to me is in danger. I hope you can help me find her."

"You mentioned a child before. Your little girl. Is that your . . . granddaughter?"

"My ward. A child entrusted to me, and I was her Keeper. She was in The Bahamas, but without a phone or any electronics, I can't know. I only know I must leave here and go to her."

* * * * *

Patrice bounded down the stairs of the Pitié-Salpêtrière Hospital, pulling the collar of her coat tight to her neck. She waved goodbye to a few coworkers, her blonde locks swaying in the chilly midday wind as she walked toward the bus stop on the corner.

A blond man in a red and black plaid coat nudged the athletic woman next to him. "That is her," he whispered. "The one with the yellow hair, coming this way."

"*Merci*, Jules." The woman reached into a shopping bag and withdrew an envelope, handing it to him. "Go back inside—but take the long way, eh?"

Jules shoved the envelope into his coat pocket. The wind blew his blond locks into his eyes. "She won't be hurt, will she?"

"Your part is done. Go now." The woman nodded to two men smoking by the far side of the hospital exit. One was dressed in a hospital maintenance uniform—a blue-gray shirt and drab, gray pants; the other was disguised as a construction worker—blue jeans, yellow hard hat, and a yellow safety vest. They dropped their cigarettes and walked behind Patrice as she made her way to the corner.

The woman put the shopping bag over her arm and raised a small radio to her cheek. "I am engaging the target. Bring the vehicles now." Dropping the phone into her coat pocket, she rushed toward Patrice. "Excuse me. Do you speak English?"

Patrice stopped, glancing at the bus stop and then back to the woman. "Yes, I speak English."

"Oh, thank goodness. I'm so lost. Can you help me? Do you know where this is?" She opened the bag to reveal a tablet playing a video. On the screen was an image of a blonde-haired woman with a gun to her head.

Patrice leaned forward, her eyes wide. *"Qu'est-ce que c'est?"*

From behind her, the maintenance man and the construction worker grabbed Patrice's arms.

She gasped, looking over both shoulders and struggling against the grip of the assailants.

"Patrice Chevalier." The athletic woman stepped forward, her nose an inch from the nurse. "Silence. *Le silence.*" She grabbed the nurse by the chin. "If you say one word, the man with the gun kills your mother. Nod if you understand."

Shaking, Patrice nodded.

"Remain silent, and this will all be over quickly. Nod again if you understand."

As a van drove up to the curb, Patrice nodded a second time.

"Good." The athletic woman said. "Keep your mouth shut and get in the van. We don't want to hurt you, but if you say or do anything, my man on the video will splatter your mother's face all over the screen—and you will be next."

The van doors opened. The men pulled Patrice inside and shoved her to the floor. As the woman boarded, the maintenance man closed the van door and they drove away. The construction worker handed the woman a blindfold.

"This is necessary," she said, giving the blindfold to Patrice. "Put it on. Cover your eyes. And remember, if you speak, the first bullet kills your mother at her apartment in Sèvres. The second bullet kills you."

Tears welled in Patrice's eyes as her trembling hands slid the blindfold over her eyes.

"Give me your phone," the construction worker said.

Patrice took her phone out of her pocket. The man took it and turned away.

The van swerved around a few more turns, then came to a stop.

"Take your blindfold off," the woman said.

Quivering, Patrice pulled the fabric down past her chin.

The van door slid back to reveal an ambulance, its doors open and a fat man lying on a stretcher, bandaged around both arms and legs.

"Right. Bring her to me," he growled in a thick British accent.

The maintenance man grabbed Patrice and dragged her to the van door.

Narrowing his eyes, the British man glared at the nurse. "You been watching a woman in your hospital. An old bird, in a special wing."

Her mouth hanging open, Patrice looked at the woman who had kidnapped her.

The man in the ambulance scowled. "Tell her to answer me, Miss Franklin."

The female kidnapper nodded to her blonde hostage. "You may answer Mr. Hollings' questions, Patrice."

"*Oui.* I—I did," Patrice whimpered.

"Aye, you did, flower," Hollings said. "Where might she be now?"

"I don't know."

"Shoot her mother. Put a bullet in each foot. See if it jogs the sweet young lass' memory."

"No!"

Hollings' face turned red. "Then stop messing about and tell me where the old bird is!"

"I do not know. While I was watching the woman, a doctor came and spoke with her. Then, they move her from the ward. No one says to me where they take her."

"Aye. And this doctor—does he know where the patient is?"

"I . . . I don't know. I never saw him before."

The fat man shrugged. "Shoot her. Kill the mother and bury the lot in the garden."

"Please!" Patrice cried. "I am telling you the truth!"

Hollings narrowed his eyes, staring at her. "Aye, lass, maybe you are. Now, where might I find this doctor?"

"I don't know that, either—please don't hurt me! I don't know where he is. I never saw him before. He is not on our staff. He—he left the hospital, and that is all I know."

"Bugger all! She's useless." Hollings growled. "Put her on the street. Let her go."

Franklin nodded, turning to the construction worker. "She can have her phone back now."

He handed Patrice the phone.

Franklin put her hand to Patrice's cheek, stroking the blonde hair away from the nurse's eyes. "You did well, little nurse. You get to live. And if you want your mother to stay alive, get out of this van and start walking—and don't look back."

The maintenance man shoved Patrice out of the van. She fell onto the cold, hard asphalt of a vacant lot. As she scrambled to her feet, the van and the ambulance sped away.

Trembling, Patrice brushed bits of gravel from the palms of her hands, walking until she was sure the vehicles were out of sight, then raced to the nearest open business—a small grocery—and threw open the door.

She collapsed to the floor, shaking and crying.

"Mademoiselle!" The grocery clerk ran to her side. "Are you all right? Are you sick? Is there something we can do for you?"

"No, please—thank you." She cowered against the wall.

My mother.

Patrice dialed the phone, her heart racing.

"Oui allo, Patrice!" her mother shouted.

"Oui, mama!" A tear ran down Patrice's cheek. "Are you okay? Did they hurt you?"

Her mother was sobbing. "What is happening!"

"I don't know." Putting a hand to her head, the nurse crouched down and peered out the store window. "Some people attacked me outside of the hospital. Kidnappers. They wanted information on a patient, and—"

Kitt.

They wanted information about Dr. Kittaleye.

"Mama, I must call you back."

"No! What is happening!"

Patrice ended the call and dialed Kitt.

* * * * *

Standing outside the van parked around the corner, Franklin smiled at the bandaged fat man in the ambulance. She held her laptop up to him. "You see, Mr. Hollings? You scare someone and then see who they contact—after you install a call tracer in their phone." She patted the back of the construction worker. "Neat trick, right? I learned it from a guy I used to work with. Maybe you've heard of him—The Greyhound?"

"Bah. The Greyhound is . . . silliness. A romantic figure made up by desperate people, nothing more. He don't exist."

"Whatever you say, since you're signing the paychecks now."

"Yes, I am." Scowling, Hollings sat up on the ambulance stretcher. "And who does our pretty young nurse call after her dear mother?"

Franklin studied the laptop screen. "She is now speaking to . . . a phone registered to Djimoa Kittaleye, somewhere in east Paris. We will have the exact location of the phone momentarily." She turned to the maintenance man. "Do a search for the name. Keep it local."

He typed on his computer. "Kittaleye. Doctor of Psychology, interning at the Pitié-Salpêtrière Hospital."

"Brilliant," the fat man said. "Start the engine. I want both of my hands 'round that doctor's manky throat before the nurse can finish warning him about us."

"As you wish." Franklin climbed into the van. "The doctor is near the intersection of Rue Cabanis and Rue Broussais. It's . . . a mental hospital.

The Sainte-Anne." She pounded the back of the driver's seat. "Go! Go!"

* * * * *

Kitt lowered the phone, her face white. "Patrice says she was kidnapped, and the people who did it will be looking for me. They—they put a gun to her mother's head!"

"Yes." Helena walked to the window and eased back the edge of the curtain. "I'm very sorry for the deception, dear, but if I had stayed at your hospital, you might be dead now."

"She said to go, to get out of town and hide somewhere."

Outside on the street, a van and an ambulance screeched to a stop.

"I'm afraid it's time for a decision," Helena said. "I must leave here and go to the child. And if you are to remain safe, you must come with me. But we must leave now."

Kitt stared at the floor, unfocused, shaking her head. "I—I have a friend who lives in Berlin. Maybe I could go there, hide . . ."

Picking up the doctor's long black coat and stylish knit hat, Helena put her hand on Kitt's shoulder. "I can't protect you in Berlin, Doctor." She grabbed Kitt's scarf. "Now, take off those boots, dear, and hurry. We haven't much time."

* * * * *

The elevator doors opened, followed by the *click-clack* of high heeled boots going across the tile floor.

Glancing up, the young lady at the desk scowled. With her phone pressed to the side of her head, the woman in the long black coat walked briskly across the lobby, the ends of her scarf bouncing around the back of her waist.

Claude leaned on the counter, whispering to the clerk. "That American cowgirl isn't right for those boots. She can barely walk in them."

"Cowboy boots for a cow." The clerk frowned. "At least we are rid of her, and I say good riddance."

"Oui." Claude called after the woman. *"Au revoir, mademoiselle, et bon débarras."*

Stifling a giggle, the clerk put her hand over her mouth. "Quiet. She will hear you."

"So what? The stupid cow doesn't speak French."

Without looking back, the woman waved, her other hand still holding the phone tight against her face. She pushed through the exit and headed outside into the cold.

"See?" Claude chuckled. "Typical dumb American."

* * * * *

At the vending machines outside of room 1918, a slender young black woman in ripped jeans approached the maintenance worker. He emptied a garbage can into a large, round container.

"Sir," she said, "can you tell me how to get down to that adorable little courtyard?"

The woman's French was good, but not great, and contained a distinct American accent. He'd never seen her before, but she was far too young to be a patient.

"Yes, *mademoiselle*."

She smiled. "Oh, you speak American."

He pointed to a sign marked *Escaliers*. "At the bottom of these stairs is the access. To the right is a door to the lobby. To the left is the door to the courtyard."

"Thank you. You're very helpful."

"But *mademoiselle*, outside is very cold. Do you have a jacket?"

"I don't." She brushed a strand of black hair from her eyes. "I lent mine to a friend earlier."

* * * * *

As she climbed into a taxi, Helena took off Kitt's hat and scarf. *"Faites le tour du bloc, s'il vous plaît."*

"Oui, madame." The driver started the car and drove around the corner.

Helena crouched as they passed a parked ambulance and van. At the end of the street, she peered between the front seats and tapped the cabbie on the shoulder, pointing at a young lady in ripped jeans. "This is my friend. *C'est mon ami, monsieur."*

The cab slowed to a stop.

Kitt ran over and got in, rubbing her arms. "Whew! It's cold out there."

"Yes, dear. Here's your coat." Helena slipped her shoulder out from the heavy garment.

"No, you hang onto it, I'll be all right. But you can have your shoes back." Kitt blew warm air onto her hands. "Now what?"

The old woman gazed into Kitt's eyes, her tone calm and flat. "Now you decide if you'll help me."

"I . . . can't." Kitt looked down. "I'd like to help you, ma'am. Honestly. But it's impossible." The young doctor turned her face to the window.

"With all I've shown you so far, if you still feel that way . . . then there isn't much else I can say." Helena handed Kitt her phone. "See if you can ring up your friend in Berlin. You must leave quickly."

Kitt stared at the phone in her hand. Frida would let her come and stay until she could make a plan for herself—but what would that plan be? Walking away from her job? Her career?

"No, dear," Helena said. "You wouldn't be walking away from anything. You'd be moving *toward* something, and you'd be helping me find my little girl."

Kitt recoiled, staring at the old woman. "What? What would I be moving toward?"

"The truth, Djimoa Kittaleye. The reality of who you are, and why you came looking for me." Helena clasped her hands in her lap. "Besides, do you think the man with the black mask—the one you have nightmares about—that it will all stop at the Berlin city limits?"

CHAPTER 6

Hamilton DeShear held a wiggling worm in one hand and a fishing hook in the other, as the charter boat drifted gently on the turquoise waters of the Caribbean. Clutching a bright pink fishing rod with silver sparkles under his arm, he leaned against the railing and brought the worm up to the hook. A warm breeze pulled at the legs of his board shorts— and also the straight blonde hair of the little girl next to him.

She stretched her yellow, one-piece bathing suit and let it snap back to her belly, idly repeating the action again and again. "Are you quite sure you're doing that right?"

"Yep." He held the hook out to her. "You wanna try it?"

Constantine took a step away. "I don't like touching the worms. They're squirmy. I don't trust them."

"Hmm." DeShear pierced the worm and slid it over the hook. "You're gonna have to learn to do this if you intend to keep fishing. Guess they didn't have this part in your video game."

Jaden Trinn emerged from the lower deck hatch, wearing a black bikini. "I wouldn't trust a worm either, Constantine." She went to the side of the boat and picked up her fishing rod, her long dark hair flowing over her tan, toned back. "But there are better baits than worms."

"Usually," DeShear said, admiring Trinn's long, tan legs.

"Sorry, boss." The captain sat perched on the front of the boat, rolling up the sleeves of his blue-striped shirt. "I grab the wrong cooler this morning. But my friend, he bringing us the good bait. You don't worry."

DeShear shrugged. "Hey, accidents happen, Laquan. We used plenty of regular bait yesterday with Captain Mateo. At least you had some worms. And now we have extra beer, so it's not all bad."

"If anyone wants to drink beer at seven in the morning." Trinn smirked, lowering her voice. "Too bad Mateo got sick. He was a much better captain."

DeShear handed Constantine her fishing rod. "There you go. If you hook anything really big, make sure you bring it *in*, and it doesn't take *you* out to sea."

Constantine lifted her chin. "I was best in my class at swimming. I could hold my breath longer than anyone else, too. Almost three minutes. I'm an excellent swimmer."

"Well, I'm not." DeShear liked Constantine's British accent, but her formal manner of speaking and extensive vocabulary were still a constant surprise. "So, don't go overboard. If you go in, then I have to go in, and I don't want to go swimming right now."

The five-year-old scrunched up her face, gazing at him in the bright morning light. "You'd go in after me?"

"Yep. Where you go, I go, kid." He wiped his hands on a rag and draped it over the railing. "That's the deal. If you fell overboard or got lost in the mall or anything, I'd look for you and I'd find you—no matter what. Remember that. We're a team, and my goal is to keep you safe. There's no telling what's out there."

"Tiger sharks out there." The charter boat captain hopped across the front deck and swung himself into the wheelhouse. His unbuttoned shirt flapping in the breeze, he took a toothpick from his breast pocket and stuck it between his teeth.

Trinn glanced at the captain. "What'd you say?"

"Tiger sharks." Laquan pointed west, toward the gently rocking horizon. A series of small islands jutted from the water. "Off the reef, just there. The cruise ships dump their trash before daylight break, so the sharks, they come looking every morning."

DeShear smiled at Trinn. "Stay out of the water until after they've eaten their breakfast, then."

"They half the size of this boat, boss," Laquan said. "Believe that."

Constantine put a hand on the rail and looked over. "Tiger sharks are of the genus *Galeocerdo*. They prefer deep water. This doesn't look deep at all." She turned to the wheelhouse, holding her hand to her forehead to block the sun. "Captain Laquan, how many fathoms of depth are we?"

"Fathoms?" He chuckled. "A good word for a little fisher-girl. The depth finder says one hundred feet, young miss."

"A hundred!" Trinn peered over the side. "It's so clear. I'd have thought it was twenty feet to the bottom. Maybe thirty, tops."

"One hundred feet, ma'am. For sure. The instruments don't lie." The captain narrowed his eyes, staring over the bow of the boat. "In Bahamas, you got the best water in the world."

Trinn peered into the crystalline waves. "What are the dark spots on the bottom?"

"That be the rocks, missus. Maybe little sea grass bed."

"Davy Jones' locker." DeShear nudged Constantine. "Don't snag your line in there."

"Could it be dolphins?" she asked.

"Not there, girl," Laquan said. "Look here."

"What is it, Captain?"

He pointed. About fifty feet away, a dark fin broke the surface in a graceful arch.

"A dolphin!" Constantine gasped, dropping her fishing rod and rushing to the starboard side of the boat. She grabbed the rail and jumped up and down. "Look! Look! Oh, I do like them so much! Captain Mateo said they had names. Do you know its name, Laquan?"

"Sure, little miss." Another fin crested the water closer to the boat. "This gal is call Pinky Tree. She got a scratch on her back, look like pine limb." A second dorsal fin followed, its owner's backside glinting in the sunlight as it rolled through the waves. "See how that boy got a rip in the back of his fin? His name Mastiff. He a big fella, king of the ocean."

A smaller dolphin popped its head out, then ducked under with a splash. Constantine squealed in delight. "Do you know the names of all the dolphins in these waters?"

Laquan adjusted the toothpick in his teeth. "For sure, little miss. A captain got to know everything in his ocean. Every rock, every coral, every animal."

Trinn reached across the vinyl bench seat and lifted a towel off her phone, snapping a few pictures of Constantine and the dolphin fins beyond her. When the passing visitors disappeared, she lowered her phone and checked the time. "Constantine, you'd better change into your clothes. We need to watch the sun out here."

The girl's face remained pressed against the rail. "Aww."

"Hey, we had an agreement." Trinn set her phone next to a stack of faded life jackets on the bench seat. "I love that your cheeks have a rosy glow, but you remember your sunburn from the other day?"

Constantine's shoulders slumped. "Melanoma is relatively prevalent for fair-skinned people who spend time in the tropics."

"I'll take that as a yes. Okay, then. There's a shopping bag on the table down below, with a new t-shirt and shorts from the hotel shop. The puppy print ones you liked. You can change in the bathroom."

Constantine shuffled away from the railing. "On a boat, the bathroom's called 'the head.' Did you cut the tags off the shirts? They itch me."

"I did. Scoot. We'll put on more sunscreen when you come back. And I got you a hat, too. It's in the bag."

Frowning, Constantine descended the stairs. "I don't fancy wearing a hat."

"I don't fancy skin cancer." Trinn slid her fishing rod out of the holder and cranked the reel, pulling in her line.

"Use that front berth, little miss," Laquan said. "The door is a bit fussy, so you pull it shut tight." He held up the radio receiver. "Boss, my friend say he coming right quick now. We see him any minute."

"Sounds good." As Laquan started the boat's motor, DeShear slipped his arms around Trinn's waist. He nuzzled her shoulder. "Having fun?"

"I am." She leaned back, kissing him. "It's beautiful weather again today. What about you, Hank? Relaxing yet?"

"I will be soon, I promise."

"Are you worried about Helena?"

"A little," he said. "We didn't hear from her yesterday. She'd usually at least call Constantine, and she has that follow up procedure soon."

"We'll call the hospital when we get back this afternoon." Trinn patted his hand. "Constantine seems okay today."

"Yeah. After last night, I wasn't sure we should come out." He took a deep breath and rested his chin on Trinn's shoulder. "All that screaming about 'They're killing her." Who do you think 'her' was?"

Trinn sighed, placing a hand over DeShear's. "It might be PTSD. She witnessed some horrific events in that Château. She saw her friends massacred. Maybe we should find someone to talk to her."

"Yeah . . . I'm not sure I trust some Bahamian therapist. In the Caribbean, the head shrinkers shrink heads for real."

"Boss!" Laquan jumped off the upper deck. "You take the wheel. I cast a line to my friend."

DeShear craned his neck, peering over the bow. A boat with a red hull approached. "Autolycus II" was painted in faded white letters across its bow.

Trinn patted his hand. "Go and steer the ship. We can talk more about this later."

"Okay." DeShear crossed the deck and climbed the ladder to the wheelhouse. Corroded fish finders and an old GPS dotted the area above the cracked, faded fiberglass dashboard, all held in place with a variety of rusted screws.

Laquan waved to the red boat as he lifted a coiled-up rope from his deck. The Autolycus II pulled alongside and Laquan tossed the line to them, then ran to the front of his boat and threw another line over. Several men in the red boat grabbed the ropes and pulled the boats together, nose to tail.

"Nothing like fresh bait, boss." Laquan tied his line off. "We fix you up good now."

A stocky, muscular man in a dirty yellow tank top hauled a large cooler off the Autolycus II. He balanced as the boats rocked, then stepped over the rail and landed onto Laquan's rear deck, slamming the cooler down. Standing, he glared at Laquan, sweat brimming on his forehead. "Best help with these, Conchy Joe. The ice melt in this hot sun."

Laquan scampered toward the cooler. "Yeah, Rally. You fix us up. Thanks, mate."

Rally looked at Trinn, his eyes lingering on her legs. "Her boongie big, bey."

Trinn picked up her towel and wrapped it around her waist.

Licking his lips, the large stranger slowly turned back to Laquan. "Got a few nice lobster in there, too. If you want, I can cook up some nice dinner tonight for the lady."

DeShear stepped to the rear of the wheelhouse. "She can take care of her own dinner plans, friend. Thanks for the bait."

Rally lowered his eyes back to Laquan. "All straight now, friend?"

"I straight now, Rally." Laquan shifted on his feet, the toothpick bouncing back and forth in his mouth. "Was a leg short, but you fix me up."

"No. We not quite straight yet, friend. You got the sail? For Jonah?"

"Right right! The sail is below. All fetch and ready."

With his eyes fixed on Laquan, Rally shouted. "Jonah! Come and get the sail."

Laquan glanced at DeShear. "I get them a sail for their other boat, boss. We trade out here, is all. We don't be a minute."

"It a nice sailboat, sir." Rally smiled at DeShear. "Maybe you come take an evening cruise with us. Bring the lady, watch the sun set."

As a deck hand jumped on board and went below, Rally leered at Trinn. "He a low fence, your captain. He mix up like conch salad. Forget your bait and ruin your trip, pretty miss. But we fix you up good now."

Laquan stepped between them. "You—you fix me up, right right. Thanks, mate."

The boat motors idled, their hulls bumping together with the waves.

Rally glared at Laquan. "You perfect in your pocket?"

"Yes, man." Laquan wiped the sweat from his brow and glanced at the hatch. "All good."

Jonah hauled a large, rolled up sail up from below, and put it on his shoulder. It dangled past his waist, front and back. Putting a foot on the deck of the Autolycus II, he lunged across and carried it below deck.

"Well, thanks for the fresh bait, mate." Laquan patted Rally on the shoulder.

Rally glared at him. "You all *kapoonkle* up, boy. Me and you ain't no company."

Laquan pulled his hand away, looking down.

As the deck hand untied the lines, Rally turned and spit over the rear railing of Laquan's vessel. "Enjoy the bait, friend. All fresh caught." He looked Trinn up and down. "And a good day to you,

Miss. And you, sir." He nodded at DeShear. "Safe travels."

DeShear chewed his lip. "Thanks for the bait."

Rally crossed over to his boat. The engine revved and the vessel pulled away, cutting through the turquoise waters and sending a wave of white out from its bow.

As Laquan rummaged through the bait cooler, the phone in the wheelhouse rang.

"Grab that for me would you, boss?" Laquan held up a handful of frozen shrimp from the cooler. "I need to get these on ice or they be nothing but chum. Got fish goo all over my hands."

DeShear stared at the other fishing boat as its white wake rolled over the water. He glanced at Trinn. "Everything okay?"

"Yeah." She pulled her towel tighter around her, scowling. "That guy was creepy, but I'm fine."

The phone rang again.

"Boss, the phone."

"Yep, got it." DeShear went to the dashboard and picked up the handset. "Hello?"

The phone line was filled with static. "Is this Hamilton DeShear?"

"Yeah." DeShear recoiled.

How did someone find me out here?

"You're a private detective, right?" the man said. "I need you for a case."

"Well, I'm kind of on vacation. Call me again in a week."

The accent isn't Bahamian. Maybe French.

"This is a missing persons case, Mr. DeShear. I think you'll be very interested in it."

A small knot formed in DeShear's abdomen. "Okay, I'll bite. Who's missing?"

"The little girl we just took off your charter fishing boat. I believe you call her Constantine."

DeShear dropped the phone and leaped from the wheelhouse, grabbing the sides of the hatch and hurling himself below. "Constantine?" The door to the front berth was shut. DeShear raced forward, grabbing the knob and pulling. The door didn't budge. "Constantine!" He jerked the knob. The thin door strained at its hinges.

Please let her be in there. Don't let her be gone!

"Constantine!" Gritting his teeth, he pulled again, grabbed the top edge of the door, and broke it open.

Splinters fell from the door latch as he peered inside.

Constantine wasn't there.

A tiny, yellow one-piece bathing suit lay crumpled on the bed, next to the empty shopping bag from the resort.

"Constantine!" DeShear scanned the small berth, yanking the thin mattress from its frame. The storage underneath was filled with mildewed boat lines and threadbare life preservers.

He whipped around, inspecting the dimness of the lower deck. None of the cabinets were big enough for her to hide in; the only other door was to the bathroom. Heart pounding, he raced forward, the flimsy wooden door swinging open and shut with the rocking of the boat. DeShear heaved the door to the wall and looked inside.

She wasn't there.

His pulse throbbed in his ears.

I missed her. She's above deck.

Somehow, I didn't see her go up.

Gunshots rang out. The window next to the bathroom exploded. DeShear hit the floor, glass falling next to him. Another shot put a hole in the side of a cabinet. Sunlight streamed inside.

Two more shots fired, followed by a thump from the deck above.

They're trying to kill us all.

"Trinn!" he shouted. "Get down!"

A chorus of gunfire erupted, filling the walls of the lower deck with holes. Covering his head, DeShear buried his face in the floor. Wood and glass fell around him, followed by pots and pans from the galley, broken coffee cups and fishing reels. Dust and smoke filled the cabin.

When the firing stopped, he leaped to his feet and bolted up the ladder onto the main deck.

The red hull of the Autolycus II bounced over the water, its large motor churning the sea into a white froth.

Trinn lay on the deck, alone, blood seeping over her fingers as she clasped them to the side of her bare midriff. A trickle of blood rolled down her forehead.

"Jaden!" DeShear rushed forward and dropped to his knees, sitting her up and pulling her hands away to inspect her wound. The reek of gasoline filled the air. "Jaden, can you hear me?" Blood trickled from the bullet wound in her side.

Trinn lifted her head, her eyes half open. "I . . . I think I got shot." A trickle of blood ran down her forehead.

DeShear wiped the sweat from his brow.

Constantine is gone. I have to go after her.
But Trinn might be dying.

He pushed her thick hair back to expose a small laceration. "You banged your head on something, too." Grabbing the towel from the bench seat, he pressed it to her side. "Did you see Constantine? Is she on deck up here somewhere?"

His eyes darted over the boat.

Constantine is nowhere in sight, and Trinn is gushing blood.

What do I do? There's no time.

"Constantine . . ." Trinn winced. "She went below. To change."

DeShear shook his head. "They took her— Laquan's friends from the other boat. They had to."

"What!" Trinn leaned forward, grimacing.

"Easy." DeShear put his hands on her shoulders. "Laquan must have gone with them."

We need to get after that boat.

"Did you see anything?" he asked.

"I don't know." Her words came in short bursts as she fought the pain. "When the shooting started . . . I was casting my line. I . . . don't know if I got shot and hit my head or . . . or if it happened the other way around." She leaned her head back, gasping. "I might have blacked out for a second."

"Okay." He glanced at the red boat, speeding away in the distance. "Don't—don't try to talk."

This is bad. Jaden looks rough.

But Constantine's on that boat. Every second we spend here, we're losing the trail.

"Hank, I've been shot before." Trinn gasped. "I'm not dying, I promise. Go after her."

"Yeah, I know you're tough. You'd say that no matter what."

Trinn groaned, wrapping the towel around her side and holding it in place. "Maybe I would, but you have to believe me now. I'm going to pull through this. It's not a fatal wound."

He clenched his jaw, staring at the blood streaming from her side.

"Don't waste time coddling me while Constantine disappears! I won't forgive you if you do that. I love that girl. We have to protect her."

"Okay." DeShear nodded. "Just sit tight." He scrambled to the railing.

As the wake from the Autolycus II reached them, DeShear's charter boat rocked, sending a small wave of gasoline and blood into his knees. Smoke billowed from the bow. Crouching, DeShear peered over the rail. The Autolycus II grew smaller in his sights, but no further gunshots came. Scrambling up the ladder, he jumped into the wheelhouse.

"Do it." Trinn reached up and grabbed the railing. "Let's go!"

DeShear grabbed the wheel and slammed the throttle forward. The engine roared, lurching the boat ahead. He spun the wheel as the bow lifted over the waves.

In the distance, the Autolycus II grew smaller.

"Hang on!" he shouted to Trinn. "This is going to be pretty rough."

"I'm good." She squeezed her eyes shut. Each smack of the hull made her moan.

DeShear raced after the Autolycus II as it headed toward the tiny islands.

They're going to try to lose us in those little islands.

A muzzle flash came from the rear of the red boat. The windshield in front of DeShear shattered.

"Stay down!" He crouched behind the dashboard. "They're shooting again."

"It's just a scare tactic." Trinn hauled herself up, gasping as she sagged onto the bench seat. Her hair whipped around her face. "Most kidnappers want a clean getaway and ransom money. Don't lose them."

He nodded, staying on their trail. The red boat rounded the first island, disappearing behind the brush and low trees. "I'm not sure what we're going to do when we—"

The fiberglass deck in front of him popped like fireworks. Bullet holes riddled the deck. DeShear looked around. More muzzle flashes came from the island, and their bullets slammed into the boat's hull.

DeShear spun the wheel to swerve away, but the engine sputtered and cut out.

"Why are you stopping?" Trinn flung herself to the deck.

"I'm not." DeShear scanned the tiny island for the gunman. "The engine died. Stay down."

Trinn lifted her hand, rubbing her fingers together. "DeShear, there's gas everywhere back here. It's all over the deck." She glanced at the engine. Several bullet holes dotted its side. A trickle of fluid spilled onto the deck. "We're a sitting duck."

"Stay low. If they were kidnappers who wanted to collect a ransom, they wouldn't be shooting at us. So who are they?"

A gust of wind carried the smoke toward them from the bow. It turned black, billowing upwards. Orange flames leaped from the bullet holes in the front deck.

"That's not good." As DeShear jumped down from the wheelhouse, more smoke poured out of the lower hatch. "They sabotaged us. They planted fires somehow before they left."

The leaking gas splashed back and forth with the motion of the boat, washing over Trinn's feet. "Hank! We need to get off this thing!"

"Over the side." He reached to the bench seat and grabbed a life jacket. Smoke engulfed him. He coughed, crawling to Trinn and slipping the jacket over her arm and around her back. "Keep the boat between us and the shooter on that little island." He helped her put her other arm through and clipped the front strap of the old vest. "Ready?"

Trinn gritted her teeth. "Yeah. Help me up."

"We go fast, okay? Don't give the shooter a target." He slid his hands under her arms. "One . . ."

The thick, hot smoke engulfed them.

"Two . . ."

DeShear lowered his head and inhaled deeply.

"Three!"

Lifting Trinn, DeShear took one step and lunged over the side of the boat. The warm waters of the Caribbean crashed around them, a cloud of bubbles rising toward the surface. His shirt and shorts pressed tight to his skin by the water, DeShear broke the surface and grabbed the back of Trinn's life jacket, swimming away from the burning boat.

CHAPTER 7

"Still with me?" DeShear said, treading water. Trinn's head bobbed with every passing wave. "Jaden?"

She groaned, lifting a hand and letting it flop back with a splash. "I'm just . . . I gotta . . ."

"Okay." DeShear pushed through the waves, swimming with the tide. "I've got you. Just talk to me so I know you're awake. I need to put some distance between us and that fire in case it explodes." He pushed through the crystalline water, pulling her by the rear of the life jacket.

"I notice . . . I get shot at a lot around you, DeShear." Eyes closed, a thin smile crossed Trinn's face.

"I noticed you get shot at a lot when I'm not around, too." He swam harder, kicking with the current. "All that smoke will alert other boaters in the area. Maybe the Bahamian Coast Guard. We just need to sit tight. How's your side?"

She groaned. "Saltwater . . . feels so good in an open wound."

"Yeah. Sorry."

Laquan's boat was black with smoke. Huge flames covered the craft from front to back, curling upwards into the sky.

DeShear kept swimming, letting the current help move them away from the burning boat—and the gunman somewhere on the other side.

"Hank." Jaden's face was barely out of the water. "Slow down. Save some energy."

"I'm fine."

"I thought . . . you weren't a good swimmer," she whispered. "You told Constantine . . ."

"I lied." He pulled them through the water with strong strokes. "I was on the swim team and put myself through college working as a lifeguard."

"Then I'm in good hands."

"Maybe. College was a long time ago."

"Hank." She placed her hand on his arm, her eyes barely open. "I . . . stashed some cash . . . the planter box, in front of the hotel. $20,000. If you need it, it's there for you."

"Stop that. You can access it yourself. You're going to make it."

He rolled onto his back, breathing hard as he continued swimming with one arm. Laquan's boat was nothing but an inferno. The upper deck was gone, its fiberglass melting from the heat and collapsing onto the lower deck. Just the burning shell of the hull remained, and a column of thick black smoke stretching upwards across the pale blue horizon.

Panting, DeShear slowed his strokes, certain they were far enough from the gunman.

No one could shoot this far with any accuracy.

He floated on his back and closed his eyes, catching his breath. It had been a while since a gunshot.

His mind flooded with images of Constantine's abduction. The second boat being conveniently nearby after their charter captain accidentally forgot the bait cooler . . .

It was all a set up.

The need for a sail—in the middle of the ocean.

How could I be so stupid?

Constantine has been kidnapped because I let my guard down. Who knows what they'll do to her?

A knot grew in his abdomen.

I have to find her. Whatever it takes, I will save that little girl.

"Hey." Jaden's voice was weak. "Watch it."

DeShear lifted his head from the water. "Watch what?" A wave splashed over his face, filling his mouth. He spit the briny water out, holding his face higher.

Trinn frowned, her eyes closed. "You're . . . kicking me."

DeShear opened his mouth to speak, but stopped. He wasn't swimming at all. He was just floating and trying to catch his breath.

"Hank." Trinn jerked to the side. "Stop."

A jolt went through DeShear's insides.

Kicking?

Bolting upright, he plunged his face under the waves. As the tiny bubbles floated past his view, long, black shadows darted back and forth beneath the surface. Some far away, some not far away enough.

Sharks.

He pulled Trinn close, pressing his hand to her wound. "Hey, let me help you. We need to keep pressure on this."

She yelped.

He put his face in the water again, looking at Trinn's side. Blood clouds curled away between his fingers like thin wisps of red smoke.

Something crashed into him, knocking him upwards. The dark gray V of a fish tail rushed past. DeShear glanced around. A dozen or more sharks circled around them, rippled with the patchy, striped pattern of a tiger shark.

He held his breath. Another dark gray predator turned toward him. Pushing the water down with his hand, he lifted a foot and kicked at the shark's snout. The impact was solid, launching DeShear in the opposite direction and turning the toothy beast away—for now.

He flung his head back, breaking the water and gasping for air. Trinn's head bobbed on the side of her life jacket.

Another shark brushed DeShear's hip.

Sharks sample an unknown item with test bumps.

If they're testing me, they're testing her.

Pretty soon the tests will turn into exploratory bites—especially if the prey is wounded and weak.

Heart thumping, he put his face back in the water. A small shark darted forward, its large black eyes coming toward Trinn's waist. DeShear punched at it, landing a blow along the side of its head.

The fish's skin was like a college linebacker wrapped in sandpaper.

Lifting his face again, DeShear gasped for air and peered at the brush on the distant island. The gunman hadn't fired in a while.

Maybe he's enjoying the show.

Doesn't matter. A chance of getting shot is better than the certainty of getting eaten alive.

DeShear turned around, swimming toward the tiny island. "Jaden, I need you to kick. Swim with me. Can you do that?"

Her head lolled on the side of her life jacket.

Another shark bumped DeShear's leg. He plunged his face under again, kicking at anything that came close. His pulse throbbed in his ears.

They're testing more forcefully. They're getting aggressive.

He thrust hard, pushing them forward. "C'mon, girl. Move your arms and legs. We gotta get to that island."

"Ow!" Trinn thrashed in the water.

The tiny island bobbed on the horizon. Waves splashed over his face.

The sharks are coming too fast. There are too many.

We'll never make it to shore.

Heaving himself forward with every stroke, DeShear dragged Trinn through the waves, staring past the sinking fishing boat. Its hull slipped lower, the black smoke turning white as the saltwater crested the sides and pulled it under. A moment later, only a giant cloud of smoke filled the air where the charter had been.

Straining, DeShear swam harder. The sun shined bright in the clear skies.

He put his face in the water again, kicking at another shark and turning it away. It moved a dozen feet with a flick of its powerful tail, then circled back.

DeShear swallowed hard.

Push. Keep going. Keep fighting.

He broke the surface for a breath of air. A red streak shot across the rising white column of smoke. The tip of a flare glowed bright against the sky.

DeShear glanced to his left. The blue and white hull of a Royal Bahamas Defense Force craft sliced through the water. He threw his hands in the air, shouting. "Here! We're over here!"

The patrol boat continued on its path, headed toward the sunken fishing boat and the cloud of steam that still bubbled up from the water. Another shark crashed into DeShear's leg. He submerged and kicked at it, but it had already passed out of reach.

DeShear surfaced again, splashing and churning the surface, turning the water around him white. "Here! We're over here!"

A shark bumped his arm, knocking his grip from Trinn's life jacket. He threw both hands in the air, kicking hard to stay afloat as he waved. "Over here! Hurry!"

The patrol boat's engines slowed, its bow turning toward him. DeShear swung his arms back and forth. "We're over here!"

The ship revved its loud engines, heading toward them. DeShear swam to Trinn and pulled her close, hugging her forehead to his cheek. "They see us." He gasped, strands of hair in his eyes. "They see us! They're coming, Jaden. Hang in there."

As the vessel approached, a crew member slid behind the gunnery mount at the front of the boat. He swung the barrel of the weapon around and pointed it in DeShear's direction.

"Hey! We're friendly!" A mouthful of saltwater washed into his face. Choking, he hollered. "Don't shoot." The crewman lowered his head to the gun sights, firing off a few rounds. The water around DeShear erupted in splashes. Another wave hit him in the face. He threw a hand in the air, waving as he coughed. "Don't shoot!"

The craft approached, its loud engines cutting back and sending a massive wave over Trinn and DeShear.

"Come, mate." A crewman tossed a life ring into the water. Its red and white rope sailed over DeShear's head as the float splashed behind him. "Grab on," the man said. "We pull you fast."

The man at the bow gun kept his head to the barrel, moving the sights back and forth over the water.

"Don't you mind him, friend. He taking care of tiger shark for you. Come. Hold tight the rope. We got you, fella!"

Grabbing the rope, DeShear put his arm around Trinn's waist and let the ship's crew pull them to safety.

CHAPTER 8

Helena instructed the cab driver to take them to the Palace of Luxembourg. As they arrived at the edge of the expansive gardens, a tour bus dropped off a pack of gray-haired people with cameras and brochures, most of them wearing blue jeans and sneakers.

Kitt paid the fare, then caught up to Helena at the garden gate. "What now?"

The old woman walked along the gravel path in front of the massive limestone buildings. Tourists snapped pictures of the manicured gardens and grounds. "We have a bit of a dilemma. I must go overseas, and I'd like your assistance in collecting my little girl. But I don't have a passport or any identification. It was all taken from me before I arrived at the hospital."

Kitt rubbed her hands together, blowing on them. "That will make things a little more difficult. Maybe they did that for your protection. I don't suppose it would be a good idea to go back to my apartment at the hospital and get mine. Not with kidnappers out there looking for me. They might be watching my friends' places, too."

"And your phone. How else could they find us if your friend didn't tell them?"

A group of teenager girls clustered together in front of a fountain. A petite red head on the end jostled her phone, holding it at arm's length as her friends smiled for the selfie.

"I think Patrice did what she could without giving me up," Kitt said. "But you're right—they found me somehow."

"Perhaps turning off your phone for a while would be a good idea, dear. What can be done to organize a passport?"

Kitt took out her phone and powered it down. "There was a guy I worked with at the hospital." Her breath made little clouds as she spoke. "He asked me out, but he was kind of weird and had a reputation for being a little shady, so I said no. But he might be able to do something."

Helena stopped walking. "He can get us passports?"

"I don't know." Kitt grimaced, staring at the massive ornate palace. "I heard he sold drugs, and somebody told me his friend sold fake IDs to underage kids. But . . . the friend might know something about getting a passport."

Helena tugged the collar of the coat close around her neck. "He stole drugs from the hospital and sold them?"

"He sold recreational stuff to college kids as a side business."

"Goodness." The old woman clasped her hands in front of her, gazing at the massive fountain. A few ducks huddled together at the far side, waddling toward a group of tourists.

They walked among the topiaries and planters, stopping at a long, rectangular basin—a reflecting pool, with a wall of carved statues at the other end.

Kitt stared into the rippling water.

I hate the thought of contacting a creepy guy to get introduced to an even creepier guy.

But Helena seems to believe the little girl is in real trouble.

And I can't think of any other way.

Kitt sighed. "It's a long shot, but the friend might be able to get us passports, or he might know someone who can. I can't begin to guess what something like that would cost, but it's a start." She looked at Helena. "Let's get a taxi and see if we can find him."

A chill swept across the stone pool, carrying the spray from the churning fountains. The old woman's wrinkled fingers held the coat tight around her. "Will you come with me?"

Kitt took a deep breath and let it out slowly, rubbing her temples.

Everything inside her said to say no.

But it wasn't that easy.

"It's been a long, strange day, and you're a very unique woman . . . but the things you've said, they've all been true." She pursed her lips and glanced at Helena. "Let's just say . . . for now, I'm willing to talk about it some more. How's that sound?"

"That sounds brilliant." Helena smiled. "Let's find a taxi."

* * * * *

Kitt took Helena's hand as their cab approached the rear lot of the Pitié-Salpêtrière Hospital. A few smokers were visible across the large lot, near the exit door and along the delivery area.

Sitting in the warm taxi, Kitt checked the driver's meter again, checking the time. "He'll come out soon. He always makes an excuse to come out during smoke breaks. It gives him a chance to chat up the nurses and admin staff. Then he'll network for more business." She tapped the window. "See those boys by the dumpsters? Those are customers, waiting." Digging in her purse, she pulled out some cash. "Let's go."

As the cab drove off, Kitt walked to a row of bushes, rubbing her arms. Helena stood next to her. "Take your coat back, dear. You'll freeze."

Kitt shook her head. "Keep it. I'll be all right for now."

Nodding, Helena looked toward the hospital loading dock. "Doesn't security see what's going on? I'm sure they have cameras."

"I think he pays them to not see him out here." Kitt shrugged. "That's good for us. We don't need to be getting spotted."

"I should say not." Helena glanced around. "I hope—"

"Shh." Kitt pointed. "See the boys going out of their hiding spot? He must be coming." She took Helena's hand. "Let's head there. If we stay along the bushes and fence, we shouldn't be too obvious to anyone. Hurry."

Helena rushed along the sidewalk. "These old bones don't move as fast as you do, dear. Especially in cold weather."

"You're doing fine." Kitt kept her eyes on the rear of the hospital. "We need to get there before he finishes and goes back inside."

A blonde man in hospital scrubs walked toward a cluster of several shorter boys, his coat slung over his shoulder. They grouped together, looking around as they spoke.

One by one, each of the smaller boys peeled off and disappeared behind the dumpsters.

"Hurry, ma'am." Kitt walked faster, letting go of Helena's hand. "He looks like he's finishing business."

"Run on ahead, doctor. I'm right behind."

They neared the end of the hedge row and a set of several dumpsters. The last of the boys finished interacting with the blonde man and walked quickly across the lot in the opposite direction. The blonde man counted his money and shoved it in his pocket, looking around the back lot.

"Go on, Doctor," Helena said. "Before he goes back inside."

Kitt walked faster. "Are you sure?"

"Yes, dear. Please."

The blonde man turned and headed toward the large steel doors.

Kitt broke into a run. *"Attendez!"* She waved her hand, sprinting past the dumpsters. With his hand on the door latch, the blond man stopped and peered over his shoulder. She waved again, crossing the lot to him.

He let go of the handle and turned to her. *"C'est à moi que vous parlez?"*

"Oui." When she reached him, she stopped and put her hands on her sides, gasping. *"S'il vous plaît, j'ai besoin de vous parler."*

"Then we speak in English, *Docteur*." He chuckled. "Your French is very hard on my ears."

Kitt inhaled deeply, trying to catch her breath. "You know me?"

"Oui. You work here. Or, you did. I think I saw an email earlier saying you had been terminated. Insubordination, I believe."

Kitt shook her head. "That figures."

Helena walked up, her hands clasped in front of her.

"This is my friend," Kitt said. "She needs help, too."

"It will be my pleasure, madame." He smiled broadly, putting on his red and black plaid coat. "My name is Jules. How may I be of service?"

* * * * *

The ship's medic lowered his stethoscope from Trinn's chest. "She's in a bad way, friend."

Jaden's face was nearly white as she lay on a cot in the lower deck of the Defense Force boat. An IV tube dangled from her arm, running to a saline bag clipped onto the boat's ceiling. A crewman with a rifle stood guard at the front of the berth.

Still dripping, DeShear held on to a cabinet, a towel around his shoulders. He was exhausted physically and mentally, but his mind raced with information about Constantine's abductors. The red boat. The faded paint. The faces of the crew—any details could be crucial.

But the sight of Trinn, unconscious and weak, blurred his thoughts.

He swallowed hard, unable to speak, staring at her face as the medic tucked a blanket around her and dabbed her face with a damp cloth.

"Some blood loss, and very dehydrated. We have a helicopter standing by at the dock." He faced DeShear, sweat glistening on his forehead. "What about you, friend? How you come to be swimming today?"

The boat sped through the water, jostling Trinn's IV line and heart rate sensor.

DeShear shook his head, trying to focus. "I— I told you, we hired a fishing charter, and the captain met a friend of his to get bait." He pressed the towel to the side of his face, his stomach in knots. "Next thing I know, our little girl is gone and the boat's on fire. You have to send a boat or a plane to scour the area, please. They can't be too far yet."

A lieutenant climbed down the ladder to where DeShear stood. He pulled his uniform collar away from his neck and wiped the sweat with a white handkerchief. "But we don't find your captain. This . . . Laquan fella. Not a hair."

"When I came above deck," DeShear said, "he . . . was gone."

"And your woman." The lieutenant narrowed his eyes. "She is shot and bleeding on the deck. Unconscious, and covered in gasoline."

"That's right."

"So, nobody left on board *unharmed*—except you."

DeShear frowned. "Look, I told you, the crew of the Autolycus II shot our boat up. I was just lucky."

"Lucky. Hmm." The lieutenant stroked his chin, stepping toward Trinn's stretcher. "When we dock, we go talk to Magistrate. We see how lucky he think you are."

"Send another boat out," DeShear said. "Laquan's out there somewhere. They escaped on a boat with a red hull—the Autolycus II, about thirty-five feet long."

The lieutenant's eyes stayed on Trinn. "We already sent another boat to your wreck site, mister. And a third." He wheeled around, glaring at DeShear. "They found some charred fiberglass from the boat's hull, but they don't find your Captain Laquan. Maybe the sharks get him—like they almost get your lady friend."

"I don't know." Sweat formed on DeShear's brow. "I was doing my best to keep us from getting introduced to the sharks."

"My man says when he spotted you, you were not close to the woman. You swam up next to her only after we saw you."

"I was holding her. But . . . we got knocked apart."

"By the shark."

"That's right."

"Yes. You already tell me that story upstairs." The lieutenant walked past DeShear. "I think my boss, he needs to hear it. About how we found a man in the water, his woman almost dead, his little girl gone and his captain missing, his boat all burned up . . . and a magical story about guns and kidnapping and mischief." He faced DeShear again, leaning close, his voice a whisper. "That is some wild story."

"I—I'm telling you the truth." A bead of sweat rolled down DeShear's cheek. He leaned on the cabinet, his head buzzing. "We . . . we went fishing, and—"

"Fishing!" The lieutenant pointed out the hatch to the open sea. "This is Bahamas, man! We don't get no trouble like that. I worked on this ocean fifteen years. When we find a wreck, we find supplies from the boat. Life vests, fishing gear, coolers, trash, shoes—but not when we found you. We didn't see no bait cooler in the wreckage, no beer cooler. We didn't find no trash, we didn't find no sail."

"The kidnappers took the sail."

"You said your charter was supposed to go all day, but my men didn't even find your picnic lunch." He paced back and forth, stroking his chin. "Maybe the fire got it, mister. That fire sent a column of thick black smoke into the sky and burned everything up— all the evidence that supports your story."

"Maybe it . . . floated away." His shoulders slumped. "I don't know."

"Maybe." The lieutenant nodded. "Maybe it burned, maybe it float away—you think so? But I think maybe you killed the captain and the little girl. And maybe you shot the woman and burned the boat, but she didn't die yet. Maybe my men found you on the water right before you finished her off."

DeShear balled his hands into fists. "No."

"Tell me now!" He pounded the wall. "Make it easy on yourself."

"We were attacked!" DeShear shouted. "They shot at everyone."

"Not the child."

"They kidnapped her! They called me on the ship's radio."

"A ghost ship!" The lieutenant's forehead glistened with sweat, a vein throbbing in his neck. "No one ever heard of this ship, Autolycus II. But it called you on a radio that burned up in the fire? Either way, nothing exists now. No radio, no ghost ship."

"Why would I put myself in the water with the sharks?"

The lieutenant gritted his teeth, jabbing DeShear in the chest. "You watch yourself, mister. You are not in United States now. Here, on the water, I am the law." He looked DeShear in the eye, lowering his voice. "I think there a reason this all happened, and I think I'll keep looking until I find out what it is. Maybe you knew a big smoky fire would get seen quick-quick from my men and you only jumped in after you saw them coming."

"No!"

"I think yes. The woman, she is in bad shape. All dehydrated. How did that happen to her and not you?"

"She hit her head."

"Yes. Very bad luck happened to everyone—everyone but you. But now you listen to me. I know these waters. I've lived on these waters my whole life. If the sharks didn't eat that captain and little girl, we're gonna find them. They'll come floating up, bloated and nasty, and drift into the shipping lane or catch on the reef at low tide . . . but we're gonna find them, mister. Then we'll see what kind of story you tell." He looked at the crewman at the front of the berth. "Put the handcuffs on him. Lock him to the rear deck."

"No," DeShear shouted. "I didn't do anything!"

The crewman stowed his rifle and pulled out a pair of handcuffs.

"We're gonna take you to the Magistrate," the lieutenant growled. "See what he thinks of your story. Me, I'm done with you. My guess is, he sends you to Pearl Island. Twenty years of busting rocks for the new road from Freeport to East End Lodge."

"I didn't do anything."

"Then you will fit right in." He sneered. "Every man on Pearl Island is innocent. Just ask them, they'll tell you." Laughing, the lieutenant climbed the stairs to the mid deck. As the boat lowered its engines, he looked over his shoulder at DeShear. "Pray your lady doesn't die from her gunshot, or Pearl Island gonna be a sweet dream compared to where the Magistrate sends you."

The boat sidled up to a dock at a large marina, and the crewman brought DeShear up from below. A helicopter sat waiting on a field in front of a resort, its blades chopping the air

As Trinn was loaded onto a stretcher, two police officers stepped forward.

The lieutenant glared at DeShear. "These bobbies take you to tell your story again, mister lucky man. Maybe you convince the Magistrate your fairy tale is true."

The police officers grabbed DeShear by the arms, pulling him toward a waiting squad car. DeShear yanked an arm free, turning toward the helicopter. "Trinn!"

The medics opened the helicopter door, collapsing the folding legs of the stretcher and lifting it onto the edge of the cargo bay.

"Trinn!" DeShear strained against the officers.

"Hold him." One of the officers reached for his baton.

DeShear jerked his arm free again, twisting away and falling to the ground. He rolled away, putting his hands on the grass and thrusting himself to his feet.

The officer unclipped his baton and raised it over his head. "Stop!"

DeShear raced for the helicopter. The medics slid Trinn's stretcher into the cargo bay and secured it. The pilot stood behind them, holding the cargo bay door.

Lowering his shoulder, DeShear rammed the pilot and knocked him to the ground. The door bounced into the medics. Grabbing it, DeShear heaved the door open and shoved the medics aside.

"Jaden—you have to find the old woman. You know the one I mean." The medics grabbed DeShear. "You have to get to her," he said. "If they found Constantine, they'll find her. She's not safe. None of us are."

The medics pulled him away from the door.

"Trinn, can you hear me?"

As the officer with the baton reached DeShear, the pilot joined the fray, wrapping his arms around DeShear and dragging him away from the helicopter.

"Trinn!"

The pilot drove a fist into DeShear's gut as the baton cracked against his skull. He fell to the ground, peering into the cargo bay door.

As the door slid shut, Trinn's hand lifted from the side of the stretcher. She gave him a thumbs up.

The police and crew of the Defense Force boat descended on DeShear, beating him until he stopped fighting.

CHAPTER 9

The Honorable Charles McCullough swept through the hot, humid hallway, the dark robes of the magistrate flowing behind him. Outside, the setting sun cast long shadows over the grounds. "Lieutenant Moray. A word, if you will, please."

The Defense Force lieutenant jumped up from the wooden bench in the hallway, leaving a bloody DeShear on the floor at the feet of two armed crewman.

As the door shut to the Magistrate's tiny stuffy office, he stepped behind his cluttered desk, eyeing the second door to the anteroom. It moved slightly in the breeze as the magistrate's small fan spun near the window, exchanging the stale office air for the cooler breezes that came with the sunset.

Lieutenant Moray stood at attention in front of the desk.

"I have a concern, Lieutenant." McCullough removed his white wig and placed it on the stand on his credenza, rubbing his ebony scalp. "You have brought me an issue that would be best not to deal with at the moment."

Moray remained at attention. "Sir?"

"Your prisoner. This . . . Hamilton DeShear." He fluffed his robes, fanning himself. "Our immigration records show he is in our country under a provision of the British and French governments—a matter of some secrecy that I am not fully privy to and that *he* may not even be fully aware of. However, the issue is before us nonetheless."

"I don't follow, sir."

"No, I suspect you don't." McCollough tilted his head back, taking a deep breath. "What is your reckoning of this man—this Hamilton DeShear?"

"He says he was in a boating accident, Your Honor. I have reason to believe otherwise."

"Based on what evidence?"

Moray frowned. "His story is so full of holes, it is more like swiss cheese than an alibi. When his woman regains consciousness, she'll tell us what happened. Then we hang that mister by the neck from the yardarm."

"Hang him?" Taking a handkerchief from his pocket, McCollough wiped his brow. "That's what you think we should do?"

"Yes, sir."

"That's because you're a bloody fool, Moray!" The Magistrate threw his handkerchief onto the desk. "Did you not listen? The man is on the island at the request of—and as a favor to—the governments of Great Britain and France!" He pointed to the door. "And he's in my hallway, beaten to a pulp. This is quite a mess you've created and brought to my door."

Moray shifted on his feet.

"I think you should clean up your mess, Lieutenant." McCollough glanced at the anteroom door. "I think this whole unfortunate incident would be better if it had never happened—do you take my meaning?"

"I do, sir." Moray swallowed hard. "But how?

Folding his arms, the Magistrate paced back and forth in the tiny office. "Have you filed a report?"

"Not yet, sir. We came straightaway after subduing the prisoner at the port."

"Subduing." McCollough snorted, putting a hand to his lips. "Here is what I propose. I shall call your superior and have the crews of the three boats split up and reassigned. From there, it will be a simple matter of getting rid of the final piece of . . . *evidence*." He peered at the lieutenant. "A man goes on a fishing trip, he gets lost at sea, and no one knows what happened. But he never came here, understand?"

The lieutenant shifted on his feet.

"Do you understand me, Lieutenant?"

"I do, Your Honor."

There was a knock on the door. The magistrate's clerk stuck his head in. "Sir, I have the information you requested."

"Good, Prenley. Come in."

A petite man with round spectacles entered the office. "My associate at the customs house says the passports were for three people—the man, the woman in the hospital, and a small child."

"We already knew that, you imbecile." McCullough waved a hand. "What is the reason for their special provision?"

"I haven't learned that yet, sir." Prenley adjusted his glasses. "But I was able to gather something else that may be of interest to you. It seems the girl is the benefactor of a legal trust."

The Magistrate eyed his clerk. "Is that so?"

"And I found this next bit to be especially intriguing," Prenley said. "According to my man, there was quite a good bit of paperwork filed in London. The net of it seems to be that in the event of the child's death, the new benefactor is the current executor of the trust. A Mr. Hamilton DeShear, of Tampa, Florida, in the United States of America."

McCullough's jaw dropped. "Cor, blimey."

"He killed the lot to take the girl's inheritance!" Moray pounded his fist into his hand. "I knew it."

"Prenley . . ." The magistrate looked at his clerk. "How much?"

"The filings are a bit dodgy on that, sir." The clerk adjusted his glasses again, peering at a piece of paper in his hand. "The price of stocks fluctuate, you know. But I was able to get an estimate from a friend at the London Exchange."

"And?"

"In U.S currency, the girl is worth approximately . . . three billion dollars, sir."

"Three . . ." The magistrate collapsed into his chair. "Blimey."

The lieutenant winced, sweat rolling down the side of his face.

"Three billion dollars." McCullough stared at the ceiling, but his focus seemed far way. His hands fell to his sides. "All entrusted to a little girl."

Prenley nodded. "And her trustee, sir."

"That's good work." The Magistrate sat up, straightening his collar. "Fine work, my boy. Now be a good lad and wait outside for us. I've, uh . . . not finished with the lieutenant."

"Yes, Your Honor." The clerk opened the door.

"And Prenley."

"Sir?"

The magistrate leaned onto his desk. "Not a word of this to anyone."

"Right, sir." The door shut.

McCullough stared at Moray. "Well, this changes things, doesn't it, Lieutenant?"

"Yes, sir," the lieutenant said. "I . . . I shall apologize to the prisoner at once—I mean, apologize to Mr. DeShear at once and—and take him to hospital, of course. Then, I'll . . . resign my commission."

"What!"

Moray knitted his hands together. "A man with that kind of money could squash me like a bug, sir."

"Are you mental?" The Magistrate stood. "What about your suspicions of him being a murderer?"

"It seems a man with three billion dollars and the connections to get a special provision may very well be a man who gets away with murder, sir."

"Interesting." McCullough stroked his chin. "I was thinking just the opposite."

"Sir?"

"Look here." He cracked the door open an inch. "See him there, on the floor? His shirt is straight from the shop at the resort—and well enough. But his shoes are from a discount house. This is not a man with three billion dollars."

Moray peered over the magistrate's shoulder. "No?"

"No. He doesn't know about the money yet. He can't." McCullough stood, closing the office door. "Prenley asked about this DeShear fellow at the resort. He's a low life private investigator who didn't have a bank account on the island until a man from Lloyds of London delivered a reward to the hotel a few days ago. He'd been scraping by until then. He and the woman have paid for everything in cash. Not very typical for an American on vacation. Now, what to do?" He picked up his gavel and twirled it between his fingers, glancing at the anteroom door. It swayed a bit, barely moving in the breeze of the little fan. "I think we carry on."

Moray gawked at the Magistrate. "Sir?"

"Yes, I think we make this whole mess go away." He paced around the little office again. "Gather him up, disperse the crew, and take him to one of your special garbage disposal places—by yourself, of course."

Shoulders back, the lieutenant kept his eyes straight ahead. "I don't think I know what you mean, sir."

"Don't take me for a fool, Moray!" McCullough wheeled around, glaring at the lieutenant. "You've worked the seas for more than a decade, and I've worked the courts for twice that. I'm sure you're aware that our tiny tourist trap occasionally needs to make a problem disappear. Simply collect that bit of rubbish in my hallway and move it to another locale. One with an . . . *understanding* of such things. And whose officers of the guard will dispose of an issue for a small fee."

Moray looked at the Magistrate. "Haiti?"

He waved a hand. "Doesn't matter to me. Just make your issue go away. I'm not having a billionaire bring in a high-powered defense team from the United States to embarrass me and this entire island nation on television, I can tell you that. I'm a year removed from my pension. I shan't be swindled out of it by the likes of him—or by your incompetence. No, your prisoner needs to remain just that—a prisoner. He needs to go far, far away, and quickly." He gazed at Moray. "Tell me, what does a trip to Pearl Island cost?"

"About a thousand dollars U.S., sir."

McCullough nodded. "Then for two thousand, you should be able to find the ugliest, nastiest place there is on earth and get him there by first light." He sat down, folding his hands on the top of the desk. "And I should never hear the name Hamilton DeShear again.

* * * * *

The Magistrate peered through his window as Lieutenant Moray loaded a semi-conscious DeShear into a Defense Force truck and drove away.

He stepped away from the window, wiping the sweat from his brow.

The anteroom door opened, and an Asian man in a cream-colored suit emerged, fanning himself with a beige Panama hat.

McCullough sat behind his desk. "What do you think?"

"It's hard to say, Your Honor." The man loosened his tie from his sweat-soaked collar. "I was a bit confused at that last part. Send the man away who controls the money?"

"Seems perfectly rational to me, Mr. Twa. The girl is of value, not him. If he dies, she retains the money. Surely we can deal with that." The magistrate reached into his lower desk drawer, retrieving a bottle of Hennessy and setting it on the cluttered desk.

"Better than using her for a harvest?" Twa sat in one of the old wooden chairs and crossed his legs. "I think not, Charles. Right now, her stem cells and bone marrow will bring millions each month. In a few years, there will be eggs that will be worth tens of millions."

McCullough set two shot glasses next to the cognac. "Which is still less than three billion, by my calculation."

Twa looked away, fanning himself. "My investors will not be happy."

"I think you're missing the bigger picture, Armen. Constantine is a genetically engineered human with genes that will never get cancer, never get Alzheimer's . . . Her stem cells and bone marrow will cure diseases, her children will carry her magnificent cerebral enhancements. People will want that. Rich people. So, I think you should present your investors with a new proposal—a few billion today *and* all their millions from bone marrow and stem cells each month, *plus* tens of millions more when she becomes of age."

"I see." A smile stretched across Twa's face. "They might go for that."

"I'm sure they will." McCullough filled the glasses and set one down in front of his guest. "And all I ask is a ticket off this rock and a modest finder's fee of ten percent. Surely, the great and powerful Armen Twa can arrange that."

"Ten percent of several billion dollars? That is quite a fee."

"It is indeed." McCullough picked up the other glass and leaned back in his chair. "Take the girl as you originally planned, and keep her there while you talk to your investors—or should we auction her to the highest bidder?"

"My dear friend, let us move slowly now. The Pacific rim is not like the Caribbean. There are ancient customs to be considered. Governments to bribe. Powerful people that must be bowed to. What you are proposing crosses into . . . dangerous territory."

McCullough scowled. "No more dangerous than it was when you came to me and asked for my help in finding the girl. I've done more than my part by arranging for her to be collected by smugglers and having the proof destroyed, as well as dispatching that fool Moray to rid you of the current pebble in your shoe—your Mr. DeShear."

"You are well connected after so many years of sending smugglers to jail from your muggy little courtroom. We appreciate it." Picking up his glass, Twa raised it to his lips—but stopped. "What about the woman?"

"A loose end, nothing more. Moray said she lost a lot of blood." The Magistrate downed his drink in one gulp. "I think it will surprise no one when she dies in her sleep tonight."

CHAPTER 10

In the front of the taxi, Jules typed a text message and sent it.

"Is that to your friend?" Kitt asked.

Next to her in the back seat, Helena sat quietly, kneading her hands as the cab bounced over the uneven street of outer Paris.

"Oui. And you are in luck, *Madame Docteur.* We can get a passport for you and your friend. Maybe it cost a few Euros, but such is life, eh?"

"Did he say how much?"

Jules turned to face her. "As you may think, these things, they are not cheap. But let us wait until we have the price, then we can negotiate. I'm sure your salary will be able to pay what is required."

Kitt snorted. "You aren't familiar with Dr. Dechambeau's pay scale."

The residences became smaller and smaller, until the car was driving through the open fields of farmland.

Helena shifted on her seat. "Is it much farther?"

"It is just here." Jules nudged the driver. *"Arrêtez la voiture près de l'ancien bâtiment. Il y a un pub. Garez-vous derrière."*

"Oui, monsieur." The cab slowed down, and the driver put on his turn signal.

Kitt understood enough of the brief conversation to know that Jules has said to park behind an old building, and that there was a pub. She craned her neck to see over the driver's shoulder. A few structures were up ahead—a large old building and a few smaller ones.

That must be the place.

Located so far from everything, the old building didn't seem like it was a business of any sort. Weeds grew around the sides; the windows were dark.

"Are . . . we meeting your friend here?" Kitt put a hand to her lip.

"Yes, yes." Jules leaned toward the windshield, licking his lips. "We meet in the back."

The cab parked behind the building. Jules counted out some cash and handed it to the driver. *"Pas besoin d'attendre. Gardez la monnaie."*

The driver grinned. *"Oui, monsieur. Merci beaucoup!"*

The hairs on the back of Kitt's neck stood up.

Keep the change. No need to wait?

What if his friend doesn't show?

Jules opened the door and stepped out, walking to the far side of the gravel lot. A rusty, broken down tractor with a missing wheel stood in the corner. "Come, ladies."

"Do we go?" Kitt turned to Helena. "Is it safe?"

Trembling, the old woman shook her head. "I don't know, dear. But I must do whatever I can to get to my little girl."

The driver looked at Kitt in the rearview mirror. "If you wish to wait in the car, *c'est très bien*—but the fare, it must continue, *mademoiselle*." He put his hand on the meter.

"My friend comes now, *docteur*." Jules pointed, climbing onto the tractor. "Come, see."

The driver looked at Kitt. *"Mademoiselle?"*

Sitting on the tractor, Jules looked past the old building and waved his arm in the air. *"Tiens, mon ami!"*

She turned around and peered through the back window. No cars were visible in the fading light. The knot in her stomach grew.

"Mademoiselle." The driver frowned. *"S'il vous plaît. Décidez."*

Jules continued waving. *"Tiens! Tiens!"* He hopped off the tractor.

Kitt looked through the rear window again. The dust from the old road cast a white-gray cloud into the air as a vehicle approached. A truck possibly, or some sort of van.

"I guess his friend is here." She faced Helena, swallowing hard. "Do you see anything? Anything at all?"

"I'm sorry, dear."

Kitt took a deep breath and clasped Helena's hand. "Then we—we'll go together. It may be our only chance."

Opening the door, Kitt lowered a foot onto the gravel and crept out of the cab. As Helena followed, the noise of the approaching vehicle grew louder.

"Yes, yes. Come." Jules walked toward them. "There is nothing to fear here. We are all friends." He smiled the same way he did when he was doing his drug deals behind the hospital. "This is simply how we must do these things."

The setting sun shrouded the car in a brown silhouette against a bright yellow background, with acres of tilled dirt beyond.

As the van stopped, the side door slid open. A wide smile crossed Jules' face. "Thank you for coming, my friend."

An athletic woman carrying a shopping bag stepped from the van.

"Ladies," Jules said. "Allow me to introduce you to Miss Franklin."

The woman pulled a gun from the bag and pointed it at Kitt and Helena.

Jules laughed. "She will be taking very good care of you!"

CHAPTER 11

DeShear's ribs throbbed and his shoulders ached. The pulsing pain from his lower lip was only exceeded by the pounding in his head. His wrists were handcuffed over his head and tied to the side of the wheelhouse railing. Wincing, he got his feet underneath himself and managed to ease the pressure off his arms for a few moments.

"Your diesel is coming now, Louis." Moray's brother lifted a fuel hose from another boat and dragged it to the rear of the vessel. "We'll fix you up quick-quick. Get you out of here."

"Aye, mate. Thanks much." The lieutenant looked at DeShear. "And you're doing good, mister. Keep quiet or my baton will come visit you again."

As the other boat pulled away from the dock, DeShear stared at Moray in the near-darkness. His captor, now in plain clothes, was only visible through one eye—DeShear's other eye was too swollen to see out of. The lieutenant stood at the helm of his scuba diving boat, checking the gages, his military baton resting on the far side of the dashboard.

"He's lying to you," DeShear wheezed, his lungs shooting pain up his sides with every breath. "Your Magistrate. Whatever he told you about me, it isn't true."

Moray's sweaty brow shined in the green light of the instrument panel. "What you say don't make a difference, mister. I know what I know, and the Magistrate agrees." He went to the rear of his boat, where a row of scuba diving tanks had been lashed to the stern, and peered into the fuel tank. "Fill both tanks tonight, Monty."

"Long trip, eh?" Moray's brother said. "I won't ask where you're going. I'll just ask you to be careful."

DeShear blinked hard, trying to get the blood out of his eye. "What is it you think you know, Lieutenant?"

"I done told you once." Picking up a clipboard, Moray made a note and returned to the wheelhouse. He tossed the clipboard onto the dusty dashboard next to his baton holster. "Now, we don't talk about it again."

A bead of sweat rolled down the side of DeShear's face. "What if I can prove what I said?"

Grabbing a diving mask off the dashboard, Moray carried it to the rear of the boat and put it in a bucket of sudsy water.

"Oh, you don't care about the truth," DeShear said. "You just care about getting paid."

"Stop your talking. It will be time to go soon." Moray folded his arms, gazing toward the ocean. "It's rough water out there. You'd best hang on tight or you'll get hurt."

"Thanks for the warning. Where was that when I was at the helicopter?" Grimacing, DeShear shifted his weight. The steel handcuffs dug into his wrists. "You know, you and your boys had a good time using me as a punching bag when there were four of you. What about when it's just one? How tough are you then, Lieutenant?"

Moray shook his head. "Get your last digs in, mister. These engines are loud, and we're running at top speed tonight."

"Moray, did your Magistrate tell you I had $250,000 in the hotel safe?"

"Ah, such lies." The lieutenant chuckled. "I'll be happy when you stop this yakkety yak."

DeShear wiped his cheek with his shoulder. "He didn't, did he? But he must have known. It was the talk of the hotel. How do you think he found out? Why else would he ask you to get rid of me? So he can keep the cash all for himself."

"Such fantastic tales you tell, mister. You must be part sailor, to spin stories that good."

"Of course, you can't trust me," DeShear said. "But can you trust him? Your Magistrate? If I'm telling you the truth, you could be a rich man. And if I'm lying, you're out an extra hour of time." He stared at Moray. "I don't know what he's paying you, but it can't be $250,000 a night."

"Maybe you have money, maybe you don't. Nothing says it's gonna be there when I show up." He walked back to the wheelhouse, looking at the instruments on the dashboard. "Maybe the police will be waiting there for me. What about that?"

"Yeah, that's a problem," DeShear said. "If you go alone. But if I went with you—"

Moray whipped around, glaring at DeShear, his nose an inch from his prisoner's face. "Then you holler in the lobby about how I kidnapped you and I get all kinds of locked up. No thank you, mister. I'll be just fine on my boat tonight." He lowered his voice. "Long trip, but in the morning . . . *you'll be gone.*"

Sighing, DeShear sagged into the wall, his head hanging. "Pearl Island?"

"Ha. No, friend. That's a dream now. A bad island is taking you." Moray sat in the captain's chair, resting an elbow on the dashboard. "Haiti, at a little place called Jean-Rabel. I hear, down in Jean-Rabel, the sun is so hot, it fries a man's skin right off, quick-quick. They got a work camp where they bust the coral with a hammer. Gets so a man's arms get big, but his brain gets small. All day, a man be hammering. Then, at night, that's the real fun. Them old boys at Jean-Rabel, they play them some guntuu. You know guntuu?"

DeShear looked down. "Can't say I do."

"Ha, mister." Moray smiled. "This is the best part about Jean-Rabel. They bring the *acullico*—the coca leaf—from central America. Honduras, Nicaragua . . . and them boys chew it all day. Don't get hungry, don't get tired, just work on busting that coral. Comes night time, the bobby place bets and the men go at it. Two by two, they fight—bare knuckle—until just one is left at the morning. That man, he's the winner. He gets a cold drink, mister. That, and a day in the shade, to watch the other men bust the coral." Moray picked up the pencil from the clipboard and tucked it behind his ear. "After two, three weeks, a man says he'd rather die than go bust the coral anymore. Can't take no more guntuu. He just sets his hammer down and walks into the sea, don't never come back no more." He leaned forward, whispering, pointing the pencil at DeShear. "That's your home, come tomorrow. And I'll be glad to see you go, mister. Because I think you killed that captain and that girl, and you tried to kill that woman. And I want you to think, every day when you're busting the coral with your hammer, and every night when you fight in the guntuu, *Moray put me here*." He glared at DeShear. "You think of me every night until you walk into the sea and never come back no more."

Monty lifted the fuel hose. "Boat's all filled up, Louis. Both tanks."

Putting the hose back in the pump, Monty stared at DeShear then put his hand on the ignition key.

"I have a story for you," DeShear said.

"I already heard your story, mister. It's time you stopped talking now."

Heat rose to DeShear's cheeks. "There's a little girl out there, and she's alive. I don't care what you do to me. I don't care about the money in the hotel. But she's out there, and I'm going to find her." He leaned toward the lieutenant, straining against his handcuffs. "If that means I have to go through you and every man on Jean-Rabel, that's what's going to happen. But that girl is in danger because of me, and I'm going to find her and get her out of it."

Moray's eyes remained fixed on the dark water stretching out in front of his vessel. "That's a fine speech, mister. But like I said . . ." He slipped the baton out of the holster and raised it over his head. "It's time you stopped talking now."

CHAPTER 12

Miss Franklin sat backwards on a folding chair near the front of the old building, her gun in her hand, staring at her two hostages. Her other associates were somewhere else in the warehouse, but Jules had long departed.

Franklin leaned to the side, taking a phone from her back pocket. "Hello?" She listened for a moment, then ended the call. "They're here." Looking past where Helena and Kitt sat, Franklin called out. "Mr. Washington, go ahead and open the big door. Mr. Jefferson, there's a yellow electrical cable over there somewhere. If you wouldn't mind locating that . . ."

"Yep. Got it," a man behind them said.

The door opened with a rumble, and a chilly breeze swept through the vacant building. Franklin stood, crossing her arms. A light passed over her, throwing a large shadow onto the stone wall behind her. Kitt peered over her shoulder as a flatbed truck loaded with wooden shipping crates rolled to a stop. Dust followed, carried by the wind.

A thin, dark-haired man got out of the passenger side of the truck, walking toward Franklin. He stopped, gazing at Helena and Kitt through Coke bottle glasses, putting his hand to his mouth. "Is . . . is this them?"

Franklin glared at him. "Just set up your stuff, Doctor."

"Yes, ma'am." He rushed to the back of the truck, glancing again at the two prisoners. "Yes, yes. Right away."

Washington and Jefferson walked to the vehicle, hauling the boxes down.

"Careful!" The doctor gasped. "Careful, you . . . *apes*. That is full of very delicate instruments."

Behind him, Franklin huffed. "You wanna unload it yourself?"

The doctor peered at her, his hands trembling. "No. No, ma'am, I do not."

She walked toward him. "Doctor, my friends and I are here as a favor to Mr. Hollings. When he gets here, I'm sure he'd like to see everything operational and ready to go."

"H—Hollings is coming here?" The thin man backed away. "Doctor Dechambeau didn't say anything about that."

"It must've slipped his mind. Now, I'm going to go make some phone calls outside. How long does this stuff take to set up?"

"Oh, an hour, miss. Maybe a little more. We need to calibrate the—"

"Hollings will be here in thirty minutes." Franklin glanced at her phone. "I'd say he'll want it up and running by then. I'm sure you don't want to disappoint him" She brushed past him, tucking her gun in her belt.

"Yes, yes, ma'am. Yes." He turned to Washington and Jefferson. "You heard her. Move it!"

Jefferson squared his shoulders, narrowing his eyes.

The doctor backed away. "Uh . . . please."

Another vehicle drove toward the flatbed, washing it in light. Kitt turned to see an ambulance. The driver turned off the headlights and cut the motor.

"Boys." Franklin walked to the ambulance and opened the door. "Little help, here."

Washington and Jefferson went to the ambulance and lifted out a fat man on a collapsible stretcher.

"Sorry, doc," Franklin said. "Hollings got here early."

The driver climbed out of his seat, going through the ambulance and grabbing a folding wheelchair. Jumping to the ground, he opened the chair as the fat man swung his legs over the side of the stretcher. With Washington and Jefferson under each arm, the fat man slid into the wheelchair and pushed himself away from the vehicle. The doctor reached into the van and withdrew a walking cane, placing it gently onto the arms of the wheelchair, then scurried away.

The fat man rolled to the front of the old building, turning to stare at Miss Franklin's two guests. A smile crossed his portly, unshaven face as his eyes met Helena's. "Madam." His British accent was thick. "How nice to see you again."

Helena sat silent, her hands trembling in her lap.

The man's gaze went to Kitt. "And you would be Dr. Kittaleye. It's a pleasure, lass. I've come to learn quite a bit about you these past few days."

The knot in Kitt's stomach surged again.

I'm sure I've never met this man before. How would he have heard anything about me?

"Aye. Received a great deal of information about you, I have. From your new friend Helena. Or as I like to refer to her, Keeper 27." He pushed his wheelchair closer, leaning forward and letting his stale breath assault Kitt's nose. "And in just a few minutes, we'll be learning a good bit more."

"We got kind of a late start," Franklin said. "Dr. Freeman here says he needs an hour to set up."

"Freeman." Hollings scowled, drumming his fingers on the cane. "Worthless as the spots on a goat's rump. But he knows how to run the equipment, so he gets to stay a while longer." He glared at Helena. "Now, it's my understanding you two are in need of passports. And just where might you be wanting to go, old woman?"

Helena remained rigid. Her eyes were open, but unfocused, staring toward the stone wall at the front of the building.

Hollings chuckled. "Do you see how she does that, Miss Franklin? Quite a trick, wouldn't you say?"

"What's the trick?" Franklin lowered her head to see Helena's face.

"She's gone standalone. It's like sleeping, but it don't generate no dreams. She's doing that to avoid answering me."

Franklin waved her hand in front of Helena's face. "How long does that last?"

"A few minutes, a few hours . . . a week—it lasts as long as the stubborn cow wants it to, but don't worry. I've a remedy. Do you have your firearm on you, Miss?"

Franklin nodded. "I do."

"Aye, very well. If you'd be so kind as to place it at the back of this young doctor's head." He smiled at Kitt. "Fully loaded, of course."

"Of course." Franklin pulled her gun from her belt and walked behind Kitt.

"Now . . ." Hollings rubbed the scruffy stubble on his chin. "It's my thinking the old bird will awaken herself right quick if you were to pull that trigger, Miss Franklin—such a loud noise and all, eh? The thing is, will she do it *before* you pull the trigger?"

Kitt swallowed hard. "Please, sir . . ."

"That's it, flower." He winked at Kitt. "You tell your friend to wake up."

"Don't hurt me," Kitt pleaded. "I—I don't know anything."

"That's where you're wrong, Doctor." Hollings drummed the cane again. "You know what she knows—if you want to. Has the old woman been acting at all like she could read your mind?"

Kitt sat frozen, her mouth hanging open.

"Yeah, I'd say she has, based on that look on your face. What you don't know is, she ain't been reading nothing. It's *you* what's been *telling* her. Bit of a difference, but same result." He raised a finger, jabbing it toward Kitt. "And right now, you're telling her you're about to get your pretty little brains blasted all over the floor of this barn. We just need to see if she hears you." He glanced at Franklin. "Best cock that pistol, Miss."

Franklin cocked her handgun.

"Aye, that's it." He lifted his chin. "Bit more drama if she feels the cold steel of that muzzle up against her head, eh?"

Franklin pressed the gun to the back of Kitt's head.

"And now, ladies and gentlemen . . ." Hollings held his hands out, brandishing his cane like a ringmaster at a circus. "On the beat of three, I shall watch as the lovely Miss Franklin pulls the trigger on her .38 caliber handgun and ends the young doctor's life in a most horrific fashion. Eyeballs will bulge, mates. Hair goes flying in chunks—skull attached, naturally. Maybe a few teeth will land at your feet, all bloody and pulpy and the like. And of course, lots of chunky, gooey brains, bleeding like bits of wet sponge right here on the floor—so those of you in the first row, eyes open, eh?" He peeked over his shoulder at Washington and Jefferson. "Don't want to stand too close, boys. Mess up your trousers." He put his cane in his lap and rolled his wheelchair backward a few feet. Lowering his voice, he peered at Franklin. "Have you ever smelled fresh brains, miss?"

"Missed out on that, somehow," Franklin said.

"Barely a smell at all." Hollings' voice was lyrical, like he was spinning a story for a child at bedtime. "Like a whiff of bread baking at a neighbor's house down the lane, and carried to you on the wind—but with a hint of the stench from back of the butcher's shop. Best see that you don't get none on you, Miss. Hard to get out, for all the oils." Looking over his shoulder again, he waved the cane at the others. "And you'll be next, you lot, if you don't get that gear set up. Now get to it!"

Washington resumed unpacking Dr. Freeman's equipment. Jefferson set up a folding table and placed a computer on top of it.

"Back to you, lass," Hollings said. "It's counting time. If I get to three before your Helena pipes up, Miss Franklin stops all your worries the hard way—with a 200-gram piece of lead." He sneered, rubbing his hands together. "Ready, steady . . . One."

Gasping, Kitt clasped her hands together. "Please, no."

"Two . . ."

The men stopped unpacking the crates, staring at the scene. Kitt turned to Helena. "Help me! Please!"

Hollings leaned forward, grinning. "Thr—"

Helena blinked, her eyes fluttering open. She faced her captor. "Mr. Hollings?"

"Yes, Keeper 27?"

She straightened up, her hands still in her lap. "How may I be of service?"

Hollings sat back in the wheelchair. "When my men get that gear set up, you're going to strap on a cap like the old days and let me see what's been going on inside that old gray noggin of yours. Then we'll find the little girl and get everything back on track."

"Do you mean to run things, then?" Helena asked.

"Me? Run Angelus Genetics and Hauser's operation?" Hollings laughed. "No. We both know I don't got the brains for that. But as it turns out, a wealthy Asian investor does—and he's keen on following through on a deal what was set up between him and Dr. Hauser but ain't been fully transacted, as it were. Maybe you know him—Armen Twa."

Helena didn't react.

"Playing your game again, eh? That's fine. Once we get the machines set up, you'll tell me what I want to know, rest assured." He glanced over his shoulder, shouting. "Doctor Freeman!"

The doctor appeared, brandishing a large syringe.

Hollings chuckled. "Would you administer the sedative to my old friend, please?"

Helena gasped, recoiling. "No!"

Dr. Freeman rushed forward. Franklin grabbed Helena's arm from behind, holding her still as the doctor plunged the needle into her arm and emptied the barrel.

"No!" Helena shrieked, kicking her feet, her eyes squeezed shut. "Oh, no, no!"

"Oh, my, yes. Yes indeed, madam." Hollings stood up, leaning on his cane. "Now, there'll be no more games—will there, Keeper 27?"

CHAPTER 13

The doctor held up a pen light and shined the beam into Trinn's eyes. "How does that feel, young lady? Does this bother you at all, hmm?"

"No. It's okay." Trinn's head rested on the hospital pillow. She held still, not staring into the light, her eyes focused on the wall behind the gray-haired physician. "How long was I out for?"

"A few hours." He snapped off the tiny beam. The nurse turned on the overhead lights as the doctor wrote on the chart. "But that is a good thing. You are recovering nicely, Miss. You have a strong system and you're healing well—but you needed your rest, and you got it." He set the chart on the mattress, smiling at her. "In fact, I've never seen anyone rebounding so quickly from a gunshot wound. Youth and good health are wonderful gifts. Enjoy them and don't get shot again, okay?"

Trinn smiled. "I'll do my best."

"Your fluids are good." He went to the countertop, writing on the chart again. "Your heart, respiration—all good. I think we'll take one last X-ray, then let you go back to sleep. In a few days, we can let you go back to your hotel."

"A few days?" She put her hands on the mattress to sit up. DeShear's instructions flooded back into her consciousness.

Find Helena. If they found Constantine, they'll find her.

"No, I can't wait a few days." Trinn threw the sheets back. "Doctor, I have to—"

"You were shot, madam. You mustn't make light of it. We've operated to restore the integrity of the bowel, but you were lucky. The bullet passed through without hitting any major organs. We've cleaned you up and stitched you up, but that doesn't mean you're ready to run off and go . . . parasailing, or some such nonsense. We need to keep you here for a few days' observation and make sure no infections arise. Then you can be on your way."

"Okay. Sorry."

Quiet down and play along for now. Look for an opportunity to slip out, then take it. Don't raise eyebrows.

Get out, and get to Helena.

But no hospital would let me walk out the front door right now. Not without raising a lot of attention . . .

"How is the pain in your side?" The doctor sat on a stool by the counter and turned around to face her. "We can put you in a wheelchair and roll you downstairs to the X-ray room."

"I'm pretty good with pain." Trinn sat upright, wincing as she swung her legs over the side of the bed. She tucked the edges of her hospital gown around her thighs.

"I see." He glanced at the nurse. "Genevieve, bring the wheelchair for our patient, please."

"I can walk," Trinn said.

"I believe you can, Miss. But my job is to get you healed completely, not to let you see how quickly you can rip your stitches and return to surgery. You will have plenty of time for showing off later—after you have been released from the hospital. Agreed?"

"Okay."

"Yes, I'm quite the spoilsport. You'll thank me later."

The nurse opened the door, pushing a wheelchair.

"Off you go now," the doctor said. "Time for some pictures."

* * * * *

Prenley adjusted his glasses, typing on his computer. A New York driver's license photo of Jaden Trinn appeared on the screen. "There we are." He turned the computer around and displayed the photo to his hired man. "Now, this nice lady is currently located in room 212 of Monarch Hospital. You'll go up the stairs from the main lobby and down the hall to the right." He handed over a wad of currency. "Any questions?"

The man counted the cash. "There's only a thousand here."

"Surely you've done work for my boss before, Nigel. You get the other half when the job is completed." He slid a hospital identification and a set of folded scrubs across the desk. "This will get you past the admitting nurse. Any thoughts on . . . how you'll do it?"

"She's dehydrated, lost blood from a gunshot. I think a quick respiratory attack will do nicely. A pillow over the face until she stops kicking."

Prenley made a claw with his hand. "Make sure none of your DNA ends up under her fingernails."

Nigel ran a hand over his beard. "With a bird like this, it's best to sit on top of her as I administer the procedure—stuff her hands under my knees before she knows what's going on, and use the body weight so she ain't able to get up. Then, it's all about pressure to the nose and mouth—under the pillow, of course."

"Of course." Prenley turned his computer off. "Come 'round in the morning for the balance of payment. And use the anteroom entrance to His Honor's office. Then take a little vacation."

"That, I will." Nigel stood. "I'll be off to Jamaica for some fun with the ladies, play a bit in the casino, and have me a time."

"Just make sure you do a thorough job of things tonight. It needs to look like she succumbed to her injuries."

"Oh, don't you worry none, Mr. Prenley. I know my job." He shoved the cash into his pocket. "Your Miss Trinn is as good as dead."

* * * * *

In his newly-acquired hospital scrubs, Nigel ascended the stairs to the second floor of Monarch Hospital. The hallway was quiet and mostly dark. He crept toward room 212, readying himself for the assault that would take place.

The plan was simple. Overwhelm and asphyxiate.

As he walked, the room numbers went by.

Room 208 . . .

His target was already wounded and possibly sedated, so she wouldn't cause much trouble.

Room 210 . . .

He checked his watch. If things went quickly enough, he'd still be able to grab a pint at Hawley's Tavern before last call. It would be mostly shrimpers, but maybe there'd be a local dealer looking to make a late night score or a freelance escort headed to the casino parking lot—anyone who wanted some additional muscle and had a few bucks to pay for his time.

The door to room 212 was closed when he reached it. He put his ear to the door frame. No noises came from inside. He glanced over both shoulders, wrapping his fingers around the doorknob and clutching it hard but turning it gently, so it wouldn't make any noise when he turned it.

He pushed the door open an inch, peering inside.

The room was dark and still.

The mattress near the foot of the bed was bare except for a single sheet. The other sheets were piled to the side. No feet were visible. The top of the patient chart showed over the foot of the mattress, but there didn't appear to be a patient in the room—from what he could see.

He pushed the door open a bit further, leaning forward as he looked around.

The bed was empty.

Not a problem, if she's still in the hospital.

He walked to the end of the bed and pulled the chart, holding it sideways so the street lights from outside could cast enough light onto the file to make it readable.

The patient had been taken to X-ray.

He set the chart down, viewing the little room. Jaden Trinn would be back from getting her X-rays soon enough. Where would the best place be to wait for her? Not the nurses' station. They didn't know him there and he didn't need more questions.

What about in the room? There was a small, wooden wardrobe. As long as Miss Trinn hadn't brought a lot of clothes, he could fit inside and pop out after she fell asleep.

Or perhaps the men's room. None of the nurses would go in there, and maintenance had likely finished their work for the night. Depending on where it was, he could peek in on his victim and commence his work when the time was right.

He peered out the door. The restrooms were less than fifty feet away.

Perfect.

He checked the room again. Simple mattress, sheets, pillows. The bed would be a cinch to get into, and once his victim was asleep, she'd be easy prey. A pillow over the face, a little applied body weight, some kicking and struggling . . . then, the gradual relaxation as the fight left the body and death stepped in—followed by the satisfaction of a job well done.

Nigel smiled.

A few more minutes wouldn't hurt. Hawley's would still be open afterward.

"There," a woman said. "That wasn't so bad, was it?"

Nigel crept to the door, leaning forward just enough for one eye to see a nurse pushing a woman in a wheelchair.

"The X-ray or the wheelchair ride?" the dark-haired patient said. "I can walk."

"I'm sure, but you must let me do my job, miss."

Nigel took a step back, his heart pounding. X-ray? This would be Jaden Trinn and her nurse, then. He looked again. The dim hallway showed enough of his intended victim's face for him to conclude it was the same as the driver's license Prenley had showed him.

Now, where to hide as she was delivered back to her room?

The wardrobe? Behind the door?

Either way, he'd have to be quick unless he wanted to take care of two victims—and the nurse would be much harder to explain.

His mind raced.

The wardrobe. Stay quiet until the nurse goes and Trinn is at rest. If discovered, bash the nurse in the face to knock her out, and get Trinn subdued and smothered as fast as possible. Stash the nurse outside with a half-burned cigarette and nobody's the wiser.

A victim of a random mugger, while upstairs her patient expired from her injuries.

He grabbed a knob on the wardrobe, pulling gently to avoid making any noise.

"Do you mind?" Trinn's soft voice bounced off the empty hallway walls. "I'm not a fan of bedpans."

"Oh, no bother, miss."

Nigel stepped to the door. The women had stopped at the restrooms.

Trinn stood, opening the door to the ladies' facilities. "I can manage."

The nurse nodded. "I'll be here. I still have to wheel you to your room when you've finished. Hospital rules."

Nigel ran his fingers over his beard, considering a new plan.

Wait behind the door. They come back, the wheelchair comes in. Clobber the nurse, strangle the patient while she sits in the chair. A forearm lock—easy enough.

It'll leave bruises, though.

He viewed the wardrobe.

Might still be my best bet. Don't want two victims when I only need one. Trinn will be asleep within the hour. I can wait.

A phone rang at the other end of the corridor. Nigel checked the hallway. The nurse walked toward the nurses' station, disappearing around the corner.

Even better. Nip into the ladies' loo and catch Miss Trinn as she comes out of the stall. Or even in the stall. Might even be able to use a pillow and hide any marks.

He grabbed a pillow off the hospital bed.

Might help keep things quieter, anyway.

And if the nurse comes in, deal with it. Might even help the cover story, her finding Trinn dead on the floor of the loo—as long as I've left the premises.

Which meant going now, before the nurse ended her call.

He stepped into the hallway, carrying the pillow.

The nurse's conversation seemed to involve checking some records on the computer.

She'll wait outside for Trinn to reappear, and when that doesn't happen, she'll come in to find her patient dead on the floor. If I can do the job before she finishes her chat, I'll be home free. If not, I'll hide in a stall until she comes in, then slip out after she runs to call for help.

He put a hand on the ladies' room door, easing it open and stepping inside, the pillow clutched to his chest.

The sink area was empty. Bending down, he peered under the stall walls.

No legs.

Standing, he furrowed his brow.

The window at the end of the restroom was open, a gentle breeze blowing in. He walked toward it, opening each stall door as he did. There was no one in the restroom but him.

Lowering the pillow, he peered out the window.

A naked woman raced toward the row of small houses on the other side of the street, her dark hair bouncing over her shoulders. She slipped behind the first residence, grabbing clothes off the clothesline in the back yard, and disappeared into the darkness.

Nigel stuck his head out the window.

A gutter pipe ran along the side of the building. Halfway down, a hospital gown flapped in the breeze, stuck on a loose screw.

CHAPTER 14

The cap resembled an old football helmet from the 1920s—thick leather bands and a strap under the chin—but the wiring and large computer monitors gave the appearance of a makeshift television studio or computer lab. Three tables had been placed in a triangle around Keeper 27: one behind her, where her inquisitor Hollings could view the monitor placed on it; one behind him where she could see the monitor, and one on the side, near Kitt, with a larger monitor, so the others present could watch the interaction.

On all three, Helena's face was displayed, the top of her head covered by the thick leather cap. Wires emerged from the side of the device, running across her shoulder and onto the floor, where they connected to several massive electronic components in beige metal housings.

A light sat on Hollings table, illuminating the old woman's head and shoulders. Dr. Freeman sat next to the bandaged fat man, biting his nails one after the other as he hunched over a computer and adjusted the resolution feed for the monitors.

Freeman glanced at Hollings, his voice quivering. "H—Have you ever done one of these remotely before, sir?"

The end of Hollings' cane *whooshed* through the air, slamming into Freeman's back. "Shut up, you imbecile!"

Freeman cried out, freezing in place, his eyes squeezed shut and his hands hovering over his keyboard. Gasping, he resumed working, his eyes staying down.

Kitt cringed, wrapping her arms around herself and bringing her knees up. Helena sat still, unflinching.

"You can't say nothing around the old woman." Hollings gritted his teeth. You can't *think* nothing around her. We're here to get information from her, not give it to her, and each question you ask . . ." He pointed at Helena and Kitt. "Offers a bit of the puzzle to them, don't it?"

Freeman kept typing on the computer.

"Right," Hollings said. "You sodding fool. Another peep and I'll have these other lads take you outside and give you a proper thrashing. Just work the computer." He returned his gaze to Helena. "Wakey, wakey, there, old girl. Time to get started."

Helena stared straight ahead, her eyes focused on the wall behind Hollings.

Frowning, Hollings rubbed his chin. "Seems our sedatives have taken hold. Well, if everything's all sorted, then let's begin."

Freeman put his hand on the mouse.

"Initiate the program, Doctor Freeman," Hollings said.

Freeman clicked the mouse and lowered his hands to his sides.

On the monitor, the face of an old man with thick, white hair appeared. He peered down his nose through black framed glasses. Deep wrinkles etched the skin around his eyes.

Hollings looked at the screen. "Hello, Doctor Hauser."

The old man on the screen looked at the questioner. "Hello, Mr. Hollings." His gaze then went to Helena. "Hello, Keeper 27."

Helena continued staring straight ahead.

"It's the sedatives." Freeman shook his head. "Doctor Hauser, I think they've—"

The end of Hollings' cane *whooshed* through the air again and came crashing into Freeman's back a second time. The thin man howled, scrunching his shoulders and bringing his hands to his chest.

From the screen, Dr. Hauser glared at Freeman.

"Sorry for the interruption, sir," Hollings said. "We needed this dimwitted bloke for setup."

Hauser eyed Kitt. She cringed. The words "facial recognition" flashed in the corner of the screen. Hauser nodded to her. "Good evening, Dr. Kittaleye." The word "loading" flashed next.

Kitt shook her head, trembling. "What— what's going on?"

"Djimoa Kittaleye." Hauser's gravelly voice came from the speakers on the table. "Born in

Uganda, emigrated to the United States with parents Tinoa and Malo at age eleven. Early testing indicated a strong aptitude in science and a predilection for medicine, and your parents directed your studies accordingly. You received multiple degrees from New York University, and were most recently interning at the Pitié-Salpêtrière Hospital, in Paris." He raised his hands, tapping his fingers together. "And now you are here with us."

"Why?" Kitt trembled. "Why am I here? What do you—"

"All in good time, Doctor. Perhaps if we begin with your friend, you will understand better." His gaze went to Helena. "Keeper 27, would you be kind enough to explain?"

Helena did not move. Dr. Hauser narrowed his eyes and tipped his head back, peering down his nose at her.

"Please don't—don't hurt her." Kitt swallowed hard, her hands shaking. "The sedative is obviously affecting her ability to respond."

"Is it?" Hauser said. "Let us see. Mr. Hollings, put the neuroreceptor imagery on the screen for Doctor Kittaleye."

Hauser's image faded. The screen displayed a view of the front wall of the warehouse. The top of Freeman's and Holling's heads were visible at the bottom of the screen; the flatbed truck was off to the right side.

"Doctor Kittaleye," Hauser said. "If you would turn Keeper 27's head to the left, I believe all will be explained."

Kitt stared at the screen.

Hollings looked at her. "Turn the old bird's head, lass. You won't hurt her."

Kitt raised her hands, leaning over and putting her finger's on Helena's jaw and at the back of her head. The old woman's skin was thin and soft, like warm rose petals. Kitt slowly rotated Helena's head to the left.

The image on the screen moved to the left, displaying the dirty floor of the empty warehouse.

Kitt recoiled. "Is there a camera on the leather cap? Did you—"

"There is indeed a camera," Hauser said. "The best camera ever designed—the human eye, in telescopic vision. Keeper 27's eyes, to be precise."

Kitt gazed at Helena, her mouth hanging open.

"We collect the electronic impulses from every neuron in the brain, presenting them here, on the screen, in a visual format much like we were seeing the things happen with our own eyes. We see what she sees, we recall what she recalls. We access that which her long-term memory has stored, and replay it the way she remembers it happening—and most of all, we can access her thoughts, in real time, before she has a chance to try to hide them. This information is interpreted and presented on the monitors in much the same way we would process it if we were receiving it ourselves—each of us, in our own heads—from her brainwaves. With this technology, we shall investigate the stores of information Keeper 27 had gathered. As we scan the levels, we can access that which she holds most precious and dear, as well as the things she wishes to keep from us."

"That's . . . not possible," Kitt said. "How could you expect to—"

"We receive the neuroimpulses at almost the same time she does. The only difference is a slight delay as the transmission data travels through the wires and the computer's processing system, approximately three nanoseconds."

"But why would you want to do that? It seems . . . intrusive. A violation."

"If you will indulge me, I shall answer with a demonstration. Doctor, suppose I ask you to *not* think of an elephant. What is the first thing you think of?"

"An . . . elephant."

"Precisely. You instantly imagine it, though you were told not to. Perhaps your personal vision is of a cartoon elephant with a yellow blanket on its back and a basket for carrying riders. Before you can consciously push it from your mind's eye, the image appears in your thoughts. It is an impulse you can neither resist nor prevent, and it happens instantaneously. An additional nanosecond might bring forward a childhood memory of a day at the zoo, handing an unshelled peanut to a slippery gray snout, that grasped it and tossed into the giant animal's open mouth. If I were to ask a sixty-year-old woman where she hid her diary as a teenager, her neuroreceptors would bombard the screen with a visual of her teenage bed, the front corner under which she had hidden it. Before a subject can change their answer and lie, they have yielded the truth."

"Now envision that technology as a scanning receiver and not a clumsy leather cap. A technology so sensitive it could pick up specific transmissions from a subject anywhere in the world, on any question desired, with no way for the subject to even be aware that anyone was asking. Wars would be prevented. The army with the technology would receive and understand the battle plan as it was being plotted—and have their answer ready before it ever deployed. Peace would be achieved before a single shot was ever fired. Cancerous cells would announce themselves and their locations. The stress of a looming aneurism would be broadcast to medical receptors and the patient invited in to have it dealt with before it ever happened."

"And you are doing these things?"

"We are. We have. We were merely . . . *interrupted* for a time. But now we will re-engage in our pursuits—which will require all of our property be returned to us. For that, we require the assistance of the Keepers."

The image of Dr. Hauser froze. The lights in the warehouse flickered, and the monitor flashed dark for a moment. The whirr from the computer fans slowed as clicking noises came from the back of the warehouse. As the fans engaged again, the monitor came back to life.

Hauser's image emerged on the screen. ". . . property be returned to us. For that, we require the assistance of the Keepers."

The image stopped, the words "initiate program" flashing over it.

"What's happened?" Hollings gripped his cane and glared at Freeman. "What've you done now, you useless git?"

"It's the program," Freeman said, typing frantically. "It's locking up. We—we don't seem to be drawing enough power in this old barn."

Miss Franklin walked toward the vehicle. "There's a generator in the ambulance. Runs on diesel. One sec and we'll have it running." She glanced at her helpers and snapped her fingers. "Boys?"

Rising from her chair, Kitt held her hands to her mouth. "He—he's not real? I thought he was on camera somewhere, talking to me."

"He's real enough, lass," Hollings said. "We'll get a more stable power supply, and he'll pick that old bird's brain clean."

"It's . . . artificial intelligence?" Kitt inched toward the monitor. "A computer program?"

"It's much more than that, Doctor. An entire human consciousness, downloaded into digital form. And not just any human, but one of the greatest minds to ever walk the earth. He wants his little girl back, and Keeper 27 is going to tell us where she is."

"You called it 'he.' It's a computer. The program glitched and it repeated itself."

"No, lass. This here is just a tiny piece—a starter program. The real deal is elsewhere, stored on a series of mainframe computers, holding the conscious, digitized mind of Dr. Marcus Hauser. And he is every bit as alive as you or me."

CHAPTER 15

As the generator hummed in the corner, Freeman restarted the program. The entire time, Helena hadn't moved.

"That's her game, the old witch." Hollings frowned. "Trying to not be awake enough to give up the little girl."

Kitt stared at her friend. "How?"

"We shall simply ask her." Dr. Hauser's face reappearing on the screen. "And as noted, before she can deceive us, the information we desire will generate through her white matter receptors, and we shall have it."

Hollings rubbed his beard stubble. "Takes a bit of warming up, sometimes, young doctor. Not every subject is exactly forthcoming."

The white-haired man on the screen looked at Helena. "What Mr. Hollings is implying is, some subjects resist the process in a variety of maneuvers. Eventually, however, we are able to run the maze, as it were. Keeper 27 shall prove no different." He tilted his head back and peered down his nose. "If we can turn consciousness off, as we do with anesthesia for a patient undergoing a major surgical procedure, we can turn it on. It's a process of engaging the right systems in the right order. And as we engage the desired systems, we simply bypass the ability to resist."

"You said she couldn't resist," Kitt said. "How can she bypass the system, then?"

"By thinking of no thought. By disengaging certain cerebral functions from their ability to be transmitted. It is a process referred to as standalone. But it will not be successful, as you will soon see, Doctor Kittaleye." Hauser raised his hands, tapping his fingers together. "Keeper 27, you were admitted to the Pitié-Salpêtrière Hospital."

Helena stared straight ahead. The view of the front wall remained on the screen.

"Keeper 27," Hauser said. "You viewed a car crash. A woman died."

Helena didn't move. The screen stayed filled with the front wall.

"Keeper 27, I wish you to think of Constantine. Where is she?"

The screen flickered, going gray, then filling with a clear blue sky and a tall, stone chateau. It lasted only for half a second, then the stone wall of the old warehouse reappeared.

Hauser smiled. "You see, Dr. Kittaleye? The proper path leads to the correct destination." His gaze returned to Helena. "Keeper 27, do you love Constantine?"

The young face of a girl with long hair and blue eyes appeared on the screen. Behind her, a pale blue sky.

The image faded; the stone wall of the barn returned.

"Keeper 27, how did Constantine cut her knee? She bled quite profusely. Were you negligent in your care of her?"

Helena quivered.

"She was three years old at the time. How did it happen?"

A spiral staircase appeared on the screen. It was made of stone, and an orange traffic cone stood at the base. A janitor's mop and bucket rested nearby, the steps glistening with water. Children's voices filled the air, the words "Hide and seek" echoing through a dark corridor.

Helena trembled, her eyes remaining fixed on the wall in front of her. On the screen, the same wall came back into view again.

"Aye, old woman." Hollings leaned forward, whispering. "It's working."

"Too inefficient," Hauser said. "The sedative has lowered her resistance, but not enough. Perhaps a more . . . *cortex-driven* approach is required, appealing directly to the deepest emotions." He looked at Helena. "Keeper 27, how did Constantine learn of John-Thomas' death?"

Helena groaned as if she had been punched in the gut. The vision appeared on the screen. A green field, with brown patches. Children running along a tall stone wall. A table of science experiments laid out along the far side of the grounds.

"Specials, my lovelies." Keeper 27 clapped her hands, looking out over the compound. *"Come now, dears."*

The children rushed to her, lining up to enter the building.

They took their seats, one by one, waiting for the instructor to begin.

Helena closed the door, gazing at the clear blue sky.

Behind her, a shot rang out—the clear, unmistakable sound of a gun being discharged. As she turned, Mr. Parker lowered his handgun at the far side of the compound, just in front of the Rituals building. He shoved the gun into his belt and waved for a tansuit to bring a cart.

Shaking, Keeper 27 looked on. She clasped her hands in front of her smock.

The tansuit pushed a collector's bin to the Rituals building, disappearing around the side. A moment later, he returned, wheeling the bin toward the row of other carts filled with the trash to be disposed of for the day.

Keeper 27 kneaded her hands, walking to the bins.

Each cart was designated with its materials. Glass. Paper. Plastic. Metal. Others carried scrap wood from the construction area, or burned items from experiments.

The last cart in the row was marked *"general."*

Clutching her stomach, Keeper 27 approached the last cart and peered inside.

The five-year-old body of John-Thomas lay on the bottom of the cart, a hole in the side of his head.

The child was still and quiet, with his eyes wide open and flies crawling over his stained red cheek. The old woman spoke to him, unable to control herself, wishing he would answer. He did not smile when she called him, and he did not move when she touched him. Tears welled in Keeper 27's eyes. "Get up, John-Thomas, get up!"

But he didn't get up. He just laid there, all still, until they wheeled the bin away like the boy was a bit of trash.

On her chair in the abandoned building, a tear rolled down Helena's face. Kitt reached out to take Helena's hand.

"But Keeper 27," Dr. Hauser said. "The answer you've given is Constantine's recollection of the events. She was nowhere near the bins that day."

Helena broke her frozen gaze, staring at Hauser on the screen.

"Constantine was in Rituals. It was you who saw the boy's body, not her. How did she learn of his death? Did you tell her?"

Helena trembled, the words barely passing over her lips. "No."

"No." Hauser nodded. "She saw it for herself, didn't she?"

Kneading her hands in her lap, the old woman shook her head. "No."

"She witnessed it—through your eyes, Keeper 27."

"No!"

"She saw what you saw—a child in the collector's bin, with a hole in the side of his head and blood running down his cheek."

Tears welled in Helena's eyes. "No."

Kitt yelled at the screen. "Stop it. Stop this—this torture!"

"And when you called him," Hauser's gaze was unwavering. "Whose voice did you hear? Whose words were being spoken?"

She shook her head.

"Tell me."

"It can't be!" Helena squeezed her eyes shut, tears streaming down her cheeks. "It can't be!"

"Who spoke the words? Who begged John-Thomas to get up?"

She put her hands to the side of her head, grimacing. "I can't."

"You can," Hauser said. "You will. Who spoke the words? Who stood there crying and begging the boy to get up?"

Helena doubled over, howling in pain.

"Who called out to him?"

"Constantine!" She threw her head back, her mouth hanging open. Tears streaked her cheeks. "My Constantine."

"She said it."

"Yes," Helena sobbed.

"But how?" Hauser raised his hands, tapping the fingers together. "She wasn't there."

"She saw through my eyes," Helena whispered, defeated. She could hold back no longer. "She witnessed it all. She saw everything."

Hauser nodded. "And when you do standalone, you see what she sees, don't you?"

"At times, yes."

"Yes, you do." Hauser's gravelly voice filled the warehouse. "Sometimes at night, sometimes during the day, but what you wish to know from that child—my property—you can access at any time. That's right, isn't it, Keeper 27?"

Helena kept her head down, sobbing.

"Dr. Kittaleye, do you now see how powerful these instruments are?"

Kitt wiped a tear from her own eye. "I'm not sure I understand. If your goal is to hurt an old woman, you succeeded. Otherwise—"

"Constantine witnessed the actions that Keeper 27 acted out," Hauser said, "as if Constantine was there herself."

"The girl on the screen?" Kitt said. "In the vision—she used the device you're using now?"

"That technology wasn't operational yet. Constantine pulled the information from the air, all by herself, as her Keeper witnessed it." He narrowed his eyes. "And we will use that same ability, in reverse, to find her and bring her back to me."

The screen went dark.

"What!" Hollings jumped up, leaning on his cane. "What's happened?"

Freeman studied his computer. "It's the power again!"

"Right." Hollings pointed his cane at Washington and Jefferson. "You lot, get on them cords and see that our electric flows undisturbed.

Climb the power pole outside if you have to, but keep that current flowing."

"The old woman is trying to block us," Freeman said.

"Ruddy old bird." Hollings clenched his cane, glaring at Keeper 27.

Miss Franklin stepped between them. "I might have a solution, Mr. Hollings. What is—"

"Hold, lass." Hollings took Franklin's arm, glaring at Helena. "Let's . . . come over here, out of earshot of that one. She can listen in from fifty feet away." As they walked past the ambulance, he called over his shoulder. "You two—Washington and Jefferson! Check every outlet, every connection, inside this building!"

Hollings and Miss Franklin disappeared behind the ambulance.

Kitt rubbed Helena's hand. "Are you okay?'

The old woman remained rigid, staring at the wall.

The two thugs walked to the far wall of the building, crouching near an electrical box. Dr. Freeman sat back, frowning, then turned and went to the large processing units on the floor.

Kitt patted Helena's arm. "Ma'am? Are you . . . can you hear me?"

Helena smiled. "Quite clearly, dear," she whispered.

* * * * *

Mr. Hollings stopped walking when he reached the far wall, his back to the others. Miss Franklin stood next to him.

"She can get people's thoughts if they're too close," he said. "But she can't read everybody. She can't read me, and she don't seem to read you. And so much the better, but still—best to be cautious."

Franklin nodded. "I was going to suggest another act of gunpoint persuasion, but I'm thinking you have something else in mind."

"She'll open up. That old Keeper loves the little girl more than anything in the world. Do anything for her, she would. We use that." He leaned on his cane. "Ask the right questions until she gives up the location, then we move quick."

"So you . . . you'll meet with Armen Twa?"

"Oh, I certainly will, miss. He's too smart to have Constantine with him when we first meet, though. He'll set a rendezvous place for the exchange to happen. Somewhere safe, in his territory. But if that Asian arse thinks he's going to steal Dr. Hauser's property and then try to sell it back to us, he'd better think again. Not on my watch."

"He's arrogant." Franklin smiled. "I like that. Arrogance blinds a man."

"Aye, it does, miss." Hollings rubbed his chin stubble. "So, I'll play along with the arrogant Mr. Twa for now, but we can't let him know anything until we have the girl. We play dumb and let them set a meeting, but by then we've already gotten the location out of Keeper 27. Constantine will know where she's being kept, how many men are guarding her, the lot—so Keeper 27 will know it, too. Which means *we'll* know it. Then we can hide a squad of your people at the meeting spot ahead of time. When you and I arrive to meet Twa, your team jumps out with guns blazing and kills them all. Armen Twa and his whole Pacific Rim gang of thieves, gone in one fell swoop."

"They'll never see it coming."

"Nope," Hollings said. "They'll be as you done said before—blind with arrogance. Suits me fine, as long as they're blind."

* * * * *

Kitt sat in her chair, scared and frustrated, her head in her hands.

What does any of this have to do with me?

Helena whispered, "Jaden Trinn is an agent for the United States government. You must contact her boss with the words *'Mao Oui.'* "

Kitt looked up. "Helena, I don't understand. What's going on?"

"I never said I couldn't read Mr. Hollings. He only assumed it. Now, when I tell you to, you must go. And remember—contact Jaden Trinn's boss and tell him what you know."

"But I don't know anything!"

"I understand, dear. Get ready."

"What?" Kitt gasped. "Where? For what?"

Helena nodded. "Look with me."

Washington and Jefferson had their backs to the hostages, working on a power line. Dr. Freeman was facing the other way, taking apart his processor. Miss Franklin and Mr. Hollings were on the other side of the ambulance.

No one was watching the hostages.

"It's your chance," Helena whispered. "Get up and walk quietly to the back. As soon as you get through that door, run. The trees on the other side of the fields will hide you, but to reach them in time, you'll need to run as fast as you can."

Kitt put her hand to her mouth. "I—I can't. They have guns."

"You have a weapon more powerful than any gun, dear. Your brain. But right now, it's your legs we need. Go."

She lifted herself up a few inches, then sat back down. "I'm afraid."

"Of course you are, dear. It wouldn't take courage otherwise."

Kitt's gaze went to Dr. Freeman, then to Washington and Jefferson, then to the ambulance.

"Go now," Helena said in a whisper.

Holding her breath, Kitt got up from the chair. She turned to the exit, her heart pounding. Each step was an eternity, each gust of wind outside caused the old roof to creak, sending a shudder down her spine. As the cool air of the parking lot brushed past her cheek, Kitt stepped onto the gravel—then burst into a sprint.

Helena saw it on the screen inside. The gravel lot gave way to the road, and then to the dirt field.

Freeman dislodged a hard drive from the processor, standing up. The vision of Kitt running across the field displayed on his monitor. "Hey!" Freeman wheeled around, glaring at the empty chair next to Helena. "Hey!" His eyes went to the back door. "Hey, she's getting away!"

The others rushed forward. Kitt was on every screen, bounding over the tilled dirt.

"After her!" Hollings glared at Washington and Jefferson. "Get that scrawny doctor and bring her back! Now! Get!"

Miss Franklin went to the ambulance and took out two guns, tossing them to her henchmen. "If you can't catch her, at least make sure she doesn't get away."

Weapons in hand, the two thugs raced out the door.

Helena continued viewing the screen. The men scrambled across the field, chasing Doctor Kittaleye as she disappeared into the brush on the horizon.

CHAPTER 16

Moray's diving boat bounced through the darkness, its engine roaring at top speed. Gripping the wheel, he checked his radar and GPS. The screens bathed him in green light. "This is near where we found your fishing charter," he shouted.

DeShear gazed into the black night. A crescent moon hung low on the horizon, casting a white reflection onto the water beneath it. Above it was only stars.

I have to disrupt this guy's plan and get back to looking for Constantine. There has to be a way, but how?

Let him talk. Get to know him. Let him get to know you. Then ask for his help. He's got a boat. Maybe he'd look for Constantine if the price is right—but it can't look like a bribe.

If he thinks I'm telling the truth, there's a chance. Start by having a conversation and let him warm up to you. It could work.

"This area looks different at night," DeShear said. "How can you tell it's where my charter went down?"

"GPS, radar. . . At night, we take these extra eyeballs, but I know this water. Your wreck is—"

A tiny fluorescent line rocketed across the bow, almost hitting them. It was like a miniature sparkler from the Fourth of July, but traveling in a straight line—and very fast. A second one followed.

"Tracer rounds!" Moray ducked, cutting the throttle and heaving the wheel to the right. "Somebody's shooting at us!"

The turn threw DeShear away from the wall. He crashed into Moray, his cuffed hands still lashed to the railing.

"Back, idiot!" The lieutenant shoved him away. "Hold fast. They're shooting at us!"

A spotlight flooded the diving boat in blinding illumination. DeShear squinted, peering over the stern as a boat closed in on their tail. "You can't outrun them! They're gaining too fast!"

"We're gonna try." Wild-eyed, Moray swerved his boat back and forth in the water, gunning the throttle. "No pirates are gonna take my boat. They'll take everything and put you and me in the water for sure, mister!"

Another tracer round soared past the side of the boat. The spotlight came and went as Moray steered the boat zigzag over the waves.

DeShear looked down at his cuffed hands and fear shot through him. He couldn't duck the bullets, and if the ship went under, he'd be dragged down with it. He grabbed the railing, trying to stay on his feet. "If you don't stop, they'll just shoot us and take the boat anyway."

Moray glanced over his shoulder. Their pursuer would be on them in seconds. "Fast boat. Gotta be pirates." He reached under the console and withdrew a handgun, placing it on the dashboard, then reached under again and pulled out a rifle. "These boys are in for a surprise."

"Don't!" DeShear shouted, staring at the oncoming lights. "We don't know how many there are, or what kind of firepower they're carrying."

"I'm not giving up my boat! My brother and I worked too hard. We'll lose them in the shallows."

"You'll bottom out and scuttle this thing." DeShear winced, peering into the floodlight. The brightness blinded him.

Another tracer round soared across the bow.

"We have another option." DeShear leaned toward the Lieutenant, yelling. "Slow down and act like a private charter. This is a scuba diving boat. Act like it."

"No. They'll board us."

"Which means they'll have to slow down. Then we can see what we're dealing with. Give me a gun. We'll fight them together."

Moray's eyes were wide. "Not a chance. You'll shoot me quick-quick, mister."

"If you try to take them on yourself, you're just going to get killed—and me right after. I used to be a police officer. I can handle a weapon. With me on your side you stand a chance. Otherwise, you lose everything."

The trailing boat fired again. The bullet ricocheted off the rail of Moray's canvas bimini top.

"I'm a lieutenant in the Navy. I don't dare let them board me, and they'd better not try."

"You're in a recreational boat," DeShear shouted. "If they thought you were a lieutenant in the Navy they wouldn't be firing at you." Sea spray washed over the boat as they crashed through the waves. "They don't know you've got guns. Use that to your advantage. Act weak and draw them in. Let them board. When the moment's right, attack."

"How?"

"Stow your guns under a tarp or an old fishing net. Something they're not going to want—and then let them push you to be near it. But you can't have me in handcuffs or it's not gonna work. They'll know something's up."

"If you make a move for that gun, mister, don't worry about no pirates. I'll take you down myself."

"They're not aiming yet. If you leave me in handcuffs, I'm a dead man when the real shooting starts. Probably, so are you. I have no desire to die tonight. I'm hoping you feel the same way."

The lieutenant stared at the boat behind his, watching it weave in and out of his wake.

"Lieutenant."

Moray kept his hand on the throttle. Sweat ran down the side of his face.

"Lieutenant!"

"All right! We play it your way! But you *bungee* sideways one time and I'll kill you." He untied DeShear from the railing and pulled out the key to the handcuffs.

"Hurry," DeShear said.

Moray opened the handcuffs and shoved them in his pocket.

"Okay." DeShear rubbed his wrists. "I'll take the wheel. You stow those weapons. Then, just pretend I hired you and your boat for some night diving."

Moray grabbed the gun and rifle, crouching as he slinked to the rear of the boat. He shoved the weapons behind the scuba diving tanks.

DeShear eased the throttle back. "Don't act like a military man. You're a scuba charter captain. I'm your customer. We're surrendering. Raise your hands."

Moray lifted his arms over his head. "Remember, mister. You die if you do anything funny."

DeShear raised his hands. "I am absolutely not in the mood to be funny."

The other boat pulled alongside them. Lines sailed onto the deck. Two men with rifles pointed at DeShear and Moray. The one on the front of the boat shouted. "Stop engine! *Zet je motor uit!*"

DeShear switched the ignition off, peering at Moray out of the corner of his eye. "What language is that?"

"They're speaking Dutch," the lieutenant said. "Dirty Dutch. Broken. No schooling."

"Tie! Tie!" the man shouted. *"Bind de boten vast en beweeg niet!"*

Moray shook his head. "English, friend. *Ne parle.*"

A man in a red t-shirt at the rear of the intruder's vessel crept forward, his rifle aimed at Moray. *"Attachez les bateaux ensemble. Rapidement."*

"Oui, oui." The lieutenant nudged DeShear. "This other man speaks French. He wants us take the lines and tie the boats together."

DeShear grabbed a line and looped it around the cleat on the side of the boat. Moray tied the stern line. The two boats were side by side, rocking in the waves.

"Reculez et gardez les mains en l'air." The man in the red t-shirt aimed his rifle back and forth between his victims. Placing a foot on the side of his boat, he crossed over to Moray's vessel and landed on the rear deck. The rifle remained pointed at his two hostages.

He pulled an 18" zip tie from his pocket, looking at DeShear. *"Venez. Attache ton ami."*

"He wants you come take that," Moray said. "He says you are to tie me up."

DeShear nodded, walking slowly. "Think they understand English?"

"This man with the rifle," Moray said, "he's one ugly pogo in that red shirt, for sure. Got a face like dog's butt."

The stranger didn't flinch.

"I think they don't speak English, mister."

"Geez." DeShear winced. "Heckuva way to find out."

The pirate held out the long zip tie. *"Venez, venez. Attache ton ami."*

"That's our opening." His hands still in the air, DeShear turned slowly to Moray. "Follow me back here, Lieuten—uh, *Louis*. I'll shove him into the drink. When I do, get your rifle and start blasting at that other boat."

Moray nodded, walking to the rear of the boat.

The gunman retreated a step. *"Arrêtez! Juste vous. Juste vous!"*

"I'm American." DeShear shrugged, moved closer. "I don't speak French. Jay nay parlay."

The zip tie quivered in the pirate's hand. *"Allez-y doucement. Doucement . . ."*

The gunman couldn't have been more than twenty-five years old. His red t-shirt was torn and faded; the sea breeze carried the stench of his body odor.

His gun looks new enough, though—a military grade weapon from somewhere.

DeShear reached for the zip tie. "I'll take this and tie him up. We don't want any trouble. Take what you want, and go."

The gunman breathed hard.

Taking the zip tie, DeShear looked at the lieutenant. "Ready, Louis?"

Moray nodded again, extending his hands.

DeShear swung around and lowered his shoulder, ramming the gunman in the belly. Wrapping his arms around the man, DeShear churned his legs, driving them both into the rear deck railing. They smashed it hard, the gunman arching backwards, his arms flailing. His rifle flew from his grip as he went over backwards into the water.

Moray scrambled for his rifle. The gunman on the other boat fired. A bullet whizzed past DeShear's head. Another pinged off the railing, sending sparks into the air.

On the deck, the lieutenant spun around, his rifle in his hands. Crouching, he fired two bursts at the remaining gunman.

The attacker fell backwards, his weapon shooting wildly as he crashed to the deck.

"Grab that handgun, mister!" Moray got to his feet, leaping onto the other boat.

DeShear picked up the handgun from behind the scuba tanks, aiming it at the other boat. More shots came from the front of the pirates' vessel. Moray ducked, then leaped forward, firing half a dozen times.

Rushing forward, the Lieutenant kept his rifle aimed at the fore deck. *"Les autres, sortez! Les mains en l'air!"* He knelt for a moment, then got up and went below. "All clear, mister!"

DeShear peered over the back of the diving boat. The man in the red t-shirt wasn't there. Only a few bubbles dotted the surface.

Moray appeared on the rear of the pirate boat, his rifle butt resting on his thigh. "Where's your man, mister?"

"I don't see him. He must have drowned."

"Think so? No pirate from these waters is gonna drown." He went to the wheel and grabbed the spotlight, turning it on. "Look here."

The light made a bright circle on the water, giving it a greenish glow against the dark night. A long, dark shadow darted past, heading behind Moray's diving boat. The Lieutenant moved the light until it landed on a lone swimmer in a red t-shirt, quietly paddling away from the boats.

"That's him," DeShear said. "He's fast."

"Not fast enough, mister."

The shadow bumped into the gunman. He shrieked, kicking wildly.

"Start the motor." DeShear rushed toward the wheelhouse. "Let's get him out."

"No." Moray's gaze stayed on the water. "No time."

Another shadow crossed under the swimmer, then another. The man screamed, thrashing the water. In the beam of the spotlight, a massive tiger shark surged upwards and sunk its teeth into his thigh. The man howled, dark clouds filling the water around him. Another shark came, taking his arm and shaking its head. He screamed, throwing himself backwards, waving his bloody stump in the air.

"Help!" Saltwater filled his mouth, the water around him churning as the sharks continued their attacked. "*Alsjeblieft*!" he screamed. "Help me!"

A huge shadow flashed upwards, lifting the man from the water. Blood streamed from his mouth and down his cheeks. The white triangles glinted in the spotlight as the massive shark landed sideways, disappearing in a giant, white splash.

The waves flattened and disappeared, a few bubbles rising through the red patch. Then the water was calm.

DeShear stood at the wheel of the diving boat, panting. "We should have done something!"

"No time, mister." Moray plopped into the chair behind the wheel, his shoulders sagging. "If you had gone into that water, you'd be dead now, too. That's the way of the tiger shark."

DeShear grabbed the railing, cursing as he lowered his head. "What about your man, Lieutenant?"

"He died, mister. Everybody died." Moray dropped his rifle, his voice falling to a whisper. "And look at that, mister. They done shot up my diving boat."

The lieutenant sagged sideways and fell to the deck.

"Louis!" DeShear hurled himself over the railing, jumping onto the other boat. "Louis!"

Moray laid on the deck, blood seeping from his mouth. Two red spots grew on his shirt. Another spread over his upper leg.

DeShear ripped open the garments. Moray had been shot twice on the right side of his chest, once in the thigh.

The lieutenant's eyelids fluttered. Wheezing, he lifted his head. "You . . . got lucky again in this water, mister." He choked, spitting blood. "Again, you're the only one who didn't die."

"You're not going to die, Louis." Kneeling, DeShear pulled Moray onto his lap, cradling the lieutenant's head. "I'll drive us out of here. We'll be back at the dock in an hour. Stay with me, Louis. Keep fighting!" DeShear raced to the wheelhouse, searching the dashboard for a key to start the motor.

There was none.

"That's okay. Your boat—I'll get us out of here, Louis!" He jumped over the rail and climbed behind the wheel of Moray's boat. Heart pumping, he turned the key.

Nothing.

He glanced at the motor. Two holes were in the side, a thin line of steam rising from the top.

"We have a radio! I'll signal for help."

Groaning, Moray shook his head. "You're not thinking, mister. Call on the radio, a Defense Force boat shows up. How am I gonna explain you being on my boat?"

"Then . . . then we'll use the common channel. A non-distress frequency. There'll be a fishing boat out here somewhere."

"No, mister. You're gonna gum up the works. Everybody here fears the pirates. Nobody comes when you call. Only the Defense Force. Then, they hang me high from the yardarm."

"No." He climbed back over the railing to Moray.

"We did pretty even, mister." The lieutenant closed his eyes. "We got them pirates, but they got me."

"No. We can still both make it . . . Give me a few minutes to wire up this pirate boat so it'll run. It's fast. We can make it back to shore and get you to a hospital."

"They'll hang me, mister." Moray's voice faded. "I don't wanna go like that."

"Nobody's hanging anybody, Louis." DeShear took off his shirt, ripping it into strips. "I wasn't kidding about the girl or the money. It's all yours, Louis—$250,000." He tied a tourniquet around the leg and folded two makeshift bandages, pressing them to the chest wounds. "With that kind of money, you can hire the best lawyer on the island to defend yourself. Take all of the money. It's yours, all $250,000. Just . . . stay with me, Louis. Don't die."

Moray smiled, weakly patting DeShear's hand. "You . . . must be part sailor, mister . . . come telling a big fib like that."

CHAPTER 17

Scowling, Hollings paced back and forth in front of the table of computers, his cane jabbing the dusty ground with each step. "We ain't got enough power, we ain't got the information yet, and we done lost a hostage!" Turning, he glared at Helena. "But we still got you, don't we, Keeper 27? So unless you want your situation to take a nasty turn, you're going to tell me what I need to know. Where's your friend run off to, where's the money, and where's Constantine?"

Helena sat rigid, kneading her hands in her lap. "Of course, I shall tell you everything, Mr. Hollings." She glanced at the cap on the table. "How could I not?"

"No more games, old woman!" He slammed his cane down on the table. "You'll tell me the truth." Gritting his teeth, he grabbed the cap and pushed it onto her head.

Freeman winced, peering up from his keyboard. "Sir, we don't have enough power to—"

"Find it!" Hollings yelled. "Find the power to get these machines to run, or find another job."

Miss Franklin stepped behind Freeman, lowering her voice. "You said she was resisting before—that's why the computer wasn't working and needed more power." She made a fist and pounded it into her other hand. "Want me to persuade her a little?"

Trembling, Helena's gaze went to Hollings. "You'll have enough power now, Mr. Hollings. I won't resist. I only ask one thing in return." She swallowed hard, her hands shaking. "People are trying to harm Hamilton DeShear and Jaden Trinn. You can make them stop."

Hollings' eyed widened. His lips curled into a slow smile. "What?" He sneered. "Are you winding me up? Me, help them? Madam, it's my life's current goal to see them both dead, especially that manky little sket Jaden Trinn. Shot me full of holes, she did. Why would I ever help either one of them?"

"Because you need Constantine." Helena's voice quivered. "And I'm the only way you'll get her. If you help my friends, I'll take you to her."

Hollings dropped into the wheelchair, his jaw agape. "Cor, blimey," he whispered, rubbing his chin. "That's quite an offer, old girl."

"It's a trick." Franklin walked around to stand by Helena. "Let me work on her for a few minutes. She'll tell us whatever you want to know, I guarantee it."

"I suppose I should be right afraid of you, Miss." Helena stared up at her kidnapper. "And I am." Her eyes went to Hollings. "But I'd sooner die than let anyone harm that child. Working with you will get me to her fastest."

Franklin patted Helena on the shoulder. "Let me give it a try."

Pursing his lips, Hollings stared at his elderly hostage. The wind swept across the roof of the old building, ruffling its worn shingles and making its walls creak. "It's a trick." He pointed his finger at Helena. "I know it is. But still, if we get the girl . . ."

"I'll get her to talk," Franklin said.

"No, dear. You've misunderstood me." Helena's eyes stayed on Hollings. "I'd sooner die than let anyone harm that child."

Hollings sighed. "Aye, Miss Franklin. We can't resort to your methods." He got up from the wheelchair, leaning on his cane as he paced the floor again. "What the old bird is saying is, she'll stop breathing on her own—she'll go standalone or whatever's deeper than that until she offs herself. And then we're buggered. No amount of pain would get through. I've seen one drone stand still as another drone clubbed it right to death. Never flinched, never raised a hand. But if grabbing Jaden Trinn and Hank DeShear allow me to get that girl . . . maybe there's a way." He jerked his head toward the ambulance.

Frowning, Franklin walked behind the vehicle again.

"You." Hollings pointed to Freeman. "The old gal ain't likely to go running off, but keep your eye on her just the same. And get that bloody computer working. We ain't finished with it yet."

"Yes, sir."

Behind the ambulance, Hollings lowering his voice and addressed Miss Franklin. "The instructions were to get the little girl by whatever means necessary. This might be the fastest way."

"It might be fast," Franklin said, "but from what you told me about DeShear and Trinn, they're dangerous."

"Aye, no doubt about that. We'll need to lock them up tight—and you'll keep a close eye on them. When we have what we want, we'll snuff them out and dump them in a shallow grave. It's all the same to me." He walked out from behind the ambulance, looking at Helena. "I won't give you Jaden Trinn. She's a dead girl, that one. Shot me full of holes and left me in the trunk of a car."

"Miss Trinn didn't kill you," Helena said. "Though she had every right. And she made sure you received the medical attention that saved your life."

"Don't matter." Hollings sat down behind the table. "I might need DeShear, to sign everything over legally and whatnot, but I don't need Trinn. She ain't part of the equation."

Helena stared at him. "He loves her. So does Constantine. That makes her part of the equation."

Hollings lowered his head and balled up his fists. "A hard old bird, you are, Keeper 27—and you drive a hard bargain. Think you've got it all figured out, do you? Well, we'll see." He grabbed the cap and handed it to Freeman. "Hook her up again."

Freeman took the cap and placed it on Helena's head, then attached the wires to the computer and engaged the processors.

"Remember . . ." Hollings stared at Helena, narrowing his eyes. "Your visions didn't see all them little children dying, did it? You were right there, and you were oblivious. All you could do was watch the tansuits load corpse after corpse into the collectors' bins and wheel them off to the trash pile—while you cried in the courtyard."

She looked down. "And the person responsible died shortly after."

"No!" Hollings pounded the table. "Don't you never say that! Never! Doctor Hauser is alive."

"Then you have nothing to fear," Helena said. "He wanted Mr. DeShear alive to transfer the money and the businesses until Constantine was old enough. I'm sure he still does. Have you asked him?"

Hollings leaned back in his chair, putting his chin in his hand. "Let's get on with the matter at hand. You want a family reunion, is that it? All of Dr. Hauser's pesky little progeny, rounded up and safe for a party?"

"And Miss Trinn."

"And bloody well Miss Trinn!" He scowled. "But in exchange, I get what I want. You take me to Constantine, straight away. And if you cross me, dear lady, you'll stand front and center as I kill each and every one of your friends—while you watch."

Helena reached up and adjusted the cap. "Then we should get started. We have a long journey ahead of us."

Dr. Freeman typed on his computer. The processors next to the table whirred.

Helena took a deep breath, staring straight ahead. An image of Hollings appeared on the screen. He was slouching, his chin in his hand, as he sat next to Dr. Freeman in the old warehouse.

"I know what I look like," Hollings grumbled. "Where's the little girl?"

Helena continued looking straight ahead. The picture on the screen faded, turning a light blue-green, as if a thick turquoise fog had settled over the monitor. The color became more vibrant, twinkling with ripples of white, like diamonds scattered across a pale blue background, moving and twinkling as they passed

The color became streaked with waves, zipping across the screen; a distant shoreline came into view. Tiny islands off the bow of a fishing boat. A handsome man raised a wiggling worm toward a fishing hook as a young girl watched.

"Here. Here we go." Hollings leaned forward, licking his lips. "That's it. That's it."

The rear of the boat came into view. A beautiful, dark-haired woman in a black bikini stood on the rear deck. An African-American man in a blue-striped shirt stood in the boat's wheelhouse, looking out over the waves. He pointed, drawing the attention of the young girl. Dolphins crested the crystalline waters.

"Yes!" Hollings said. "Yes, that's it. Where are they?"

The image flashed to the little girl stepping aboard the boat when it was tied to the dock. The man had already boarded. He held her hand as she stepped down onto the deck, the woman following behind. In the distance, a large resort rose over the palm trees. And in between, the hulls and sterns of the many moored boats in the marina displayed their names—and their home port.

Andros Island Marina, Bahamas.

"The Bahamas!" Miss Franklin clapped her hands together. "Easy enough. That's a four-hour flight. Let's go. Stash the vehicles and—"

"No, not so fast." Hollings raised a hand, staring at the monitor. "We can't just buy plane tickets—she got no passport, and I can't exactly be seen in public. We'll need a jet—a big one—or we hire a charter boat. The only thing with the range for a trip like that is a blooming freighter."

"A boat?" Franklin put her hands on her hips. "That's slow."

Helena's gaze was fixed on the wall, her voice a whisper. "Armen Twa has a plane in Paris."

"Bah." Hollings tapped the ground with his cane. "I don't trust him. My mates at Port of London can get us on a freighter. But I know this old bird." He glared at Helena. "If I don't ask specific questions, she won't tell me specific answers."

"Going by boat." Franklin shook her head. "That adds days."

"Aye. But the girl's worth billions. That's worth taking days for." He rubbed his chin stubble. "Now, Keeper 27, who is in The Bahamas?"

Helena remained silent. Jaden Trinn and Hamilton DeShear flashed on the screen. DeShear hugged Jaden from behind, slipping his arms around her waist and kissing her.

"But not Constantine." Hollings grumbled. "I thought not. And where might she be?"

The screen went black.

A dark room with a stone floor and walls appeared. Water dripped somewhere in a corner, letting green moss grow on the wall. Above a wood-slat bed, a tiny window with bars on it looked out over another crystal blue sea.

On the floor of the cell, a raggedy man sat, scraggly and dirty, his long hair disheveled.

"I don't see her." Hollings leaned forward. "Where is she?"

Helena blinked a few times and the image faded.

"What!" Hollings slammed his hand into the table. "Bring it back!"

She turned to Hollings. "Constantine will be there. Soon."

"But where is that place?"

"First, we collect my friends." Helena lowered her head, staring at her hands. "I shall tell you no more until then."

"You blasted old crow!" Jumping to his feet, Hollings raised his cane and slammed it into the tabletop. "Woman, I have no time to waste on these games. Tell me where she is!"

"If you have no time to waste," Helena said quietly, "then we had better get to The Bahamas. When my friends are safe, I will tell you more. But for now, I can tell you this. You have a friend—a pilot—who runs air freight. Captain Restley. He will require $200,000 American dollars to take us all safely to The Bahamas. In cash. When you tell him you'll need an additional two days to get to where Constantine is, he will agree to do it—for an additional three hundred thousand."

"Half a million dollars!" Hollings choked, putting his hand to his chest. "Half a million dollars and two days!"

"Two *additional* days." Helena looked at her kidnapper. "But as you say, there is no time to waste. His plane is scheduled to leave for The Bahamas in four hours. If we leave now, he will let you aboard. A delay of even thirty minutes will add a week to your journey."

Cursing, Hollings smashed the cane into the table. "You old crow! I ain't got the helpers back from chasing your little doctor friend what run off, do I?"

Her face did not show the faintest hint of a smile. "I suppose you'll have to call them back and let her go."

Red-faced, he heaved his cane toward the exit and plopped back down in his wheelchair. The cane skittered across the dirt floor, coming to a stop near the wall.

Franklin put a hand on her hip. "What do you want to do?"

"Sod it!" Hollings pushed the wheelchair away from the table, rolling himself toward the ambulance. "Pack this gear. Be ready to leave in five minutes. We'll hire whatever men and guns we need once we get to The Bahamas. And let the doctor lady go. She won't be able to do us no harm from here."

CHAPTER 18

In the darkness, Moray's boat rocked gently in the waves. Louis moaned, waking up again. The makeshift bandages on his wounds were caked in dried blood, his chest slowly rising and falling.

DeShear knelt next to the Lieutenant, holding a plastic water bottle to his lips. "Here. It's the last of our water. You take it."

Louis sucked up the final sips, then turned his head away, his voice a whisper. "You are cruel, mister."

Picking up a rag, DeShear wiped the sweat off the Lieutenant's brow. "It's cruel to save your life? You're just tired. You're in a lot of pain and you're talking nonsense. When we get you to a hospital—"

"They . . . will hang me."

"Forget about where you were taking me, and why. Nobody needs to know that now. We'll tell them I'm just a tourist, and that I hired your boat to take me scuba diving at night. On the way, we were attacked, and we defended ourselves."

"You know where we were really headed." Each breath Moray took was a raspy wheeze. "You . . . could have killed me in the night. Thrown me over the side to the sharks. Why didn't you?"

"I'm not a murderer. I told you, I'm trying to find a little girl, not kill her. I was trying to save the woman I was with, too. That should be obvious to you by now. I had every reason to kill you and I didn't—doesn't that at least make you think I might be telling the truth?"

The engines of the Defense Force cutter could be heard long before the boat itself was visible. DeShear jumped up, rushing to the rear of boat, waving his arms as the beam of a distant spotlight swung back and forth over the water.

"Here! We're here!"

He knew the sailors on board the cutter couldn't hear him, but he couldn't help himself.

DeShear glanced at where the lieutenant lay on the deck. "It's almost over, Louis. We're going to be rescued. You just have to hang on a little longer."

Moray's head hung sideways, his cheek on his shoulder. "You . . . used the radio."

"That's right." DeShear continued waving. "Now, we're almost rescued."

"You saved me from dying in the night." Louis got to his feet, sagging against the railing. "So I can be humiliated and die in the daytime."

"What?" DeShear turned around.

Groaning, Louis threw a leg over the rail. "Let the sharks take me. I'm not going like this." He put both hands on the railing, leaning toward the water.

"No! Louis!" DeShear lunged for the lieutenant, wrapping his arms around him and hauling him in. They crashed back onto the deck. "You're going to stay alive, Louis." DeShear gasped. He gritted his teeth and grabbed the lieutenant by the collar. "You're going to tell the Defense Force sailors how I bandaged your wounds and gave you water through the night and saved your miserable life!"

The spotlight bathed the deck in brightness. DeShear rolled onto his back, holding a hand up to shield his eyes. Louis lay on the deck, moaning. Sitting up, DeShear waved again. "Help us! We have an injured man!"

The Defense Force cutter slowed its engines, pulling along side the two smaller boats. A man's voice came over the ship's loudspeaker. "Raise your hands. Do not move!"

DeShear stood, lifting his arms over his head. "Hurry! We have an injured man. Bring your medic."

Several sailors in white uniforms jumped from the Defense Force cutter and onto the deck of the diving boat. Another crewman stood behind a machine gun mounted at the front of the big ship, aiming his weapon at DeShear.

Two more sailors came on board. One carried a black bag, the other carried a rifle.

"This man is Louis Moray." DeShear pointed to the lieutenant. "He's a member of your armed forces and he needs urgent medical attention."

The sailor with the bag kneeled at Louis' side. The other sailor stood in front of DeShear, pointing the rifle at him. "You sent a distress call?"

DeShear squinted in the bright light. "I did. That's right."

The rifleman looked over the two boats. "How about you tell me what happened here, sir?"

"We were going night diving. Scuba diving." DeShear spoke loud enough for everyone on board to hear, including Moray. Nodding at the diving tanks at the back of the boat, DeShear looked at the sailor. "We were shot at by men from another boat. My charter captain is also in your armed forces, so he had some weapons. He slowed the boat down. They had us tie the boats together, then they boarded us. There was a firefight."

The sailor with the rifle narrowed his eyes. "You shoot the men on the other boat?"

"No," DeShear said. "The lieutenant shot one. I knocked the other one into the water. He was killed by sharks."

"Sharks." The sailor pointed. "Lots of sharks in the waters around here. Too many to go night diving."

"We didn't plan on stopping here. We stopped because they shot at us. We were headed somewhere else."

"Where?"

The loudspeaker crackled. "We have something in the water! Port side of your vessel."

The rifleman peered over the railing. "This be your man?"

"I don't know." His hands still over his head, DeShear walked to the side of the boat.

The bloated corpse of a man floated face-down in the water, bathed in illumination from the ship's spotlights. An anchor chain was wrapped around the dead man's waist. The chain hung straight down from the body, its anchor barely visible in the spotlight.

"You knocked the man into the water, but tie him to the anchor first?"

"No." DeShear winced. "That's . . . I don't—"

A crewman on the Defense Force cutter tossed a retrieval pole to a sailor on Moray's boat. Leaning over the side, the man swung outward and made a grab for the corpse.

The curved end of the pole made a small splash as it fell short of the body. The sailor pulled the pole back and moved up the deck a few feet before leaning over again. His second cast bumped the corpse's leg.

The dead body rocked back and forth.

"That's a good-sized anchor," the rifleman said. "But the body still pull it up. In these parts, the sea always give up the dead."

DeShear kept his eyes on the corpse.

The sailor's pole went out again, dropping the long retrieval hook on the side of the corpse's neck.

"Ha!" the rifleman said. "You got him."

As the sailor pulled the pole, the bloated corpse turned, nearing the boat but slipping from the hooks' grasp.

DeShear stared at the dead body in the water. It had both arms and legs.

As the corpse drifted closer, more details became clear. The spotlight illuminated the dead man's clothing. He wore a blue-striped shirt.

DeShear stepped closer to the rail, his jaw hanging open.

Laquan! The fishing charter captain!

Gasping, DeShear grabbed the railing.

How did he end up here? Dead, and chained to an anchor?

How could that happen?

When the crewman's next cast reached the body, he snagged the waist.

The corpse rolled over as he pulled it in. The dead man was wearing a black scuba diving mask. His arms, legs and clothing were streaked with a yellow paint, and the short harpoon from a spear gun stuck out of his chest.

"Shark repellent." The crewman pulled the body next to Moray's boat, pointing to the streaks of paint across the dead man's clothes. The crewman fanned his nose. "He's covered in it. That stuff sure puts off a smell."

The rifleman glared at DeShear. "You say you knock this man in the water?"

DeShear's mind raced.

Laquan was in on the attack. He had to be. He sent Constantine to the front berth on purpose, and arranged for the rendezvous with the kidnappers.

But to end up chained to the bottom, with a spear in his chest . . .

He got double crossed.

When the shooting started, Laquan must have put on the mask and doused himself with shark repellant, then went over the side—either carrying a hidden air tank or knowing one was waiting for him on the bottom.

And it was—along with someone holding a spear gun and an anchor chain.

The whole thing had to be planned pretty precisely, but I guess once they had Constantine, they didn't want any loose ends—or extra partners.

The sailor nudged DeShear with the tip of the rifle. "Sir, I asked you—is this the man you knocked into the water?"

"No." DeShear squeezed his eyes shut, fully aware that his next words were going to sound extremely bad for him. "That's Laquan. He . . . was the captain of my fishing charter a few days ago. Lieutenant Moray saved us that day."

The sailor whistled. "You sure are unlucky. Sounds like every boat you take, somebody ends up dead. Or maybe you're not unlucky at all." He called out over his shoulder. "How's the lieutenant?"

"He may not make it," the medic said. "Bring the stretcher!"

DeShear turned to Moray. "Louis! Tell them. Tell them how I saved you. Tell them I'm innocent."

The rifleman glanced at the bloody man on the deck. "Well, lieutenant?"

Louis raised his eyes to DeShear. "All I know is, he told me a big story. Looks like it didn't turn out to be true."

"Louis!" DeShear rushed forward.

The rifleman stepped in front of DeShear, forcing him back. He grabbed DeShear's arms and held them behind his back.

"Tell them!" DeShear shouted. "My charter was attacked. You picked up me and Jaden Trinn out of the water. I told you we couldn't find the captain."

"Looks like we found him now." The rifleman pulled out a pair of handcuffs. "But he's not talking."

Two more sailors carried a stretcher over to the lieutenant. Laying it down, the men eased their wounded patient onto it and strapped him in.

DeShear twisted out of the rifleman's grasp, dropping to his knees at the lieutenant's side and grabbing the stretcher with both hands. "Louis, please! You and I, we were attacked last night! I saved you. Tell them. I'm not a murderer! I just want to find the little girl."

His eyes half open, Louis turned his head to gaze at DeShear. "You saved me . . . and you ruined my life," he whispered. "Now, I ruined yours."

"No!" DeShear cried. "No!"

The sailors pried DeShear's hands off the stretcher.

"Same water . . . same story," Moray wheezed. Straining, he lifted his head off the stretcher. "You go on a boat, someone you don't like dies."

"No! Louis, tell them the truth! Please!"

"You're a murderer. You killed them all." Drops of blood flew from Moray's mouth with each word. "You never should have come back here."

The lieutenant collapsed back onto the stretcher.

"I didn't kill anyone! Louis!"

One of the sailors put his fingers to Moray's throat. After a moment, he shook his head. "He's gone."

Grabbing DeShear, the rifleman dragged him away as the other sailors lifted the stretcher onto the cutter.

The rifleman thrust his weapon sideways against DeShear's chest as two others held his arms and handcuffed him.

"You're a killer, working with these pirates," the rifleman said. "You're up to something—and we're gonna chain you up in a hot jail cell until we find out what it is."

Two other crewmen hauled the floating corpse into Moray's boat, rolling it over so Laquan's face stared up at the night sky. As they waited for another stretcher, one reached down and pulled off the dead man's black diving mask.

CHAPTER 19

In the back of the ambulance, Helena shuddered. She pulled her seat belt tighter and folded her hands in her lap.

Hollings leaned forward from where his wheelchair was clamped to the ambulance floor. "What are you up to, Keeper 27? You seeing one of your visions?"

As she stared at the ambulance wall, the metal seemed to soften and fade, a low hum growing in her ears. A dim image of a recreational boat appeared, drifting forward like it was playing on a movie screen that was immersed in a thick fog. The image became clearer, the fog lifting. DeShear struggled against two sailors in white uniforms. They dragged him from the vessel. On the boat's deck lay a man in a blue-striped shirt, soaking wet and streaked with yellow paint.

Helena stared into the vision, gazing at the man. Some type of arrow stuck out from his chest.

His arms lay at his sides, water sloshing back and forth around him as the boat rocked in the waves. Other than that, he didn't move.

She looked closer. The dead man's face was covered with a black scuba diving mask.

Slowly, Helena's gaze moved away from the ambulance wall, a hint of a smile tugging at her wrinkled lips.

Red-faced, Mr. Hollings glared at her, his lips moving.

The last of the fog lifted from Helena's eyes. The hum faded, and Hollings' words reached her ears.

"Here, you old bird. What's happening?"

"Nothing. Just some news for Dr. Kittaleye." Keeper 27 leaned back, easing into the headrest. "Her nightmares are at an end. The man in the black mask will not be able to bother her any longer."

Hollings continued ranting—*The what? The who?*—but Helena was no longer listening. She squeezed her eyes shut, clenching her hands against her belly as the other visions came rushing back.

A little girl lay strapped down on an operating table, held down by people in surgical scrubs.

"You—you don't use any anesthesia?" an attendant said.

"There was a . . . reaction the first time," the surgeon replied. "Now, we just go in cold."

The surgeon sliced the skin of her tiny leg as the little girl kicked and screamed.

Smoke rushed upward as the wound was cauterized to stop the bleeding. The stench of burnt flesh filled the air. The skin and muscles were pried open with large metal clamps, the little girl shaking as the attendants forced them into place.

Then came the drills.

"We must extract from several places if we are to reach the rich marrow," the surgeon said.

As the girl screamed, they drilled into her. Bits of bone flew from the drill tip until the holes were large enough, then a long, firm wire was shoved into her femur. The child cried, straining against her captors, but to no avail. As her tiny chest heaved, the tubes were inserted and the machine turned on, humming as the marrow was slowly sucked out. When they'd filled a two-quart bag, the procedure was ended.

The girl lay on the table, her cheeks wet with tears, sobbing.

"There," the surgeon said. "Put a bandage on the leg until we're ready to go again."

"A bandage? Doctor, surely we must suture the wound and—"

"This is a business!" The surgeon peeled off the latex gloves and walked toward the exit. "Patch her up and give her an ice cream. We drill again tomorrow."

In the ambulance, Hollings shouted at Helena. "What's that you're mumbling, Keeper 27? They're killing who?"

Helena turned away from him, wiping the tears from her eyes as the horrid vision faded.

CHAPTER 20

Trinn pulled a piece of rope through the belt loops of her oversize stolen shorts, tying it in a knot as she ran through the yards, heading toward the hotel.

Hours, the doctor said. I was out for hours!

Wincing, she held her side and climbed over a small fence, hoping to move around undetected from the street. Her t-shirt snagged, leaving a piece of white on the point of the slat and a scrape on her stomach, but she didn't slow down.

If DeShear's instructions are still in place, I need to get word to Helena. But I wasted a lot of time in that hospital.

If the plans have changed, how will I know?

She crouched by a dumpster near the marina. A chain link fence separated the civilians' boats from those of the Defense Force. On the wall outside the duty hut, under a bright street light, was a payphone.

She bit her nail, her gaze going from the phone to the street light.

No. It's too risky to try a call from here. Too much visibility.

And it might be too risky to call Helena at all now.

She considered the cash she had hidden in a planter box in front of the resort.

If I can get some money, I can get a passport and ID.

But that takes time. If Helena's at risk, I need to get to her quickly.

Sighing, Trinn closed her eyes and pressed her head against the dumpster.

A noise came from a nearby boat. Trinn ducked, hoping she hadn't been spotted.

A male and female sailor emerged from the lower deck of a Defense Force vessel, fixing their clothing.

The woman grabbed the radio from the boat's console. "Unit ten-thirty, checking in."

"All clear, Ensign Jolie," the dispatcher said. "You and Mr. Desmond can lock up your craft and head back to quarters. Only unit seven twenty-one is still out."

"Roger, base. I'll give them a quick hello." She adjusted the radio. "Unit ten-thirty to vessel seven twenty-one at sea. Come in, MacPherson."

The radio squawked. "Seven twenty-one here," a man said. "Good evening, Ensign Jolie."

The woman smiled. "That you, Michael?"

"It surely is, Miss. How are things at the marina?"

"Mighty fine, sir. Mighty fine." She winked at Mr. Desmond. "And what about your distress call? All good?"

"We riding high on the tide, sister. Caught us a murderer, maybe—that man from the other day. The one with the burning fishing boat."

A jolt went through Trinn's insides.

Burning fishing boat!

There can't be two of those in two days.

Trinn crouched lower, craning her neck toward the Defense Force boat.

"Murderer?" the Ensign said. "That's bad for business on our little island. What this fella's name?"

"You saw it on the duty sheets for the day. He call himself Hamilton DeShear, from the States. Look like he attack Lieutenant Moray on his diving boat and try something funny."

"That fella bad news." Jolie paced back and forth in the little boat's wheelhouse. "The Magistrate gonna lock him away, come morning."

"Quick-quick, you bet. And serve him right, too. The lieutenant's in a bad way. The boys want to gut this DeShear like a fish and throw him over the side."

A car's headlights washed the dumpster in light. Trinn recoiled, crawling further behind the blue steel box.

I need to get out of sight but still stay close enough to see and hear what's happening.

"We gonna sign off," Jolie said. "When you due in?"

"Be a few hours. This big boat take a while longer than your little speedy one."

"See you when I see you, then. Unit ten thirty, out."

"Good night, Ensign. Seven twenty-one clear."

The ensign locked up her boat and headed toward the base dormitories. Trinn sat on the asphalt, replaying the conversation between the sailors.

Helena might be in trouble, but DeShear definitely is.

Trinn shook her head.

She stood up, lifting the faded plastic lid of the dumpster and peering inside. It was dry, mostly empty, and not very smelly. Gaps along the warped, cracked lid would allow for observation of the boats. It'd make a good enough hiding spot until the boat carrying DeShear arrived.

She put one foot on the side support of the container, hoisting her other leg over the top.

Sorry to disobey orders, Hank. You can be mad at me later—if you live.

* * * * *

As a car went by the front of the dark little house, Nigel stared at the laundry line in the homeowner's back yard.

One, two, three, four, five.

Five pairs of clothespins—but only four t-shirts.

He ducked his head and walked under the rope, examining the second laundry line. Two pairs of shorts, and three pairs of clothespins. Stepping closer, he took out his phone and turned on the flashlight. The shorts were considerably larger in the waist than the naked woman he witnessed running across the street. Turning, he viewed the tiny yard. A third and fourth line had previously hung from the pole, but now only three did. The fourth had been cut. Part of it dangled from the pole; part of it was sprawled on the ground, its clothes laying in the short, sparse grass. Nigel bent down and picked up the end of the dismantled laundry line and stared at the pruning shears on the ground next to it.

And then she had a makeshift belt.

If she gets a pair of shoes, she'll be moving fast.

Coiling a section of rope around his fist, Nigel picked up the shears and sliced off a section for himself. He tied a knot in the middle and yanked the rope tight with both hands.

And this little garrote will go around your skinny neck when I find you, Miss Trinn.

Shoving the rope in his pocket, he continued along her trail. A small piece of torn, white cotton cloth hung from the top of the neighbor's fence.

And then you went here . . .

The next house had apparently delivered the shoes to his fleeing prey. The occupants left their footwear in a row on the back porch—two small pairs of children's shoes, one large pair of men's shoes, and an empty gap between them.

Just enough space for mama's shoes.

He looked to the next yard. It was the last house in the row.

And where did she go after that?

She doesn't know anyone's after her. She just wants to get someplace. Where?

She knows her man DeShear's been taken away.

Would she think she could steal a boat and go after him? Intervene somehow on his behalf? Or would she just run back to her hotel?

He walked to the edge of the yard of the last house, looking down the road.

She might stay off the main streets—she has so far. She doesn't want to be noticed. She's afraid of what will happen if she's spotted. That will slow her down.

He pulled out his phone to call Trinn's resort.

Put a word in the desk clerk's ear. Change the locks on her room and call me if she comes in. With no access to the room, she can't reacquire her money or clothing, credit cards, identification . . . that will limit her ability to move very far. Then it's just a matter of—"

A passing car illuminated the fence between the marina and the Defense Force boats. The black lid of a trash dumpster lowered. Under it, a glimpse of white t-shirt and long, dark hair.

Nigel gasped.

Unless there's magic in the air, there you are, Miss Trinn. Hiding in the rubbish like the irritating piece of trash that you are.

Near the marina. So you can be ready to help your man somehow when he comes back from his little boat ride.

He pressed his hand to his pocket—and the firm lump of rope coiled up inside it.

Very well, miss. Very well.

But I don't fancy jumping into that bin, do I? Might take a few seconds to climb in, and then I'd lose the element of surprise, wouldn't I? And possibly have you overtake me? No. Can't have that. Might be a broken bottle or piece of wood in there that you've fashioned into a weapon.

No, we need to get you out, not get me in.

And what would do that? A bit of fire tossed in, maybe? A Coke bottle full of gasoline, with a burning rag for a stopper? Light some newspaper and stuff it into a sack of oily rags from somewhere?

But where am I going to get that on short notice tonight? I can't exactly run off and leave your bin unattended—you might not be here when I got back . . .

Nigel rubbed his chin, viewing the dumpster from across the wide-open parking lot on his right. On his left, a door slammed. A bus boy carried a trash bag out of a seafood restaurant, tossing it into the dumpster at the rear of the building. As the boy returned inside, the dark, furry shadows of several large rats scurried across a nearby telephone pole wire. One by one, they crawled down the wooden utility pole and across the fence to the restaurant dumpster.

Free meal, eh boys?

And maybe just the way to get our Miss Trinn out of the dumpster without me going in.

CHAPTER 21

Trinn crouched inside the dumpster with her t-shirt pulled over her nose. Putting her head against the warped dumpster lid, she peered outside. The street light allowed enough illumination to see the quiet boats.

Nothing yet. But the ensign said it would be a few hours.

There was whistling and footsteps in the parking lot behind her. The gravel crunched with every step. Trinn turned toward the sound, lowering her head.

A man approached, carrying a dark green trash bag and whistling as he walked.

Trinn frowned.

Great. Of course someone has to throw trash away while I'm in here.

She hunched down, pressing herself against the front wall.

Just stay still and he probably won't see you.

The lid opened, letting in light from the streetlight. The bag dropped in, sagging sideways as it hit the floor. The inside of the dumpster was cast in shadows again when the lid banged closed, and the man walked back in the direction he came.

Trinn peered out as the stench of rotting fish guts assaulted her nose. Gagging, she faced the recent bag of deposited trash. Fish heads and entrails seeped out onto the floor of the dumpster. She exhaled, shoving the t-shirt over her nose and putting her face to the wall.

Out of the corner of her eye, the bag moved. Two lumps under the plastic, moving toward the open gap at the top of the bag. Then, a third.

She pressed herself harder into the wall. Goosebumps tingled on her arms.

No, no, no. Don't be . . .

The first massive rat leaped from the bag, covered in slime and baring its teeth.

Trinn stifled a shriek, throwing herself backwards into the corner of the dumpster.

A second and third rat emerged, dripping with slime and clawing through the goo on the floor.

As a pack, they came toward her.

"Oh, no!" Trinn clawed the top of the dumpster, trying to pick her feet up. "No, no, no!"

As the first rat snapped at her ankle, she threw open the dumpster's plastic lid and swung her legs upward like a gymnast. With both hands on the steel frame, she righted herself and balanced on the edge of the dumpster, kicking as the attacking vermin bit at her feet.

A slime-covered rat leaped at her, grabbed her calf. Its claws dug into her skin.

Heart pounding, Trinn lowered her belly onto the steel frame and slammed her leg back and forth until the rat let go, then thrust sideways off the dumpster. She crashed onto the hard asphalt of the parking lot, rolling away as fast as she could.

On her back, she crawled backwards, panting. A shiver went up her spine as she stared at the blue steel box.

"Here, miss, what's happened? Are you all right?" A man rushed forward—the one who'd just thrown the trash away. "I'm frightfully sorry. I didn't know you were . . . well, were you in the rubbish bin, ma'am? I don't—I had no idea. Are you homeless, miss? Do you need help?" He put his hand under her arm. "I'm dreadfully sorry. Please, allow me to help you up and let's get you a proper meal."

Trinn turned to face him, opening her mouth to speak. The stranger dug his fingers into her arm and yanked a rope from his pocket with his free hand. His grip shot daggers of pain up her arm as the rope uncoiled and he looped it around her head.

Barely stable on her feet, Trinn swung her face away and brought her free hand up to her neck as the rope dropped past her chin. Clawing outward, the back of her hand slammed into her throat as the attacker pulled the cord tight.

The rope crushed Trinn's fingers against her windpipe. She pushed her hand outward to keep the cord from slicing through her neck and killing her.

The attacker pulled her backwards, yanking her off her feet and dragging her across the parking lot. Trinn tried to yell for help, but nothing got past her windpipe. Flopping over, she swung at the stranger's legs and feet, the pressure building in her lungs.

"Aw, Miss Trinn," he grunted. "Is that the best you can do?" Chuckling, he pulled her along the side of the building. "Don't worry. This will be quick."

She kicked the ground, scrambling to get to her feet and relieve the pressure on her throat. She swung her free hand at his face.

The man leaned back, pulling her up and arching her over his midsection. "No," he gasped, tightening the rope around her neck. "I don't think so. Can't have any scratches, love—DNA and all that." He jerked her head back and forth. "Now, just be a good little lass—and die. That's all we want."

The pressure mounted. Trinn's eyes pulsed, her lungs aching. No air was getting in or out. Her attacker kept knocking her off balance so she couldn't get her feet down and relieve the pressure.

"That's it, girl." He groaned as he tightened the cord. "It'll be over soon."

Splotches of red and green appeared before her eyes. The street light overhead turned pink. She blinked, pushing blood over her cornea. Her mind raced.

Think, Jaden. Get an angle or you're dead.

He jerked her again. Trinn squeezed her eyes shut, her hand swinging wildly at any part of him. She brushed chin stubble, then hair, but couldn't connect.

As his chest pressed into her spine, he yanked the cord again. She twisted, sending them sideways. They crashed into a garbage can, knocking it to the ground and spilling its contents.

The rope tightened again.

"You're done, girl." His bad breath was hot in her ear. "It's almost over. The blood vessels are bursting in your eyes, and the tunnel vision's coming. That's death, love. Let Uncle Nigel put you down nice and easy. There's no need to fight. Just let it happen."

Groaning, Trinn swiped at him again, her fingertips smashing into the wall behind him.

Nigel laughed and pulled the rope tighter. Her eyes felt as though they would pop. Her vision clouded, growing dark around the perimeter like she was falling down a well.

"That's it," he whispered. "Let it come. Let death take you."

She closed her eyes and clenched her teeth, throwing her hand back again. She smacked the wall a second time. Pain shot up her fingers, making them throb.

His sweat dripped onto her cheek. "That's a good lass. I like a bit of a fight, if you must know."

Trinn's eyesight turned red, then faded to black. Her forehead throbbed, her pulse drumming in her ears.

I'm dying. Do something. Anything.

He swung her side to side again, her feet brushing ground.

Lift! Use your body weight to knock him off balance!

She grabbed the wrist of her roped hand, putting all of her weight on it. Red blotches splattered across her closed eyes. Throwing her legs upward, she kicked out, arching her back.

The motion brought them both forward. Her feet touched the ground again. Holding tight to her wrist, Trinn heaved her legs up again. The rope dug into her fingers as she leaned back and kicked her legs and torso outward.

Her stomach jolted like she was falling. They both fell forward. She turned her head as the asphalt rushed toward her. Her body jolted with the impact as Nigel landed on top of her.

"No, you don't." He was back on his feet before she was, lifting her by the neck again.

Trinn shoved her feet into the ground, forcing herself into him and knocking them both over backward. They slammed into the wall.

She could barely see. Nigel grunted, heaving her to the side. Her head crashed into the wall. Rearing back, he rammed her head into it again.

She put her hand out to stop the impact. As he slammed her forward again, her hand went through glass. She forced her eyes open.

A window.

As Nigel swung her at the wall again, Trinn leaned toward the glass, hitting the window frame with her forehead. Pain surged through her temples.

When he jerked her back, she didn't fight.

"Oh, yes?" he shouted. "Giving up, are we, love?"

He shoved her toward the glass. Trinn bent forward and lowered her head into it. The window shattered, sending a shower of glass over her head and neck. Heaving herself left and right, she dropped her weight into the broken glass, then shoved herself forward as hard as she could. The glass scraped across her collarbone, dragging her attacker's hands into its sharp edges.

Nigel howled, loosening his grip on the rope.

Trinn forced herself sideways, driving her head into his teeth. She jerked backwards and rammed him again, spattering blood over his face, then launched herself into his nose.

The crunch filled her ears, and the rope loosened again. This time, her bound hand was able to pull some slack from her throat. She sucked air into her lungs.

Nigel pulled the rope, dragging her along the side of the building. She grabbed her bound wrist and lunged forward, then side to side, left and right, front and back—anything to keep him from regaining his leverage.

"No, lassie. That's not how this ends." He jerked her off her feet. "You die. I walk away."

Trinn grabbed her wrist one last time, summoning the last bits of her waning strength. She dropped her weight onto her wrist. Nigel leaned back, counterbalancing and taking her off her feet. As she lifted, she brought her knees to her chest and then thrust her legs over her head, landing her knees alongside her attacker's ears. Upside down, she wrapped her ankles tight and jerked her thighs to the side as hard as she could.

Nigel's breath caught in his throat. The rope loosened. He put his hands on her hips, pushing her away.

Trinn clenched her legs harder, slamming them to the side again and again. Nigel dropped the rope, clutching her legs as they went over backwards.

She slammed into the ground but maintained her grip on his head, forcing her weight back and forth.

Nigel screamed, clawing at her. With a final push, she twisted and jerked, a massive crunch emanating from the attacker's neck.

His hands fell to the ground. A slow hiss escaped his lips, his jaw hanging open.

Trinn pulled the rope from her neck, gasping for air. The cord was covered in blood.

Gasping, she rolled away and got to her knees. Nigel stared out into the night, unblinking and unmoving, his head at an odd angle from his body.

Trinn sagged into the wall and massaged her throat. "That's . . . how this ends," she rasped. "You die . . . and I walk away."

Putting her hand on the wall, she forced herself to her feet and staggered down the alley.

Beams of light illuminated the wall and everything around her.

"You, there! Hold it!"

Flashlights shined into her eyes. Racing footsteps came closer.

Trinn broke into a run.

Half a dozen people in blue uniforms swarmed around her. They pushed her to the wall and put handcuffs on her wrists. Trinn gazed at the uniform of a Bahamian Defense Force soldier.

"You're coming with us," he said.

An ensign placed two fingers on Nigel's throat. "Not this one." He shook his head. "He's dead."

"You!" The soldier jerked Trinn's arm. "What's your name?"

She turned her face away.

"Never mind that." An officer stepped forward. He pushed Trinn's matted hair from her forehead, his gaze moving over her blood-streaked face and neck. He faced his soldiers. "Take her to the infirmary." As his men picked Trinn up, the officer turned and peered toward the water. "We've got a boat coming in any minute now, with a prisoner on board. We don't need any kind of distraction."

CHAPTER 22

On the second ring, Magistrate McCullough pried open one eye and glared at his phone. Next to him in the bed, his wife groaned, rolling over and pulling a pillow over her head. The Magistrate sighed, picking the phone up from the nightstand and holding it to his ear. "This had better be good," he mumbled. "Do you know how late it is?"

Armen Twa chuckled. "Oh, I think you will like what I have to say, Your Honor. I have just had a most interesting phone call. From a Mr. Hollings—I believe you know him."

"The fat old sot." McCullough snorted. "What does he want?"

"He wished to inquire about certain . . . *packages*."

"Oh?" The Magistrate yawned, closing his eyes and snuggling into his pillows again. "We move a lot of merchandise around here. What packages would these be?"

"A small, medium and large one, shall we say. Two that you sent to be . . . *disposed of,* and one that is in my possession."

"Well, too bad for your friend. I'm sure both of those packages are well gone."

"Mr. Hollings is no friend of mine, Charles, but allow me to shed some light on the situation regarding the packages. The one from Florida is being returned to you as we speak, and the one from New York is in custody of your man at the base. So it seems a deal may be in order."

Magistrate McCullough groaned, rolling onto his back and putting his forearm over his eyes. "We've been through that. Your people want the small package, exclusively. So unless your friend Mr. Hollings is willing to part with several billion dollars in cash, I don't see—"

"That is exactly what he proposed. In fact, he asked me to name my price."

Charles scoffed. "He's not the negotiator his master was, is he? What did you tell him?"

"Five billion. American."

"Did you?" The magistrate shook his head, smiling. "I bet that had the git hopping mad."

"I thought it would as well. But as it stands, he agreed."

"He what!" McCullough bolted upright in his bed, his heart racing. "Did you just say Hollings agreed to pay five billion American dollars?"

"Yes," Armen said. "He is actually on his way to you now, to perform the transaction for the two larger packages as soon as possible. Can you arrange that?"

"Arrange?" The magistrate threw the sheets back, bounding out of bed. "I bloody well don't even know where they are!" He raced to the bathroom, flipping the light switch and turning on the cold water faucet. His bloodshot eyes stared back at him, his jaw hanging open.

Five billion dollars! And I've ordered them both to be killed!

I need to get to the base and stop that order.

Breathing hard, he glanced around the room, looking for his clothes.

"Charles, I can hear you panicking. Please, calm down. As I stated, one of the packages is on the way to you." Armen Twa's tone was calm and measured, as always. "It is scheduled to arrive at the dock momentarily, if it is not there already. The other package, I believe, is at the base infirmary."

When the sink filled with cold water, McCullough took a deep breath and plunged his face in. The chill sent shivers down his spine, but he was awake. He lifted his head and grabbed a towel from the rack, drying himself as he rushed back to the bedroom. "How—how do you know all this?" McCullough asked.

"You are not the only one with Defense Force people on your payroll, Charles."

The Magistrate threw open his dresser drawer and dug for some pants. "The New York package. She's in the infirmary?"

"Yes. It seems she had a run in with your man Nigel. As a result, he will no longer be reporting for work."

"Ah, the ruddy witch. Nigel was a good man." Charles sat on the bed, holding the phone to his head with his shoulder and sliding a leg into his trousers. He leaned over and lifted the window shade, peeking out toward the base. Several sailors were tying a Defense Force boat to the dock. The rest of what he could see appeared to be quiet.

"We all get tempted to go past our prime, dear fellow. Last night, Nigel did. This morning, see that you do not." Twa's phone line crackled with static. "It is my understanding the packages are in rough shape. If it is not too much trouble, you may wish to have them cleaned up. I expect this to be a somewhat emotional transaction. Presentation will matter."

Charles zipped his fly and grabbed his shoes, heading for the door. "And then what?"

"You will wire the cash to me," Twa said. "Then, give your guests the location of the third package and send them to finalize the last part of the deal."

The Magistrate stopped walking, his heart in his throat.

If DeShear were to somehow survive, he'd be a rich man who might come looking for revenge.

I'll need a plan for that.

But right now, I'd better see this deal gets arranged the way Armen Twa and his partners want it.

"You . . ." McCullough rubbed his chin. "You aren't seriously considering giving Const—uh, *the little girl* to Hollings, are you?"

"I am seriously considering the fact that if Mr. Hollings will offer five billion American dollars for this trio of misfits and freaks, they must be worth ten. When he arrives, I will kill him and his people before they can leave the airport. We will sort out everything else after that."

In the middle of his dark living room, Charles chewed his lip. "He'll be expecting that, Armen."

"Of course he will," Twa said. "That is why he has demanded to have an insurance policy—so he feels safe. And I have agreed."

"Oh?" Grabbing his car keys and suit coat, Magistrate McCullough opened his front door and sprinted toward his old, rusty Mercedes. "And what insurance policy would that be?"

"You, Your Honor."

CHAPTER 23

Kitt knocked on the door, pulling her jacket collar up. She glanced up and down the hallway, heart pulse throbbing.

Every minute on the trains, every transfer that seemed to take an eternity, she'd been paranoid.

She didn't even know who might be after her, but she believed Helena and she'd seen enough to know someone *was* after her.

And if Gretchen let Kitt inside her apartment, Kitt had the hardest decision yet.

"Jaden Trinn is an agent for the United States government. You must contact her boss."

Standing in the second-floor hallway of her college friend's apartment building, Kitt groaned.

She'll never believe my story.

I certainly wouldn't.

What should someone make of such a story? Two calls to a generic U.S. government information site—one from the train station and one at a transfer depot— had yielded nothing.

What exactly was I supposed to do with such vague information?

But Berlin would be a safe harbor for a day or two, and that's what mattered now, while she deliberated on Helena's cryptic message.

She knocked on the door again.

Please be home, Gretchen. Please, please, please . . .

Kitt shivered in the hallway, brushing melted snowflakes from her shoulders. Berlin in February was as cold as Paris, maybe colder. Dark before dinner and often overcast all day, the city had a bleak feel outside. Inside, she knew, German hearts kept a warm house.

New York had been that way. She loved New York winters as a child, but hated them as an adult. Ten inches of new snow was a day off for schoolkids to play with friends. For adults, it was slow traffic and car wrecks on icy streets—if the car started in the first place. Walks to campus became long, cold and miserable, especially the walk home in the dark.

Kitt leaned to the door, listening. It seemed as if a TV was on inside. Some sort of sports match, but she didn't understand enough German to know for sure.

She knocked again.

If Gretchen isn't here, I'm not sure what I'll do.

The door opened, revealing a tall, handsome blond man with messy hair. "Ja?"

Warm air radiated outward from the tiny residence. Clasping her hands in front of herself, Kitt tried to remember her basic German. "Hallo. Ist Gretchen da? Ich bin ein Freund aus der Schule."

That more or less sounded correct. *Is Gretchen here? I'm a friend from school.*

Understanding the answer would be a different story. She could read a little German, but listening to and understanding other languages always gave her trouble. Everyone spoke too fast.

She could have asked for Gretchen in English—most Germans under the age of forty spoke English fluently—but trying to speak in the man's mother tongue was a way of appearing . . . sympathetic.

The blond man wiped his hand on his thick sweater, turning and calling over his shoulder. "Gretchen, einer Ihrer Freunde ist hier."

Kitt didn't catch any of that—except "Gretchen."

So, Gretchen must be here.

Her friend's voice came from a back room. "Ich komme gleich raus."

The man nodded, opening the door wider. "Sie kommt gleich raus. Möchten Sie sich setzen?" He gestured to the couch.

Kitt entered the apartment. "Oui, merci—I mean, danke schoen."

"Ich bitte Sie," he said, scratching his side and walking to the back room. There, a few words were exchanged with Gretchen—and not pleasant-sounding ones.

Kitt sat, listening to their exchange. The man was upset about something; the woman wasn't having any of it.

I've come at a bad time.

This was such a stupid plan! Why did I think showing up unannounced was a good idea? Gretchen and I haven't spoken in weeks.

What do I do if they kick me out? I have about ten euros left and no place to stay, no means of getting anywhere . . .

"Kitt!" Gretchen burst into the room, a beautiful, buxom ray of sunshine. Her smile melted the layer of frost Berlin's chilly weather had etched onto Kitt's exterior. She ran across the room, throwing her arms around her friend. "How are you? Are you in town for a seminar or something?"

Gretchen's words were thick with her accent, grown thicker since leaving school and returning home.

"I'm here because . . ." Kitt sat with her mouth hanging open. She'd rehearsed it on the train, but now it seemed too absurd to explain out loud. She looked down, shrugging. "I'm here because I'm in trouble. I need a place to stay for a day or two."

"Trouble! Oh, no. Of course you can stay here. What has happened?"

The blond man came out of the back room, putting on a heavy coat and heading for the door. "Auf Wiedersehen. Ich rufe Sie am Ende meiner Schicht an."

Gretchen patted Kitt's arm. "Hold on just one moment." Jumping up from the couch, she grabbed the man and turned him around, kissing him passionately.

Kitt looked away, shifting on her seat.

As the kiss ended, Gretchen ran her hand through the man's hair. Her voice was soft and sultry as she gazed into his eyes. "Vergeben Sie mir?"

"Ja." He blushed. "Ja, natürlich."

She watched him go, then returned to the couch. "Now that my boyfriend has gone, you must tell me all your troubles. Are you hungry? Thirsty?"

"Oh, I'm starving," Kitt said. "I haven't eaten since—I don't know when. Last night, I think." She rubbed her eyes. "I don't even know what day it is anymore."

"Do you need to rest?" Gretchen massaged Kitt's arm. "You look very tired."

"Yes, but we need to talk first." Kitt glanced around. "And we probably can't talk here in case I was followed."

"Then we must feed you. We can talk while we eat." She stood, walking to a small table where a coat laid over the back of a chair. "There's a small tavern on the corner called Der Beagle. It has good food, a big fireplace, and a very good-looking bartender."

"But isn't . . ." Kitt got to her feet, pointing to the door. "Didn't you . . . who was that guy you were just—did I miss something?"

"That was Karl." Gretchen put her coat on, digging in her purse until she pulled out her keys. "He is in law school for one more semester, and he tends bar at night. At Der Beagle."

Shaking her head, Kitt went to her friend and put her hands on her shoulders, looking into her eyes. "Gretch, you need to listen very carefully to what I have to tell you before you say I can stay here."

"You can stay here. Your problems are my problems."

Kitt winced, looking at the door. "I appreciate that, but—"

"How bad can it be?"

Pursing her lips, Kitt dropped her hands to her sides. "I'm . . . fleeing from kidnappers and I need to call the United States government about one of their agents."

Gretchen laughed. "Are you joking?" Her smile faded as she stared at her friend's face. "You're . . . not joking."

Kitt stared at the floor, her voice a whisper. "No."

Gretchen looked at Kitt, then looked at the set of keys in her hand. A motorcycle roared by on the street below.

She put her hand on Kitt's shoulder, lowering her head to look into Kitt's eyes. "If I am ever in trouble, I know I could show up at your door and you'd take me in. What kind of friend would I be if I didn't do the same? But this sounds . . . very serious. Possibly dangerous."

Kitt swallowed hard. "It is."

Gretchen nodded. "Then I hope you can understand my reply."

Kitt's heart sank. A knot formed in her stomach.

She won't help me, and I can't blame her.

"Let's go to Der Beagle," Gretchen said. "It sounds like we may need legal advice."

* * * * *

Over cold beer, hot knockwurst, and warm rolls, Kitt explained what had happened since the Chief of Medicine of the Pitié-Salpêtrière Hospital had summoned her in the middle of the night. Her interaction with Helena, and how the elderly woman had been able to describe the deaths of the two women before they happened; Mr. Hollings and Miss Franklin, and their kidnapping attempt.

But not the strange machines their abductors had hooked to Helena, and not the imagery their computer screens had displayed. A friend's trust has limits.

Karl sat next to Gretchen, his arms folded on the table, silently watching Kitt as she finished her story.

"So, I got to a train as fast as I could, and I came here." Sighing, Kitt lowered her hands to her lap. "If I say more, it might put you in danger."

Gretchen faced her boyfriend. "So? What do you think?"

"Find the right government department and make the phone call," Karl said. "What's the worst that could happen?"

Kitt put her elbows on the table, massaging her temples. "After everything that's already happened, I'm afraid to think about it."

"No, that is not the right way of thinking, doctor." Gretchen reached out and took her friend's hand. "Running is a temporary solution, at best. I agree with Karl. You will make the call as your friend Helena asked, and we will go from there. You'll be safe in our apartment. If we have to call every branch of the U.S. government, then that's what we'll do."

Kitt smiled, the knot in her stomach dissipating. "It'll just be for a few days. I'll call my mother and get some money, then start working on my passport and identification—"

"First things first." Gretchen picked up her purse. "Let's go make some calls."

Karl scanned the mostly-empty bar. "It's slow tonight. Oskar will let me leave early."

"Stay and make your money, *Geliebte*." She kissed him. "It's a simple phone call. What could happen? But we'd better call soon. There's a six-hour difference in the time. We will make the call, and then I will fix the couch up for you to sleep on. Come. We have work."

Karl stood, sliding his chair under the table. "If you need anything, call me."

"Make some money so you can pay your tuition." Gretchen wagged a finger at him. "Or you may be a bartender forever."

Kitt and Gretchen exited the pub, going onto the dark street. The walk back to the apartment was short but cold. Kitt shivered, constantly looking over her shoulders, her arms crossed over her chest.

"You never got used to this weather, did you?" Thin, whispy white clouds that drifted from Gretchen's lips with every word she uttered.

Kitt stared at a car as it passed on the street.

"In the morning, there's a nice breakfast place around the corner." Gretchen pointed. "We'll split a *bauernomelett*—scrambled eggs loaded with bacon and onions. Or some *goetta*. Very hearty."

Glancing over her shoulders again, Kitt pulled the collar of her coat close.

Gretchen slid her hands into her coat pockets, looking at her friend out of the corner of her eye. "I think Karl has the hots for you."

"What?" Kitt whirled around.

"Oh, you can hear!" Gretchen laughed. "I thought you had gone deaf."

"I'm so paranoid." Kitt ran her hand across her forehead.

"It's not paranoia when someone's actually out to get you." Gretchen took Kitt's arm and wrapped it around hers. "Let's get you inside. The sooner we make that call, the sooner you can relax."

* * * * *

Kitt stared at Gretchen's phone where it lay on the table. Next to it was Gretchen's laptop, opened to a search engine result displaying "Federal Government of the United States" and an 844 customer service phone number.

"Go on," Gretchen said. "It's not going to dial itself."

Kitt leaned back, slouching in her chair. "I just keep thinking, if I use your phone, then they have your phone number."

"I'm not in any trouble."

"No, but . . ."

Gretchen pushed the phone across the table. "Call."

"How do we even know where the call goes? I don't have a department or—"

"You're stalling. Call!"

Wincing, Kitt picked up the phone and entered the number on the screen.

The overseas line took a moment to connect, then the automated answering service came on. Kitt held the phone away from her face and pressed the speaker button.

"Thank you for contacting USA Gov," the recorded woman said, "your guide to federal government information. *Para continuar en español, presione dos.* For tax or IRS information, press one."

Kitt put her hand over the phone. "What department do you think?"

"CIA?" Gretchen shrugged. "Who works overseas?"

"For passport information, press two."

Kitt rubbed her chin. "Maybe the State Department? I have to get it right. She may be in real trouble."

"Please hold while your call is transferred to the next available information specialist."

Kitt's jaw dropped. She glanced at Gretchen. "Which department did it go to?"

Gretchen got up and went into the kitchen. "I guess we'll find out in a minute."

A woman answered, the line thick with static. "Thank you for holding. This conversation is being recorded for recordkeeping purposes. How may I direct your call?"

"Uh, thank you." Kitt shifted on her chair. "I have an urgent message for an employee, but I don't know which department she works in."

The operator spoke in a monotone. "The United States government employs over two million people, ma'am. What kind of work does she do?"

"I don't know. Her name is . . ." Kitt bit her lip, glancing at Gretchen.

Her friend nodded, whispering. "Go ahead."

Clearing her throat, Kitt sat up straight. "Her name is Jaden Trinn. I don't know what kind of work she does, but I was told to get a message to her boss, and that's what I'm trying to do."

"Can you spell the name?"

"Geez, I'm not sure of the spelling." Kitt looked at the ceiling. "I'd assume it's J-A-D-E-N, and the last name is Trinn, spelled T-R-I-N-N. But it may be a variation of that."

"Checking the main system for Jaden Trinn." The sound of fingers on a keyboard came over the line. "I'm sorry, I'm not showing a Jaden Trinn."

"What about with a Y?" Kitt asked. "Like, J-A-Y-D-E-N? Can we try that?"

"Checking . . . nothing is coming up." More keyboard noise. "I've tried several variations, ma'am. There's no Jaden Trinn in our system."

Kitt sighed, looking at Gretchen. "But Helena was so specific. She said Jaden Trinn was an agent of the United States government, and to contact her boss with the message Mao Oui. Helena's a very smart woman. I have to think she knew what she was talking about."

"Yes, ma'am," the operator said. "But we don't show a Jaden Trinn. If we can narrow it down at all . . ."

"No, that's . . . that's all I have." Kitt put her elbow on the table and lowered her chin onto her hand. "Just—there was a Mr. Hollings and a Miss Franklin, and, well . . . I don't know. I'll try to figure something out."

"Thank you. We receive calls 24 hours a day. If you need help with additional details, we have an embassy in Germany, in Berlin. Would you like the address?"

Kitt sat upright, staring at the phone. "You . . . know I'm calling from Berlin?"

"All calls are sourced and recorded, ma'am."

"Okay. Thank you. Goodbye." She ended the call, dropping the phone and glaring at Gretchen with wide eyes. "They know right where we are!"

Gretchen smiled, reaching across the table to take Kitt's hands. "But Helena told you to call them, so they're the good guys."

"Oh, if only I could be sure." Kitt pulled away, standing up and pacing back and forth in front of the fireplace.

"You watch too much TV. Karl will be home soon. Maybe he'll have some ideas." Getting up, Gretchen went into the kitchen. "Let's have a beer and do some more searches. Something will present itself."

"I can't drink." Kitt bit her fingernail, pacing faster. "I need to focus."

"It might help you relax."

"What was she telling me? 'Jaden Trinn is an agent of the United States government.' An *agent*. What qualifies as an agent?"

Putting a bottle opener to a beer, Gretchen pursed her lips. "FBI, CIA . . . Farm Bureau . . ."

Kitt went to the computer, sitting down. "Let's search departments of the U.S. government." She typed on the laptop. "And see who has agents working for them, as part of the employee's title."

Gretchen poured the beer into a glass. "She said there were two million employees."

"Yeah." Kitt studied the screen. "They can't all be agents, though. That's a pretty limited use word."

* * * * *

Two hours later, Gretchen was asleep on the couch and Kitt was still on the laptop, her eyes half open and her head bobbing. Two empty beer bottles sat on the table, next to a legal notepad filled with Kitt's handwriting, all of it scratched out.

She typed in another department, scanning the titles. Each query created more things to look at.

Her search "How many U.S. government departments have agents?" revealed nearly a hundred independent executive "units" and 220 "components" of the executive departments. A search for "List of US government agencies" yielded an A-Z index. There were thirty-seven agencies under the first part of letter "A."

Kitt rubbed her eyes.

This is useless. I must have misunderstood the message.

But if I don't figure it out, what does that mean for Helena?

She sat upright, twisting back and forth to loosen her back, and typed another department listing.

The sound of a key in the lock brought her back to full consciousness. She glanced at the door. "Karl?"

The lock rattled. Soft, metal-on-metal scraping followed. The doorknob jiggled.

Kitt got to her feet, backing away as she kept her eyes on the door. "Karl, is that you?"

She bumped into the apartment wall. Glancing outside, a car went down the dark street.

Are we too high up to jump?

The knob rattled again.

Kitt leaned over and shook Gretchen. "Wake up. Someone's trying to come in."

"Oh?" Gretchen rolled over, putting her cheek to the couch cushion. "Did he forget his key again?"

"No!" Kitt's pulse raced. "Gretchen! I think—"

The door flew open, slamming into the wall with a bang. Gretchen screamed. Two men in dark clothing rushed inside, wielding guns.

One looked at Kitt, his face drawn and grim. "Is there anyone else in the apartment?"

She backed away. "What?"

"Is there anyone else in the apartment?" he yelled.

Kitt trembled. "N-no."

"My boyfriend!" Gretchen said, her hands at her throat. "He will be home soon. There's no one else."

A third man with a gun walked through the door, holding Karl by the arm. Gretchen screamed again.

The man let Karl go. "There's no need for that, ma'am." He walked through the apartment, poking his head into the other rooms.

Karl raced to Gretchen's side. "Gretch, it's okay."

"What?" she looked around, tears welling in her eyes.

Karl put his hands on her shoulders. "These men want to talk to Kitt."

Swallowing hard, Kitt stepped away from the wall.

The stranger's accents are American, not German.

One of the men came toward Kitt, pointing his gun at her. "Dr. Kittaleye?"

Her heart pounding, Kitt put her hands in the air. "Yes."

"The apartment's clear," one of the strangers said, emerging from the rear room.

The man in front of Kitt put his gun away and flashed an ID at her. "I'm Agent Daxx with the U.S. Bureau of Diplomatic Security." He nodded to the younger men with him. "That's agent Flynn, and Aristotle Hiles from Israeli Intelligence. We'd like to talk to you about the messages you've been leaving for Jaden Trinn's boss. Will you come with us, please?"

"No." Kitt's voice wavered, her hands shaking as she spoke. "You talk to me here. He's my lawyer." She glanced at Karl, then turned back to the agent. "Now, you tell me—who is Jaden Trinn, who is her boss, and what the hell is going on?"

"Jaden Trinn is an agent with the Bureau of Diplomatic Security," Daxx said. "At the moment, her boss is the President of the United States."

CHAPTER 24

With a soldier holding each arm, DeShear was escorted through the hot, dark infirmary. His triage room was more like a prison cell than a hospital room—bars on the door and window, and the barest of amenities. The bed was a collapsible cot, with no mattress, and two white sheets folded on top of a coarse green blanket. No sink or toilet; no light. Only three walls and row of iron bars with a Defense Force guard standing at the entrance.

The soldiers released their grip on DeShear's arms, allowing him to walk the short distance to his cot under his own power. He sat, wiping the sweat from his brow.

"Rest well, murderer," the guard said, locking the door. The noise of the keys echoed down the dark corridor. "Soon, the magistrate will come. Then, you will hang." He chuckled, walking toward the end of the hallway.

DeShear jumped up, gripping the bars. He glared at the guard, his eyes drifting to the few other rooms in the wing. Two cells over, medics attended to a dark-haired woman who appeared to be asleep or heavily sedated. In between was another cell that was dark.

Lowering his head, DeShear closed his eyes and slunk to the floor. The cold, hard concrete was cool against his skin. He stared at the ceiling, exhausted.

He remembered playing two-square with Constantine the day he met her, and the fishing game on her tablet.

He remembered the way her face lit up when he told her they were going on a real fishing boat.

It seemed like an eternity ago.

The dark ceiling became a daydream of another child, years before, suffering in a hospital bed. Hours and hours of bedside vigils, holding his daughter's tiny hand, hoping things would improve and save her three-year-old life. But the disease was stronger, and one morning he realized he was holding a hand that was no longer holding his.

A few hours later, she was gone.

His daughter's face became Constantine's, laughing and playing, kicking the ball around the compound, the sun shining over the playing field.

"I won't lose another one." DeShear stared at the ceiling, gritting his teeth, his hand balled up into fists. "I won't. I couldn't fight the disease, but I can fight the people who have you." His face grew hot, his insides filling with rage. He got to his feet, a bead of sweat rolling down the side of his face. "There's a way to find out where you are. I will find it, and I will find you." Staring at the floor, he nodded in the darkness. "There's a way."

At the end of the hallway, the keys rattled. The door opened and a tall man in a suit walked in, heading toward DeShear. The Defense Force guard scurried along behind him.

Reaching the third cell, the man stopped. "Who are these people?"

The guard stepped to the man's side and snapped to attention. "Medical officers, Your Honor."

The man in the suit nodded at the medics. "Leave us."

"But, sir—"

He glared at the medical officers. "Am I not speaking clearly? Leave us. Now!"

The medics stood and assembled their things, leaving the cell and heading for the exit. The guard locked the woman's cell door.

"The light."

"Sir?"

"In her cell." The man folded his arms. "Put out that light."

The guard reached to a wall switch and shut off the lights in the cell, casting the entire ward into near-darkness. The street lights on the marina parking lot shined through the tiny windows on the far side of the ward, throwing long white rectangles onto the dirty floor.

Slowly, the man in the suit turned and walked toward DeShear. He stopped at the cell door. "This is the prisoner I inquired about?"

"Yes, your honor."

"Open the door. I shall talk with him alone."

"Sir, he is a murderer!"

"Well, he certainly won't murder me. I'm the one chance he has at leaving this island alive." He looked at DeShear. "Do you understand that, Mr. DeShear?"

Staring at the stranger, DeShear nodded, lowering himself onto the cot.

"You see? We'll be fine. Open the door."

"Your Honor, please."

"Open the door, then leave us. I wish to speak with the prisoner alone, and I shan't ask you again."

The guard stepped forward, his keys jingling in his shaking hands. The lock turned and he pulled the cell door open.

The man in the suit stepped inside, and the bars closed behind him. The guard backed away, then turned and walked back to the ward entrance.

The man in the suit peered at DeShear. The light from the tiny window illuminated his face. "Do you know who I am?"

"I was told a Magistrate was coming. The guard called you Your Honor."

"Very good." The Magistrate nodded. "So you understand your life does indeed rest in my hands."

DeShear smirked. "Yours might rest in mine as well. I'm a murderer, according to these Defense Force people."

"Be that as it may, unless you are very stupid, right now I am as safe as if I were in my mother's arms—and you don't strike me as a stupid man. Crude, perhaps, but not stupid."

"And not a murderer." He stood, clenching his fists. "I didn't do what I'm accused of."

"You are a disgraced police officer. You were fired and lost your home and your pension. You became a private detective, hired by one cheating spouse to hide in the bushes and peek into hotel windows to catch the other cheating spouse. You lived in a mediocre apartment and could barely keep ahead of your bills. Not a very dignified life. Certainly not one that instills credibility to a court of law." The Magistrate raised his chin. "Three billion dollars is a lot of money. Life changing money. The kind of money that buys dignity."

DeShear narrowed his eyes, glaring at the visitor. "I don't know about any money like that. I got a $250,000 reward, that's it. We spent about three thousand of it. Whoever does your research is mistaken if they think I've got more. I risked my life to save Jaden Trinn and a little girl named Constantine. Trinn will tell you that."

"I'm sure she will. If she lives. And the girl . . . there are several interesting stories about her. Some say you killed her. Others say she's an heiress. What do you think?"

"I didn't kill Constantine," DeShear said. "She's out there, kidnapped, and I'm just about all she has in the world. She was only in The Bahamas because of me, so I'm the reason she's in danger now."

The Magistrate peered toward the tiny window. The bars on the opening cast shadows of the bars across his face. "I believe you."

"You . . . you do?" DeShear stepped forward. "Then let me go. Help me look for her. I can pay you. I told you, I have almost $250,000. Why—"

"There's no need to look for Constantine. I know precisely where she is."

DeShear's jaw dropped. "Then—take me to her. Please."

"Oh, I shall. As I said, three billion dollars is a lot of money. A life changing amount of money."

"You want money? Fine. Take what I have. You keep talking about three billion dollars. I don't have anything like that."

"No, but you're about to." He stood, pacing back and forth in the tiny cell. "Constantine is the beneficiary of Dr. Hauser's estate, and it seems he was a very wealthy man."

"But that's not—I don't control that."

"Unless you were named as the trustee of her funds until she becomes an adult." He pointed at DeShear. "Then, you would."

"But I'm not!" DeShear held his hands out. "And it would be Constantine's money, not mine. The probate courts will see that. I won't have the money. Constantine will."

"Yes." The Magistrate nodded. "If she lives."

"What?"

"I'm an officer of the court, Mr. DeShear. I'm an expert in the law. As I said, the situation is as follows. When the child dies, the money will be yours to control."

"Why would you . . ." DeShear looked up. "Wait. 'When she dies?' You know she's alive. So you know I didn't kill her."

"I'm a simple Bahamian, but I watch the news." McCullough stared at the prisoner, stroking his chin. "A chateau is swarmed by French and American officials who discover an illegal genetics program and organ harvesting operation. Days later, a young child from France suddenly shows up on my doorstep—complete with two American guardians and a special provision from the governments of France and Great Britain. We are a tiny island with a lot of eyes and ears. We don't get a lot of visitors like that."

DeShear leaped up from the cot, grabbing the Magistrate by the collar and pinning him to the wall. "You took her!"

McCullough grabbed DeShear's hands. "I connected the dots and called some people. It's what I do. People are interested in taking her—and for whatever reason, you. I've arranged that."

Gritting his teeth, DeShear let the magistrate go and turned away. "You want money? Okay. I'll sign whatever you want, just help me get Constantine back."

"I want dignity and respect." McCullough stood up straight and smoothed his shirt. "The kind that doesn't come from decades of fighting to keep a low-level magistrate's salary, sweeping drunken tourists and disenfranchised vagrants from the streets, to receive the reward of a meager pension. But what if? What if there were a benefactor who created parks and fountains? Who carried money from the tourist centers to the hillsides where the residents live in ramshackle huts with tin roofs? What if better schools were built, and hospitals, and prime educators were brought in to wean the economy off the wallets of fat American tourists? Then, we'd have real change. And the person who made all that happen would be admired and respected. If you were to turn over the entire estate to me, I could make that happen and live a life of luxury."

"Where is Constantine while all this is happening?"

"Gone. To wherever such unlucky children go—eventually. First, she will reside in a place where people will dissect her and draw her stem cells and bone marrow until she can't walk or think. Then they'll harvest whatever eggs she gives up when she comes of age. But as soon as they use her up, they will dispose of her. Maybe someone in her new home will see her on a milk carton and call the authorities—if she's still recognizable."

"Don't. Don't do that."

"It's done. She has already arrived at her new home to start her new life. Most children in such circumstances last about six months before they give up. Very few see the age of twelve because they've committed suicide long before . . ."

DeShear rammed the magistrate up against the wall, pinning him with a forearm to the throat. "No!"

"Either way," McCullough gasped, "she's gone now. And you've been sold to the same people who bought Constantine. In fact, a bit of a bidding war has broken out. I've been assigned the role of an insurance policy. One set of buyers wants me along to ensure his safety. The other agreed. But when delivery is made, neither will have use for me—or you, I presume. So it seems we need each other."

Breathing hard, DeShear stepped away again, his eyes fixed on the magistrate.

"I shall keep you alive for now," McCullough said. "And you'll do exactly what I say, when I say it. That is the only way you'll see Constantine alive again. But I'm no fool. My estimation is, soon after the exchange is made, it'll be every man for himself. I might be able to slip away, but for how long? If some foolhardy American with a grudge is after me . . ."

"You ordered Moray to get rid of me, didn't you?" DeShear pointed at McCullough. "You knew I wasn't a murderer."

"You were an unfortunate liability who has now become a possible asset."

"You know I'm innocent!"

"Yes, you are. What of it?" The Magistrate folded his arms. "A day ago, you were worth a lot of money to me if you were dead. Now, you're worth a lot of money to me if you're alive. Your innocence has nothing to do with it one way or the other."

"They'll kill me—you said so yourself."

"Probably. And quite frankly, that's a good result for me. A disgruntled man with several billion dollars might one day come to The Bahamas looking for revenge. I can't be looking over my shoulder the rest of my days, can I? I'm a respected citizen of this community." He walked to the cell door. "Guard!"

"Wait," DeShear said. "I don't care about the money. You can have all of it, however much there is. Just get Constantine back and let us all go."

"And thus the reason for my visit tonight—to assess your vulnerabilities." The Magistrate sneered. "These are the words of a desperate man. One who'd say anything—but then as soon as he's released, would sic the Governor's corruption task force on me. Possibly just kill me in my sleep one night. No, that won't do." He faced the bars. "Guard!"

The door at the end of the hallway opened. A soldier walked toward DeShear's cell.

DeShear dropped to his knees, clasping his hands together. "Please. Help me save Constantine."

The Magistrate sighed. "Unfortunately, Mr. DeShear, you're much too agreeable right now. But I fear that won't last, and that your anger will return. No, you need to be dead or so broken that you would never, ever consider turning on me—like Lieutenant Moray, or so many others I've put under my thumb. But breaking a man requires more time than I have at the moment, and as I say, I stand to make a lot of money from delivering you to your new owners. So, enjoy your brief reunion with the child, and then your speedy death."

"No. Help me get her out of there."

The guard put the key in the lock.

"Goodbye Mr. DeShear."

"Help me please. Help me bring her back."

The cell door opened, and the Magistrate stepped out. "Perhaps you'll need to be bound and gagged for the flight." As the guard locked DeShear's cell, McCullough glanced at the third cell in the ward. "Your lady friend is already sedated. Maybe that's the way to go." He smiled, walking away. "After all, you're a murderer. Everyone knows it. Perhaps sedation, chains and a gag will be seen as merely a good precaution, even on the back of a cargo plane."

"Don't let them hurt Constantine." On his knees, DeShear gripped the bars of the cell. "I'll do anything. Just help me get Constantine back."

McCullough waved as he waited to exit the ward. "In due course you'll see this was the only way."

"No!" DeShear shook the bars. "Bring her back!"

CHAPTER 25

Ari Hiles stepped onto the sidewalk outside Gretchen's apartment. Agent Flynn followed him.

"So?" Ari asked. "What do you think?"

"My professional opinion of Dr. Kittaleye?" Agent Daxx shut the front door of the building and folded his arms. "She's nuts. She said some truly bizarre things, and our information shows her background is a little sketchy."

Ari frowned. "She studied parapsychology in college. Big deal. I think her information warrants looking into. And Jaden Trinn is a co-worker of yours. Doesn't that matter?"

"We have procedures," Daxx said. "This doctor might have gotten all her information off the internet. Since the Angelus Genetics thing went down in France, we're inundated with conspiracy theories. But here's what we know. Trinn hasn't been reported overdue or anything else. We're here because this headshrinker doctor made phone calls, not because Jaden Trinn is missing." He looked at his coworker. "Flynn, what do you think?"

"I don't know." He shrugged. "Yeah, some things happened to this doctor, but does any of it rise to the level of an investigation by the Bureau of Diplomatic Security? Not at the moment. She says somebody tried to snatch her in Paris, but she got away—okay, then that's a matter for the Paris police. If there's something there, she's an American citizen, so maybe the FBI gets involved." He put his hands out, glancing at the Israeli Intelligence agent. "We have to refer it to them, Ari. As far as the information the doctor *says* she heard from an elderly lady about Agent Trinn, she made a few phone calls—so we're here now—but she doesn't know much, and she doesn't appear to be a threat." He shook his head. "There's not really much hard information here. We'll send someone to look for the warehouse she says the kidnappers took her to. We'll see about the vehicles she says they used. Right now, we're swamped with a million other calls about Angelus Genetics—people insist their neighbors are genetically engineered drones and are going through their trash looking to send them to the mother planet! It's crazy, and this doctor's story is close to the top of my list for oddball claims I've heard this week. I say we file a 302 and follow up to see what pans out. If Trinn is missing, okay—Dr. Kittaleye will be our starting point. Otherwise, I agree with Daxx. That story she spun about telepathic machines . . . that's pretty out there."

Daxx looked at the Israeli Intelligence officer. "Ari?"

"I just—I know Jaden Trinn." Ari sighed. "She's a field agent, level three, reporting right to the President."

"You want us all to go back in and talk to her some more?" Daxx said. "Let's do it. Her story is thin at best and crazy at worst, but we'll do our job."

"No." Ari looked down. "I take your point."

"Look, Flynn and I will check into it from our end, you check into it on yours. Your agency supported Trinn on the Angelus Genetics situation. You played a key role in their takedown, so Mossad might have a lot more flexibility here than we do. If you find out anything else, call us. We'll send in the Marines, no problem. Otherwise, I think this one's done for now."

"Yeah, okay," Ari said. "Thanks."

The agents shook hands. Daxx pointed to his agency vehicle. "Can we give you a lift?"

"Nah." Ari walked backwards, hooking his thumb over his shoulder. "I think I'm gonna walk for a while and clear my head. I'll get a cab."

"Okay." Daxx waved. "Catch you later, Mossad."

When their car was out of sight, Ari turned around and went back to Gretchen's apartment. As she let him in, Kitt got up from the couch. "They think I'm crazy, don't they?"

He shrugged. "They're . . . getting a lot of extremely unusual calls since Angelus Genetics made the news."

"Great." Kitt looked at her friend. "What about you, Gretch?"

"You had a scare." Gretchen walked to Kitt, putting her hands on Kitt's shoulders. "I don't disbelieve you, but you have to admit, it was a wild story."

"And you?" Kitt glared at Ari. "Why aren't you gone?"

Ari put his hands on his hips, frowning. "Because I know Jaden Trinn. I've worked with her. She's got a direct line to President Brantley for a reason—she's helped him in the past. He trusts her. So, whatever Jaden needs, he'll have it ready. Plus, I've seen first-hand some of the things Dr. Hauser and his people can do. There are no coincidences when it comes to them. Trinn told me things about Helena and Constantine, too. If Helena said she has visions, and you saw it on a computer monitor . . . that's good enough for me. If things solidify, the American agents will be right there with us."

Kitt flopped onto the couch. "Thank goodness somebody believes me—and doesn't think I'm a nut." She faced Ari. "So what happens now?"

"I don't know." Ari took out his notepad. "Let's go over your story again. Then we'll make a call to Jaden's boss. Maybe he'll have some ideas."

Kitt gasped. "But . . . the other agent said her boss is the President of the United States!"

"Yep." Ari pulled out his phone. "Does that change things for you?"

"Wow." She put her hands on her hips, taking a long, deep breath. "Wow, wow, wow."

"Kitt . . ." Gretchen put her hand to her lip. "The—the President of the United States?"

Kitt stared at Ari's phone, rubbing her brow. "Okay, let's do it. I'm not crazy. Let's . . . let's call the President."

.

CHAPTER 26

The vehicle ceased its jolting and jarring drive, coming to a stop. The engine shut off, Constantine's seatbelt was unclipped and her blindfold removed. She squinted in the bright sunlight.

A dark-haired man with a short beard opened her car door. He was relatively handsome, and fairly young, maybe twenty standard years old, but he looked angry. "This way, girl."

Warm air rushed across Constantine's face. Not as warm as it had been in The Bahamas, nor as humid. It was moderate, and nice. She slid out of the car seat and jumped down onto the smooth, dark gray surface.

Constantine's two male captors walked ahead of her, towards a run-down wooden building with a crumbling brick fireplace. She glanced around the desolate area. It was mostly smooth gray stone with large ruts and gullies, and practically no vegetation.

The clear blue skies and wispy clouds met a charcoal horizon. No other buildings seemed to be within eyesight. There was nowhere to run to or hide in. If it hadn't been for the wind and sun, it might have been the surface of the moon.

Constantine gazed at the smooth surface under her feet.

Volcanic stone.

The female in the group of kidnappers nudged her five-year-old hostage from behind. "Walk, little one."

The captors' accents were French. They spoke in broken English to Constantine, but she understood the conversations in their mother tongue. No one had apparently told them she could speak other languages, and she let it remain a secret, but there hadn't been much talking since she'd awakened.

She remembered pulling the wooden door shut in the front berth of the fishing charter, and the hand that rushed forth when she opened the door again after changing her clothes. The rag squeezed her nose and mouth, its pungent, solvent-like smell burning her lungs and sinuses—then there was darkness.

The sore, red dot on her arm indicated a syringe had been administered at some point.

"There is water in the house," the woman said. "Rinse your mouth and drink as much as you can. I will bring you a toothbrush later, and some of the little crackers."

"Thank you." Constantine marched up the path. "I did warn you, though."

"*Oui*, you did."

Constantine peered over her shoulder at the woman. She knew her captors' voices, but hadn't seen any of their faces yet. The woman was also young, and very pretty, with blonde hair in a ponytail.

Constantine's gaze darted to the vehicle they'd arrived in. The side of the dirty, dented vehicle said Jeep Wrangler.

She looked back at the woman. "You've not done this before, have you?" Constantine held her hand up to block the bright light. "The blindfold causes confusion between the optic receptors and the ones in the inner ear. Nausea and vomiting are a common result."

The dark-haired man at the front of the line grumbled. "Quiet, you two. *Nicole, vous parlez trop. Faites votre travail.*"

Constantine translated in her head. *You talk too much. Just do your job.* And he had finally said a name—Nicole. Turning back to watch her step, Constantine whispered, "Dimenhydrinate may help next time. If you're to do a lot of this."

"*Chut, fille.*" Nicole lowered her voice. "You will get me into trouble. Go in the house, yes? It will be better when you get some food inside you."

"Nicole!" the bearded man shouted.

"*Arrête, esclavagiste!*" Nicole scowled at him, waving her arm. " *J'ai eu une longue route, aussi!*"

Constantine kept her head down. Nicole's tone was sharp. She was angry with him. *Stop, slave driver. I had a long drive, too.*

The walkway to the old building looked to have been made mainly by foot traffic wearing down the rock. The ruts and holes along the walkway had been filled in with gravel; otherwise, it looked like everything else. It was all gray, everywhere—the walk, the fill, the area outside the walk—all of it. Everything here was stone. Everything but the building.

At the house entrance, the dark-haired man flung the old door open and walked straight in, letting the door bang shut behind him. *"Boueuse!"*

Part of the painted structure was, or had been, two stories high, with some sort of tower at the back, but all of it was weather-worn and falling apart. Most of it had no roof.

The door bounced open on its rusted hinges, allowing the second man to grab it and hold it open for Constantine.

The bearded man looked around, calling out again. *"Boueuse!"*

The house was mostly empty inside, with sun shining through holes in the roof, but no water on the floor. The breeze was nearly as strong inside as it had been outside. The walls were faded and peeling, and an odd odor permeated the air. It smelled like the abandoned outhouse sites they had excavated on the older part of the chateau property—earthy, and with a hint of dry manure.

A man's voice came from the back of the house somewhere, under the two-story section. *"Je suis ici, Valentin. J'arrive. Un moment."*

Constantine nodded.

The bearded man is Valentin and he's calling the other man "Muddy."

Eating an apple, a large man came into the room. The men spoke in French.

Valentin asked if everything was set; Muddy replied that it was, "as far as can be," and said they had been instructed to not start for a few days.

Frowning, Valentin cursed and walked out the rear door. The bright blue colors of the ocean filled the door frame as he passed through.

Constantine put her hands to her belly, a nervous twinge going through her.

We're high up on a cliff somewhere.

"Girl!" Valentin shouted.

Nicole nudged Constantine again. "Go. Do not be afraid."

Constantine peered up at the young woman. "I'm not afraid."

"No." Nicole smiled. "You are very brave. But still, you must go now to your . . . *cabine de couchage.* Your sleeping quarters."

As Constantine walked across the room, the other kidnapper chuckled. She hadn't gotten his name yet, but they were being careless now, relaxing and letting their guard down, so it would only be a matter of time.

The man shook his head. *"Ses quartiers pour dormir? Sa cellule de prison, vous voulez dire."*

His words struck fear into Constantine.

"Her sleeping quarters? You mean her prison cell."

She pushed open the rear door and stepped outside. The rush of waves sounded over the stony slope. To the right, a small rock building had been erected, with a crooked metal roof and low walls. The sea raged far below, crashing into the rocks and sending out a white spray in all directions. In the distance, a few other islands rose up from the surf.

"Here, girl." Valentin pointed to the stone cabin. "Come with me." Grabbing her arm, he hauled Constantine along with him. "This will be your new home. Don't wet yourself when you see it."

She jerked her hand away. "I'm not afraid of an ugly old house. I'm certainly not afraid of you."

"No?" Valentin raised his hand and slapped Constantine across the face. "What about now?"

A firebolt of pain shot across Constantine's cheek as she tumbled backwards. Her bottom hit the hard stone surface. She gasped, recoiling from Valentin.

"Espèce d'animal!" Nicole raced forward. *"Tu frapperais un enfant?* She shoved Valentin away, turning to Constantine. "Are you okay?"

Panting, Constantine put her hand to her cheek, her eyes wide.

"This is not how things are supposed to be!" Nicole shoved Valentin again. "Get away. Go to a barn if you will behave like an animal."

Gritting his teeth, Valentin grabbed Constantine's wrist and yanked her to her feet, pulling her toward the cabin. "Put her inside and shut the door." He turned, his face red, glaring at Constantine. "Do not test me again, girl." Dropping her hand, he stormed toward the main house. "Or you, Nicole! More than one body has gone off that cliff never to be seen again."

When he reached the house, he threw open the door and shouted for Muddy.

"Go and do your job, dimwit!"

Muddy exited the main building, rushing to the cabin.

A large fence ran from the sides of the house and out to the cliffs, effectively encompassing the cabin on all sides. The top of the fence was covered in razor wire. Rusted yellow signs hung from it, with lightning bolts painted on them, and the words Electric Fence, High Voltage.

At the front of the house, the Jeep's engine roared to life, its motor revving and its gears grinding as it bounced and lurched over the primitive road. Two men were visible inside.

Nicole stood, watching until the vehicle was far away. "Jean and Valentin have gone." She sighed, squatting in front of Constantine. "I'm sorry, little one. That was . . . *injustifiée*. Uncalled for."

"He won't hurt you much bad," Muddy said to Constantine. "He need you. You doesn't going over the cliff, no."

She swallowed hard as Muddy opened the cabin door. Stone steps descended to a gray stone floor, disappearing into darkness. A tiny window on the far side illuminated a small bed in one corner, with a pile of dirty blankets on it; a metal bucket stood in the other corner.

Muddy peered into the doorway. *"Sors de là, putain."*

A thin woman with straggly black hair and too much makeup staggered up the steps. She giggled, speaking French. "He's useless. He's not a man." The woman's cocktail dress was wrinkled and her high heels were dirty. A dozen bracelets adorned each of her wrists. Tattoos covered her arms and legs.

Muddy replied in French. "Wait for me at the main house. I will get your payment." He turned to Nicole. "Take her. I will do this part."

"Are . . . you sure?" Nicole put her hand to her lip.

Muddy nodded. "You don't want to see it. Now, go."

As the women walked to the house, Muddy looked at Constantine, speaking his broken English. "Come, girl." He held his hand out. "You doesn't be afraid."

Constantine slipped her tiny hand into Muddy's massive one, a knot growing in her stomach. The skin of his fingers and palms were cracked and rough. Lowering his head, he crept down the steps.

The inside of the cabin reeked of feces and vomit, only lessened by the wind blowing through the interior. Flies hummed over the metal bucket. To the left was a small door, with another one on the rear wall. Through the second one, the giant blue ocean was visible, and the other islands.

Muddy stood in the center of the room. "This is your home, girl. You doesn't try to run away." He wagged his finger at Constantine. "That big fence, it fry you *croustillant*, and the cliffs take you a hundred feet to your death." Muddy smacked his hands together. "The rocks below are like cheese shredder, and the currents are big-strong. Push you back over the rocks again and again, until your skin is scrape off and your arms and legs get slice cut away. You doesn't go there, hokay?"

She stared out the tiny window of the rear door. The beautiful, clear sky came down to meet the jagged top of the gray stone.

"You are stay here," Muddy said. "Later will be food, hokay?"

Constantine nodded. "Okay."

Muddy walked to the steps.

"Why do they call you that name?"

He stopped and turned around, facing her.

"The other man—the one with the beard. He calls you *Boueuse*. That means muddy, like wet dirt. I learned that on a field trip. Why does he call you that?"

Muddy pulled at the hem of his t-shirt.

"I don't think it's very nice," Constantine said. "I won't call you that."

"I doesn't care what you call me, girl. Just remember what I tell you. There is no run away here. If you try, you fall to the rocks."

Muddy lowered his head walked up the steps, shutting the wooden door behind him.

A gust of wind lifted Constantine's hair into her eyes. She turned to the rear door, walking over to it and putting her hand to the knob.

The tarnished brass knob turned, and the old door creaked open.

She stood there, gazing out over the gray stone landscape, the wind blowing her hair back. In the distance, a rainbow shined between the two other islands.

"They don't lock it."

Constantine jumped, turning toward the bed. She put her hands to her belly as the pile of dirty blankets sat up.

A ragged man with a long beard stared at her, his face worn like old leather. He coughed, wiping a stained finger across his mouth, smearing it with blood.

Constantine backed away, her heart pounding, until she bumped into the stone wall.

"They don't lock it," he said. "Because they don't need to."

His voice was raspy and harsh, with a French accent. His skin was saggy and cracked—dark, from too much sun and too little care, and covered in liver spots. His head hung down on his chest, his shoulders thin and sagging. His greasy hair hung from his head in long, unkempt strands. His shirt was dirty and stained under each arm; his pants were frayed and full of holes, letting his bony knees poke through. His filthy, black-stained feet brushed the floor, his long yellow toenails chipped and broken.

He looked at Constantine with bloodshot eyes. "What that giant oaf said is true. There's no escaping here. The rocks on the ledge crumble under your feet. You will fall and you will die, like the others did. I should know. I had to recover the bodies. Terrible sight."

Constantine forced herself to breathe.

"You're the one they told me about." He pointed a long, gnarled finger at her. "From the chateau."

She nodded, her pulse throbbing in her ears. The crook of his arm was filled with a series of red dots, like those left from syringes.

The man coughed again, displaying his sparse brown teeth as he glanced around the room. "Don't worry, child. This is my Hell, not yours." He stared at her with red eyes. "But you'll be in your Hell soon enough, and yours is much worse."

DAN ALATORRE

CHAPTER 27

The ambulance parked on the side of a long runway at the *Paris Le Bourget* airport. As Hollings clutched the sides of his wheelchair, his attendants lowered him to the tarmac. His jaw hung open as he stared up at a massive plane. "Cor blimey, that's a big bird."

"It's a C-130 cargo plane." Miss Franklin heaved a backpack over her shoulder and grabbed the wheelchair handles, pushing Hollings across the tarmac. "The U.S. Air Force sold them to Brazil, who sold it to Armen Twa. Now it's our ride to The Bahamas." The aircraft's massive wings stuck out close to fifty feet on each side, with two giant propellers on each. A platform lowered from the rear of the giant plane. Service personnel jumped out of a luggage tram and unloaded various crates and boxes, pushing them up into the aircraft's belly. Franklin pushed the wheelchair toward the plane's gangway steps. "There are a few dozen seats in the front, and a nice big cargo area in the back for our guests—with plenty of welded metal hooks. just right for a set of handcuffs. Nice and cold back there, at altitude."

Hollings ran a hand over his fat, bearded chin. "I can't bloody well lock the old girl up in the back, then, can I? That sounds a bit dodgy, and she's integral to this deal."

"Not the Keeper," Franklin said. "Her friends—Trinn and DeShear. Of course, I recommend we gag them so they don't make too much noise. The old woman can sit up front with us, as long as she behaves."

"Aye. Likely, she won't do that, neither. But I've a remedy."

The pilot approached Hollings. "Sir, we are fueled and ready to depart at your request."

"Then let's get underway." Hollings stood, grabbing the rail of the steps. "And Miss Franklin, would you be so kind as to ask Dr. Freeman to come have a chat with me regarding Keeper 27 before the plane takes off? And tell him to bring his sedative syringes."

* * * * *

Hollings leaned on his cane, staring down the aisle of the giant plane. The middle section appeared to have been retrofitted to be similar to a regular airliner. Rows of four cloth seats, with ample legroom between them. The front section, just behind the cockpit, held several private suites and a board room.

Hollings whistled, gazing at the polished mahogany bedroom in the luxurious front suite. "Armen Twa travels in style."

Miss Franklin escorted Keeper 27 to her seat, helped her buckle up, then stood in the aisle next to her.

"Aye, old woman." Hollings limped toward them, leaning on his cane. "Ready for a nice long overseas flight?"

Dr. Freeman followed Hollings down the aisle.

"We've got just the thing to keep you from pulling any tricks on this flight." Hollings turned to the doctor. "If you would administer the shot, doctor."

Keeper 27's eyes went wide. "No!" She lurched backwards in her chair. "Please, no!"

Franklin grabbed the old woman's wrists, pinning them to the armrests. "Hold still. This won't hurt."

Dr. Freeman held up the syringe, tapping the barrel and easing the plunger forward. A drop of liquid glimmered at the top of the long, shiny needle.

"No, please!" Keeper 27 twisted under Franklin's grip, stomping the floor. "Mr. Hollings—you know what these do. Please don't."

Hollings leaned in, his face close to hers. "And just what *do* they do, Keeper 27? They give you the sight?"

She trembled, staring at the shot. "Please."

"Tell me." Hollings licked his lips. "What happens when a sedative is administered to your old hide? What do you see?"

"Awful things." She shook, her mouth hanging open. "Terrible things."

"Such as a group of children in caps, having the transmission cranked up so high it fried their little brains? Is that what you saw? No. You were right there and you didn't see that. Stop playing games. What do you see?"

"Please." She shook her head. "No."

"Tell me. Now." He pointed to Dr. Freeman. "The shot's coming! Talk."

Groaning, she turned away. "Please."

"Do it," Hollings shouted. "Give it to her!"

"Death!" Keeper 27 screamed. "I see death. Bullets flying, bodies falling. I see people with guns, shooting everyone and everything."

"Where?" Hollings leaned closer. "Is Armen Twa planning a double cross?"

"I can't." Keeper 27 swallowed hard, her eyes squeezed shut. "I can't see where."

"Lies!" He grabbed her collar. "I gathered fifty armed men on this plane. It's them you saw, isn't it?"

"Many will die." Keeper 27 cried. "It's terrible."

"Where?" He shook her. "Where?"

"At the airport."

"Yes, that's right." Hollings let her go, standing. "We'll have the upper hand."

"You won't." She glared at him, tears in her eyes. "The Asian man is preparing to do the same to you. He wears a tan hat with a black band on it."

Hollings nodded, rubbing his beard. "That's probably him—Armen Twa. Good work, old lass. I knew you'd be of use." He turned to Freeman. "Now give her the shot."

"What!" Keeper 27 said. "No!"

"Bah." Hollings stepped away, leaning on his cane. "I'll not be having any antics on this flight, old girl. Nor you telling your secrets to anyone who cares to listen. You know me better than that."

Franklin held the old woman down while Freeman shoved the needle into her vein. Keeper 27 struggled for a few seconds, then fell still.

"Check her pulse, you quack," Hollings said. "Make sure you haven't killed her."

Freeman put two fingers to the old woman's neck. "She's fine. Sleeping soundly. That'll last until we get to The Bahamas, at least."

"Good." Hollings turned, heading toward the mahogany suite. "Have another shot ready for after we pick up her friends, but keep it out of sight. I'll not have her acting up during the second leg of our journey, either."

Miss Franklin stepped forward, pulling a pair of handcuffs out of her belt. She slipped one cuff around Keeper 27's left wrist and ratcheted it snug to the old woman's wrinkly flesh. The other cuff went through a hole in the armrest, locking Keeper 27's arm in place. A second pair of cuffs went on the other arm and was secured to the armrest between the seats.

Franklin stood up and looked at Dr. Freeman. "Now she won't be going anywhere."

"I'd have thought the sedative would be enough."

"That's why you're the doctor and I'm the tactics expert." She slipped the handcuff key into the breast pocket of her shirt. "It's my job to make sure things stay where I put them."

CHAPTER 28

Constantine sat cross-legged on the hard stone surface, the setting sun shining on her shoulder. Long blue waves stretched out before her, gently rising and falling, as the wind blew nonstop into her face.

"Girl." Muddy walked out of the main house, carrying a brown paper bag. The old wooden door banged shut behind him. "You doesn't get too close to the edge, hokay?"

"I'm not close. I'm plenty far away. I've no interest in falling."

"You talk smart for little girl." He reached into the bag, pulling out a cloth napkin and handing it to her. Inside was a fried chicken leg. "You eat."

Constantine shoved the chicken into her mouth, greedily biting as much as she could chew. Crumbs rolled down the front of her shirt.

"You drink is here." He held the bag open. Two sodas were inside, and a bag of potato chips. "Go on. Take."

Constantine swallowed her mouthful of chicken and quickly took another bite, eyeing the soft drinks in the bag. One was an orange Crush, the other was an orange Gatorade. Under the bag of chips was a small package of Goldfish crackers.

"Are these for me as well?" She picked up the bag of smiling, fish-shaped treats.

Muddy nodded, placing the chips on the ground next to her.

"And may I have the can of Crush soda, please?"

He stared into the bag.

Constantine shifted on her seat. "I'm sorry. Was that one for you? I'll have the Gatorade, then."

The big man looked into the paper bag again, then held it open and lowered it down to her.

Constantine peered up at him. "You don't know which it is. You can't read, can you?"

Grunting, Muddy dropped the bag and walked toward the house.

Constantine got to her feet, running after him. She grabbed his big hand. "I'm sorry. I didn't mean to embarrass you. You looked right at the cans of soda. I bet you've memorized what the words Coca-Cola and Coke look like because you can't read. That's why you didn't know what kinds of sodas these were."

Muddy stopped, looking at her.

"That's right, isn't it?" Constantine asked. "You're not educated."

"I plenty smart enough for you, little girl."

"That's not what I mean." Her eyes stayed on his. "It's okay. I won't tell."

The wind lifted Muddy's hair, tossing about his temples.

Constantine tugged his hand, looking back to her spot on the stone ground. "Would you like to come and eat with me?"

He tried to pull his hand away, but she didn't let go.

"I knew a . . . a *woman* once," Constantine said. "At a chateau, where I lived for many years. She mostly watched over a group of the younger children, but she watched over my tier once. She was quite nice. She was big—like you—and quiet . . . like you. My Keeper had me help the woman in the kitchen once. I watched her put things away in the pantry. Since she couldn't read labels, she memorized the appearance of all the household goods. The commercial laundry detergent came in an orange box, diet drinks had a big "D" printed on each bottle—that confused her a bit when someone brought Dr. Pepper once—and vanilla ice cream came in a blue carton with a white orchid on it. Cherry candy was red most of the time, but sometimes she took him cinnamon candy by mistake. He didn't like that. Cinnamon candy is hot. He got very cross with her."

Muddy gazed at the little girl holding his hand. "What was the name of her?"

"I don't know. They weren't allowed to have names. Isn't that terrible? We called them The Keepers, and they took very good care of us."

Constantine looked up at him, the wind blowing her hair across her eyes. "I suppose you're my keeper now."

Muddy looked away, his gaze peering over the long blue horizon.

"Did you not get proper schooling? The tansuits where I lived didn't get any schooling. They didn't go to Rituals, either, but they weren't stupid, like people thought." Constantine lowered her gaze to the ground. "Anyway, I'm quite sorry I embarrassed you. I knew lots of very good people who didn't have schooling, and they were very good to me and the other children."

"My name is Cleo Boisseau."

"I see." She wrinkled her nose at him. "They call you Muddy because '*Boisseau*' sounds like '*boueuse*,' is that it? The word for mud? That's not nice—and not very clever, if you ask me. Sloppy pronunciation as well. I should like to call you Cleo, if that's all right with you. My name is Constantine." She moved her tiny hand up and down in his massive one, shaking hands. "I'm very pleased to meet you, Cleo. We shall be good friends." She raised an eyebrow, smiling at him. "Ho-kay?"

Muddy smiled back. "Hokay, little girl Constantine."

She walked back to her spot, the cloth napkin held in place by the chicken bone and the soda. The Goldfish crackers were nowhere in sight.

Constantine sat, patting the ground next to her. "Come on, Cleo. It's nearly dark hour. We *must* finish our dinner. Keepers are very strict about such things."

Muddy lumbered over and sat down.

"Boueuse!" Valentin shouted from the house. The back door banged open. *"Où se trouve le paquet?"*

The big man scrambled to his feet, rushing toward the house.

Constantine silently deciphered Valentin's new instructions.

A package? Is that how they regard me? I suppose they think they're smart, talking about me in code, as if—

Valentin clapped Muddy on the ear. *"Idiot! Ne deviens pas amical!"*

"You leave him alone!" Constantine jumped up, rushing toward the two men.

"No, girl." Muddy put his hands out. "You stay. I am go."

"You heard him!" Valentin raised his hand, glaring at her. "Or do I need to give you a reminder?"

Constantine tried to shove him. "You're just a bully. When they come to rescue me, you'll be sorry."

"Is that right?" He narrowed his eyes. "Well, we will see, eh? Now go to bed or I throw you over the cliff."

"You won't." Constantine stood up straight, sticking her chin out. "You *can't*. You're a mere foot soldier, following orders. You're not allowed to hurt me."

"No? Did your cheek heal so fast?" Valentin turned away. "Go to bed."

"I'm not afraid of you. Bullies are just big cowards." She took a step forward. "When . . . when someone comes to rescue me, you'll see. Then *you'll* be afraid."

Valentin sighed, rubbing his forehead. "I think no." He turned to the child. "Your precious mommy and daddy, they do not come. No one comes to save you."

"My . . . my *father* will stop you. Somehow, he will find you and this wretched place, and . . . and . . . he will put a stop to all of this. He will."

"And yet I do not fear him, little freak." Valentin smiled walking with a dance in his step. "Because your father is dead. He die in the chateau. All the news say so."

"He's not dead." Heat rose in Constantine's cheeks. She balled up her fists. "He'll come for me. You'll see. And you'll be sorry."

"You are a puny little thing, barely even human, really—a disgusting creation of science from a petri dish, and you make such a loud noise." Valentin leaned over and put his hands on his knees, his nose an inch from hers. "If I throw you from this cliff tonight, I will replace you tomorrow with another girl, *oui?* I go to a freezer and thaw her out, and a few years later she is here, just as you are. Or . . ." He turned to the main house. "Maybe she lives now, in Cambodia, or China." He pointed at Constantine. "The same look as you, I think. The eyes, the face—like sisters, perhaps. Triplets. All the same, yes?" He stood up, folding his arms over his chest. "Only, those girls don't be so loud. Now go to bed!"

She stomped to the stone cabin and slammed the door, watching them through the crack. When they had gone back into the main house, the car started and drove away.

Constantine went to the rear of the cabin, easing open the door and going back outside.

The sky cast a warm glow over the sea, turning it a golden yellow-white as the water reflected the sun's brilliant rays. From the rocks below, the noise of waves crashing on rocks came to her.

She crept toward the rocky, gray cliff, leaning forward to see over the edge.

Wave after wave smashed and churned against the rocks. The water was white with foam, rocking backward and then rushing forward again, crashing into the jagged black tips of the cliff bottom. It was an army of waves attacking a fortress of stone. Each blue soldier raced forward to challenge the rocks, confident and sure, then exploded in a spray of white and disappeared on the field of battle. Only the blue uniform remained among the white foam. A moment of silence followed—of peace—and then the next blue soldier advanced.

Each attack was the same, and yet different. No individual effort could make the rock fall, but as with the Grand Canyon, enough unrelenting effort would turn the rock to sand or wash it away completely.

Her gaze drifted along the top of the cliff's edge. The setting sun cast deep shadows into the many cracks and gullies that the molten lava had left behind as it raced into the sea. Bits of grass clung to the cliff wall.

Between them, the golden sunset illuminated a narrow pathway.

Constantine gasped, bolting upright.

She jumped to her feet, running along the cliff. A crack on the stone surface opened to a narrow gap. Rocks and gravel had filled it, pushed by the wind and rain. The fissure turned to the right, between the two stone plates, one on top of the other, leaving a ledge of about ten inches—a path—that descended steeply downward along the gray stone face.

The cliff curved inward as it dropped, so she couldn't see how far the little path went.

Not from here, anyway.

But maybe from the other side.

She held her hand up to block the glare from the setting sun, peering over the stony gray ground. The cliff curved in a C, with the cabin closest to the center.

The far point on the west will let me see what's under this side.

Constantine ran to the far side, her feet flying over the shiny gray surface. Massive waves crashed onto the rocks below.

At the westernmost point, the electric fence blocked her from going further. She turned, panting, studying the rocky cliff face.

There, bathed in golden sunlight, was the rest of the path. The sheer ledge jutted out from the side of the cliff, angling lower and lower until it disappeared into a tower of stone. Ancient lava had seeped from a fissure, oozing downward until it met the sea and turned into a giant, gray water slide.

From there, the shore of the next island seemed barely a mile away.

She clapped her hands together.

Then that's it. I shall make my escape to that island as soon as possible. Once I'm there, I can—

The ground beneath her feet trembled. A loud snap, and a chunk of stone next to her fell away, crashing into the surf below.

Constantine fell sideways, away from the new edge of the cliff, and crawled to safety. She got up when she reached the cabin, her heart pounding, adrenaline surging through her insides. Another crack echoed from the rock. She turned to see another chunk of the cliff drop away.

It was the place where she'd been standing.

She stood there, breathing hard, massaging a knot in her gut so big she thought she would throw up again. Swallowing hard, she sat down and stared at the sharp new edge of the western cliff.

I must be more careful.

She closed her eyes, taking a deep breath, and slowly walked back toward the cliff.

The sun had drifted lower in the sky. The pathway had disappeared—lost in the gray maze of stone.

Good. Then no one else will know it's there.

When I make my escape, they won't know where to look.

All I shall need is a diversion of some sort.

She pulled at the hem of her shirt, gazing at the pattern of colorful cartoon puppies chasing after their bones.

Miss Jaden bought this for me at the hotel shop.

If I disappeared and Valentin found this floating on the rocks, he wouldn't look any further.

She glanced at the cabin.

But I mustn't appear to be considering escape, or they may move me or lock me up.

She walked to the little stone building, the sun turning orange as it dipped into the water on the horizon. The temperature seemed to be the same as it had been earlier in the day, barely cooler at all. But the constant breeze made it very pleasant.

She sat down on the stony ground and waited for the stars.

When I get to the other island, I must get a signal to Hamilton somehow, so he can come and get me. He and Miss Jaden must be proper worried by now. But it can't be helped.

Twilight descended over the cabin. Constantine stared into the water below her, watching it turn from bright blue to a dark black shadow. She brought her knees up to her chest and wrapped her arms around her legs.

"You're thinking about escaping." The man from the cabin limped through the rear door.

"I'm not," Constantine said. "Valentin was very clear. I have no wish to fall on the rocks and be smashed to bits."

"You're thinking about it. All prisoners think about escape."

She peered at his silhouette in the growing darkness. "Do you?"

The man took a few more steps, turning to face the setting sun. "Not anymore."

The first few white sparkles of starlight appeared high overhead. Constantine stared into the sky. "Do you know where we are?"

"I thought a genius like you would know. Do you not?"

"Well . . ." She scooted forward, pointing. "The position of the sun at midday suggests we are near the equator. This place is not unlike The Bahamas in that regard. The climate is much more moderate. It's quite nice."

"A very nice climate. Go on."

She furrowed her brow. "The constant winds would suggest an island, as does the presence of the other visible islands nearby, but I can't see enough of their shape to draw much more from that. And I suppose the pleasant temperature limits us to the Pacific, where the climate is influenced by northern and eastern trade winds. Now, there are many islands in the Pacific, so . . . The brown shopping bag and American sodas would indicate a U.S. presence, either here or nearby . . ."

"Anything else?"

"Valentin drives a Jeep. Few non-U.S. countries in the Pacific rim would have those. They're expensive, and not very fuel efficient. I'll know more when the stars are visible, but I'd surmise we are on one of the Hawaiian islands." She turned to him. "Is that a good guess?"

"It is." He nodded. "Maui's barren west coast, to be precise. Aloha." The man hooked his thumb at the main house. "I overheard you speaking with that giant oaf earlier. About how your Keeper took care of you. That world is gone. You've . . . got a very different set of keepers now."

"Why are you here? You're a prisoner, too, right? Did you do something?"

"I did . . . and I will." The gaunt man sighed. "I'm a puppet. A lifeless marionette given one drug to make me sleep, and another drug to wake me up when they need me to work." He narrowed his eyes, staring out over the water. "One day, when I have the courage, I will end my torture by throwing myself to the bottom of this cliff."

"Is there no one who cares about you?" Constantine asked.

He peered at her. "Why did you say your father is alive? Everyone knows Doctor Hauser died in that chateau."

She pursed her lips, looking down. "I don't believe my father is dead."

"I admire your resolve—foolish that it may be. But for now, no more walks along the edge of the cliff." He wagged his finger at her. "You have just learned what can happen, eh?"

Constantine gasped, looking up. "I didn't—"

"There is no escape. Learn that now. Several people have died going over the cliff. That pathway you saw in the stone, it gets very narrow—and then it gets very crumbly. And then you fall onto the sharp rocks and you die. I told you, I have recovered the bodies."

She shook her head. "I won't try to run away."

"Don't forget, I know who you are. If your rescuers are to come, they need to come quickly. The . . . *operations* these lunatics have planned for you, it will be very hard on you. Many drills will cut into your little legs. They will slice away many sections of your head, until you are used up. Then they will discard your tiny, dead body, killed at the hand of someone who knows how to keep you alive until the harvest is complete. This is what awaits, so tell your hero to hurry fast."

Her tiny mouth hung open. "How do you know all this?"

"Because I am the man they have hired to kill you. A surgeon, paid to operate until nothing useful remains. And because I am a coward, I will do my job." He limped back inside. "There is a blanket on the floor. That will be your bed tonight."

His coughing fits resumed, coming and going until they were replaced with the sound of snoring.

Constantine sat on the stony ground, her knees to her chest. The sky grew dark around her, as the wind blew over the wide, black ocean.

She rocked back and forth, whispering to herself. "I'm not afraid of him. I'm not afraid of Valentin, either. I'm not afraid." Her voice wavered as the descriptions of the surgeries came rushing into her head.

"Many drills will cut into your little legs. They will slice away many sections of your head . . ."

She squeezed her eyes shut, her voice quivering. "I'm *not* afraid. I'm not. I'm not . . ."

The knot in her stomach got bigger. The waves below grew louder in their intensity.

"I'm . . . not afraid . . ."

She dropped her head onto her knees, pulling them tight to her chest and wrapping her arms firmly around them. "I know you'll come for me, Hamilton." Constantine's voice cracked. "You said you would, and you will." Swallowing hard, a tear rolled down her cheek. "Please come soon, Hamilton. Please come for me."

In the darkness, the five-year-old remained on the outside of the stony gray cabin, sobbing.

CHAPTER 29

Gagged and bound, DeShear trudged with his Bahamian Defense Force captors to the large plane. A soldier gripped each of his arms and a third walked behind them with a rifle pointed at their prisoner's head. The group proceeded up a metal loading platform that entered the tail of a huge aircraft. Two massive propellers spun on each wing, creating a loud hum inside.

After selecting a space between the cargo crates, one of the guards pulled a pair of handcuffs from his belt. He slipped it through a waist-level, welded steel loop that stuck out from the plane's frame. "This way," he shouted, barely audible over the noise of the engines. "You can stand or sit during the flight. Be sure to move around some, or you get a blood clot on such a long trip." As he opened the steel cuff, the other guard grabbed DeShear's arm and held it still.

"Smart man." The soldier with the rifle poked DeShear in the ribs with the muzzle. "No sense getting dead over a plane ride."

When the second handcuff was placed around DeShear's other wrist, the guard stepped away, tugging on the chain. The links clinked through the steel loop until the thick steel cuff hit it, holding DeShear in place.

The guard smiled. "Happy travels, murderer." Leaning close to DeShear, he spoke loudly. "Don't ever come back here. Next time, I guarantee you will exit the island in a different way."

He stepped aside as the next group of soldiers advanced. They carried Trinn, still unconscious and limp, her mouth hanging open.

DeShear grunted, pulling against his restraint.

Laying Trinn down, the guards lifted her hands over her head and handcuffed her the same way they had locked up DeShear. Her head hung on her shoulder, her feet sticking into the aisle.

"Move her legs," the lead soldier shouted. "We don't want anyone to trip."

A guard grabbed Trinn's ankles and shoved them to the side. Dozens of men with weapons marched up the loading ramp, passing DeShear and going into the compartment in the plane's midsection.

The lead guard grabbed DeShear's shirt collar, yanking him forward. "I heard you tried to kill this woman." He nodded at Trinn. "So we locked her up just far enough away. You can see, but you cannot touch—and she can see you. Maybe when she wakes up, she tells a different story than you tell. Maybe she tell the truth." He shoved DeShear into the wall, turning and walking away. "Of course, it gets very cold back here when the plane is flying." Stopping at the compartment door, he put his hand on the knob and let the last of the hired guns pass through. "Maybe you will get lucky and die of the cold before anyone say anything."

Chuckling, the soldier pulled the door shut.

An electric motor engaged, whining as the loading ramp raised up and shut against the hull of the plane, casting the rear section in darkness.

* * * * *

Hollings stood in the aisle, talking with Miss Franklin and Dr. Freeman.

Behind them, Keeper 27 sat upright, her eyes wide open. "They are here."

"Aye, they are, old girl." Hollings leaned on his cane. "DeShear, and that witch, Trinn. Loaded like crates with the rest of the gear. And believe me, if she wasn't being sold to Armen Twa for a pretty penny, she'd never see the end of this flight. Toss her out over the Pacific, I would, after what she done to me."

"But . . ." Keeper 27 looked around. "We've landed. Aren't we getting off the plane?"

Hollings smiled. "Dear girl, you're losing your faculties. We've only had one leg of our flight. We're gearing up for the second leg of the journey right now. You've not slept through it—yet." He called out over his shoulder. "Dr. Freeman, have you got your little black bag handy?"

Keeper 27 gripped the armrests. "What— what are you doing?"

"Well, since this is the last time we'll be seeing each other," Hollings said, "I thought I'd give you a proper farewell."

Dr. Freeman pulled a syringe from his medical case. Keeper 27 recoiled.

"Aye, that's it." Hollings chuckled. "I did so enjoy seeing you kicking and crying the last time, old girl."

"No!" Keeper 27 leaned away from the doctor. "There's no need! No!"

"Give her a right good dose, mate." Hollings opened the door to his private berth. "I don't want her waking up in the middle of the flight asking for a glass of water."

As Hollings disappeared, Dr. Freeman stepped toward Keeper 27, holding the needle high.

Shrieking, the old woman kicked and thrust backwards into her seat.

The engines revved, jolting the passengers as the aircraft lurched into motion.

Freeman came closer.

"No! No!" Keeper 27 screamed. "Please, no!"

As the needle pierced her arm, Keeper 27 howled, arching upwards in her seat. Her wrists strained against the handcuffs. Her eyes rolled back in her head as her tongue stuck out. She convulsed wildly, banging her legs into the seat in front of her.

Miss Franklin grabbed the old woman's arms, holding them down and looking at Freeman. "What's happening?"

The doctor swallowed hard, his jaw hanging open. "She—she's having a reaction."

Keeper 27 flailed in her seat.

"No kidding." Franklin frowned. "What did you give her?"

"A—a sedative." He took a step backwards. "It . . . it was the same thing as last time, I think."

"You *think*? Would you mind checking, doctor?"

Freeman shrugged. "I mean, it *is* the same thing . . . but this one came from a Bahamian pharmacy. It might contain other stabilizers."

Franklin struggled to hold the old woman down. "Come on! Do something!"

"I . . ." He glanced at a nearby soldier. "Get some blankets." He opened his bag and dug through the contents. "I've got a . . ."

Keeper 27 slammed back and forth, groaning and gagging. Pressing her shoulder into the old woman's midsection, Franklin looked at the doctor. "A what?"

The doctor shook his head. "I'm not a trauma physician! Diazepam is usually administered to alleviate a seizure, but . . . but she's reacting to the sedative I just gave her!" He put his hands on his head. "I don't have anything for that!"

"Do *something*!"

The plane tilted as it ascended, its engines roaring. Keeper 27 turned pale. Foam gathered at the corners of her mouth.

"Hurry!" Franklin shouted. "We're going to lose her!"

The doctor dug in his bag. The old woman jolted upright against Franklin, groaning, then slammed upwards again. She gagged, her hands banging against the steel handcuffs.

The soldier returned, handing Freeman two folded blankets.

"Get—get her out of there." Freeman placed the blanket on the floor. "Undo the restraints. Put her on the floor."

Franklin opened her shirt pocket and yanked out the handcuff key, undoing Keeper 27's restraints. As she put the key back in her shirt, Keeper 27 lurched forward.

"Easy. I've got you." Franklin eased Keeper 27 to the floor, putting her head on the pillow.

Breathing hard, Keeper 27 stared at the ceiling, her hands and legs twitching. Franklin knelt over her, wiping the spit from the old woman's mouth. "Hang on. We have something for you." She glared at Freeman. "Don't we?"

He stared at Keeper 27, his eyes wide, backing away. "I . . . I have nothing. My bag's been looted. There's nothing . . ."

Keeper 27 screamed and lurched upwards, arching her back and kicking her legs.

"You're a doctor!" Franklin shouted. "Do something. She's going into another seizure!"

Freeman shook his head, backing away.

Franklin put her hands on the old woman's shoulders. "I'm not going to let you die. We're just going to ride it out. If you can hear me, I'm . . . I'm going to try to help you."

Keeper 27 grabbed Franklin's shirt, pulling her down into her chest. The old woman moaned, shaking, veins throbbing on her forehead. She gagged again and again, her mouth hanging wide open.

Franklin yelled at the doctor. "We're going to lose her! Do something!"

Arching her back again, Keeper 27 let out a long moan, then collapsed.

The wrinkled fingers slipped from Franklin's shirt and fell onto the old woman's waist, then slowly slid to the floor.

Keeper 27's head sagged to the side. Her breath passed over her lips in a low, faint hiss, and she didn't take another.

Franklin sighed, staring at the old woman.

Creeping forward, Dr. Freeman knelt down and placed his fingers to Keeper 27's throat. Lowering his hand, he shook his head. "She's gone."

Franklin sat down in the aisle, closing her eyes and putting her hand to her forehead.

Taking his stethoscope from the bag, Freeman placed the tips in his ears and held the bell to Keeper 27's chest. After a moment, he took the stethoscope away and put it back in the bag, his head hanging.

Looking at her crew, Franklin got to her feet. "If I . . . could get a few volunteers to take her body to the back, please."

Several soldiers stood up.

"Lay her in the cargo bay," Franklin said. "It's cool in there. That will be best for now."

A soldier nodded. "We have a rescue stretcher in the rear of the midsection, ma'am."

"Yes, that . . . would be nice." She faced Freeman. "Thank you, Doctor. I won't be needing your services back here any longer. If you'd report to Mr. Hollings and tell him what has happened, I'd be obliged."

"Hollings?" The doctor's eye went wide. "But he'll—he'll . . ."

"Shoot you? That's probably true." She turned to one of her crew. "Please escort the doctor to the front cabin."

"With pleasure." The soldier stood up, grabbing Freeman and hauling him to the front of the plane.

The other soldier returned, carrying an aluminum-frame stretcher. It was a sturdy, basket-shaped device, made of a series of thick rods and overlaid with a canvas lining. He placed it alongside Keeper 27, then Franklin and several others lifted the old woman into it. Franklin picked up the blanket from the floor and covered Keeper 27's entire body with it. The blanket draped over her shoes, to the end of the metal piping, almost twelve inches longer than it needed to be to cover her frail old corpse.

A muffled gunshot came from the front of the compartment.

Franklin shook her head. "Sounds like we'll need another stretcher."

The private cabin door flew open and Hollings raced out, limping with his cane as he rushed toward Keeper 27. He stopped, his jaw hanging open. Inching forward, he pulled back the big blanket and gazed on Keeper 27's face. "Aye, what a mess we're in now." He covered the old woman back up and peered at Franklin. "Put her in the back, and say nothing to anyone." He looked over the crew. "That goes for you lot as well. Not a word of this to anyone until after we've concluded the transaction."

"What about Freeman?" Miss Franklin asked.

"Seems the doctor has met with a bit of an accident in my cabin." Hollings rubbed his chin. "It's probably best if he didn't continue along with us. Send a few of your people 'round. We'll dump Dr. Freeman's useless carcass into the ocean."

* * * * *

The lights flickered on in the cargo bay of the plane. DeShear got to his feet as the midsection door opened. Two soldiers carried a stretcher with a blanket over it—covering what appeared to be a body.

DeShear shook his head.

It's starting already.

Wherever Dr. Hauser and his people go, death follows.

The soldiers set the stretcher down across the aisle from him, between two crates. Two other soldiers entered the compartment, dragging a dead man in a white lab coat. They went to the rear of the plane, engaging the overhead motor of the loading platform.

Cold air rushed in as the gate lowered.

Stepping onto the platform, they grabbed the dead man by his hands and feet, swinging him back and forth between them. On the third swing, they let go, sending his limp, lifeless body into the pale blue sky.

DeShear looked away.

The soldiers raised the loading platform until it shut again, then walked back to the middle section.

"Savages!" DeShear cursed as the door shut behind them. Lowering himself back to the floor, he stared at the blanket covering the other corpse. "Why did they toss one body and not the other?"

"Thankfully, they did not." Keeper 27 pulled down the blanket.

"Helena!" DeShear glanced around, lowering his voice. "What are you doing here? What happened?"

"A bit of deception, I'm afraid, sir. I shall tell you all about it." She smiled, holding up the handcuff key she swiped from Miss Franklin's shirt pocket. "But first, do you know how to use one of these?"

CHAPTER 30

The morning sun found Constantine still outside the cabin, curled up on her side, asleep.

She lifted her head, blinking. The ever-present wind blew her hair into her eyes. Jutting out over the crystalline blue waves, the edge of the cliff was as daunting as it had been the night before when it almost took her life.

I must be more careful.

Constantine sat up. "In fact," she said to herself, "I've been behaving like a proper child. My Keeper would say, 'Young lady, this is not how I raised you.' She'd expect me to rise to the challenge."

She got to her feet staring at the edge of the cliff.

"We must make a plan, mustn't we, Keeper 27?"

Mimicking Helena, Constantine answered herself. "Yes, dear. Very good."

I must have a way to get down to that path without being noticed.

They leave me alone a fair bit. Perhaps after breakfast they'll go—and I can sneak away.

A jolt went through her.

You're being quite silly in your thinking. Who's to say they don't take you to some ghastly surgical center straight away this morning?

She crept toward the edge of the cliff as the big, blue waves crashed below. The little path wasn't visible yet. The dark gray stone, with all its gullies and ruts, hid it well—and the others never ventured close enough to the edge to see it.

Good. No one will know where I've gone.

She observed the main house. There hadn't been engine noise or any slamming of doors to indicate Valentin or the others were around.

Well, then. I suppose there's no time like the present.

She marched east along the cliff, toward the crack in the rock.

Gazing into the gray gap, she put her hands on her hips. The surface was shiny, as if it hadn't been there very long—but "very long" could be ten years or a hundred on a geological scale.

She balanced on one foot, easing her red sneaker down to the shiny gray gravel. The rocks shifted under her shoe, but didn't collapse or fall away.

And we've begun.

Turning sideways Constantine squeezed into the gap. It was tight for three or four steps, but the gap widened as she went lower, until it opened onto the cliff face and the morning sun. There, it was like a ten-foot-wide cave, high enough for an adult to walk around on or for a child to hide in.

To her right, the little shelf-path disappeared around the corner. Ten inches wide, maybe more, that stuck out from the sheer face of the high cliff.

Constantine squinted in the bright light. The waves were louder here, where the sounds carried straight up the stone surface. She ran her tiny fingers over the gray rock. It was rough to the touch, and wet. Cool, like the stone cabin had been, but not cold.

Putting her rear to the stone cliff wall, she stepped sideways along the path. It seemed much higher now. Far below, a wave crashed onto the rocks. It exploded with a *boom*, sending white foam in all directions.

Constantine gasped, pressing herself backwards.

The next wave crested and smashed into the rocks. Another boom and another spray.

"The rocks below are like cheese shredder," Cleo had said. *"And the currents are big-strong. Push you back over the rocks again and again, until your skin is scrape off and your arms and legs get slice cut away."*

Panting, she clung to the rock wall, slowly turning around so she wouldn't see the bottom of the cliff. Her cheek to the stone, she stretched her hands out wide, inching along the narrow path.

Go slow. There's no hurry. You must keep your balance.

The waves crashed below.

Keep moving. Steady as she goes.

The rock path shined with wetness, maybe from the sea spray or a light rain.

She stretched her foot out to the path, easing her weight onto it.

The little red sneaker slipped to the edge. Constantine's stomach lurched as the rock wall moved away from her face. She gasped, throwing her hands out, clawing at the stone as she went backwards.

A hand clasped onto her shoulder, jerking her back onto the ledge.

The surgeon from the cabin glared at her with bloodshot eyes. "Step with me! Now!" He pulled her toward him. "This way. Slowly."

Trembling, Constantine obeyed the doctor's commands. Sea spray surged upwards with every wave, coating her in a fine mist as the churning water far below grew in its intensity.

"Come!" He shouted, pulling her. "Keep coming!" His grip stretched her t-shirt as she inched along the ledge. "Yes. Good. That's it!"

At the opening, he stood to the side of the crack. Wet with sweat, he held her as she squeezed sideways into the gap and climbed back up to the top.

He followed, reaching up when he was halfway through, and hauling himself over like he was climbing out of a swimming pool.

The doctor rolled over onto his back, his thin chest rising and falling with each hard breath. "The wind." He gasped, pointing toward the water. "The sea changes constantly. And that affects the waves." Propping himself up on one shoulder, he peered at

Constantine. "Which affects the rock, yes? Understand?"

Her heart still pounding, Constantine nodded.

"Come." The doctor got to his feet. "It is time for breakfast, and we can't be seen here." He put his hand out and helped Constantine to her feet. "Are you okay, girl?"

Breathing hard, she nodded again.

"Good." He limped toward the cabin. "You don't do that again."

Constantine turned toward the stony edge as the sound of another booming wave crashed into the rocks. Drops of water shot all the way to the top of the cliff.

Trembling, she backed away before turning and running to the cabin.

* * * * *

The doctor sat on the bed, holding a plate with several breakfast pastries on it. A small, metal coffee cup sat at his feet. He held the dish out to Constantine. "Eat."

Taking a danish, she looked around for a place to sit. She picked the spot on the floor where the blanket had been laid, using it as a cushion. "When did these come?"

"Right when you started your little adventure." He set the plate on the bed and picked up a croissant, sniffing it. "You are small, but you are not invisible. You are lucky they didn't see you."

"I suppose so." She scrunched up her nose. "But they must have noticed I wasn't here."

The doctor set his pastry down and pointed to the small door next to the rear exit. "I told them you were in the toilet."

Constantine took a small bite of her danish. It had an apple filling and seemed to have been baked recently. It wasn't hard, or stale-tasting. "I should thank you." She glanced toward the main house, lowering her voice. "For keeping me from falling just now."

The doctor bent down and picked up his coffee, taking a sip. The breeze from the ocean pushed his greasy hair around his temples.

"Anyway," she said, "I don't wish to appear ungrateful. So, thank you. Doctor . . ."

The surgeon stared out the rear door.

"It does seem curious, though. If you're going to kill me anyway, why didn't you just let me fall?"

"No more talking." His eyes remained fixed on the door. "Eat."

She took a few bites of her danish. "You don't feel good, do you? Is it the drugs you mentioned? Did you take something to make you sleep last night?" When he didn't answer, she finished her breakfast. "If you're not hungry, I'll have yours. I'm famished."

She got up and walked to the bed, reaching for the croissant. The doctor's hand shot out, grabbing her by the wrist.

He glared at her. "That one is mine."

"Yes, of course," Constantine said. "Very sorry."

He let go of her hand and picked up the croissant, but didn't eat it. Rubbing her wrist, Constantine walked to the rear door. "How do you know the fence is electrified?"

The doctor looked at her. "What's that you say?"

"The fence. It has signs on it that say High Voltage, and Cleo said it would fry you if you touched it . . . but as far as I can see, there's no electricity out here. There are no power lines running to the main house, and there are no utility poles nearby. I suppose a battery system is possible, but it would have to be very large. They can't have buried a cable in this rocky ground, and I haven't heard a generator."

He stared at her from the bed.

"Did you not ever check?" she asked.

Grunting, the doctor got up from the mattress. "Valentin was right. You talk too much." He brushed past her and walked outside.

The back door of the main house banged shut. "Constantine!" Nicole bounded over the gray stone yard, carrying a plastic shopping bag. "Have you finished breakfast?"

"Yes, Miss Nicole." Constantine went to the front door of the cabin.

Nicole trotted down the steps, swinging the bag.

"Thank you for breakfast, miss. It was very tasty. I do like apple."

"Très bien." Nicole smiled, holding out the bag. "I have brought you some different clothes.

They are used, but clean, *oui?* I think they will fit you."

Constantine checked inside the bag. A bright red windbreaker with a white collar sat on top of a pair of jeans. Lifting them revealed a pink t-shirt, socks, and underwear. She looked up at Nicole. "They're very nice, miss."

"Let us try on the jacket. I think I guess the right size for you."

Nicole helped Constantine slip into the windbreaker, zipping it all the way up to Constantine's neck. The child pranced around the cabin, spinning in circles with her arms out. "It's lovely, miss! Thank you."

"Good." Nicole beamed. "Would you like to go for a walk?"

Constantine raised her eyebrows. "Is that allowed?"

"I am sure a short walk will do no harm. A young girl needs exercise, yes? And Valentin is not here. Come." Nicole held out her hand. "Walk with me."

They crossed the stone yard together, hand in hand, only letting go to allow Nicole a chance to take a key from her pocket and open the big lock on the back door. Once they were inside, she re-locked it and they passed through the dingy interior of the main house.

Beyond the house was a tall mountain, green and lush, with a rainbow shining behind it. At the bottom of the slope stood a desert. Small, brown bushes stuck up from the rough gray rocks.

Nicole walked uphill, to the left. "Come on. Time to exercise."

Constantine ran to catch up with her, taking Nicole's hand again. She had to take two steps for every one of Nicole's, but she didn't mind. After a few minutes, they were at the top of a small plateau. The mountain rose up behind them and the bright blue waters stretched out below, as far as the eye could see. The other islands appeared majestic in the morning light.

Nicole put her hands on her hips, her blonde ponytail waving in the wind. "What do you think?"

"It's quite spectacular." Constantine faced the beautiful scenery, keeping Nicole in the corner of her eye. "I might say this island looked like heaven if I wasn't supposed to die here."

"What!" Nicole whipped around, grabbing Constantine's shoulders. "Who told you that? Was it that horrible Doctor Solaine?"

Constantine nodded. "He said he was a surgeon and that he would drill into my legs and cut into my head. He said people would make him do that again and again until there was nothing left of me—and then I would die."

"Oh, no, no, no." Nicole hugged Constantine, pulling her close. *"Chut, fille."* No more of that talk. I would never let you suffer so."

"No?"

"Never. There will be a procedure, yes. An operation, to draw some bone marrow and stem cells. But I would never let them continue with their horrible plans. It will never be like Doctor Solaine told you."

Constantine buried her face in Nicole's waist. "Oh, thank you, miss."

"I will save you from that, eh? I know where Valentin has hidden a gun." She stroked Constantine's hair. "After the first procedure, they will relax. Then, I will steal his gun and sneak you out. We will escape to this beautiful place together, *oui?*" She kissed the top of Constantine's head. "And then I will shoot you, girl. You will not suffer, I promise."

Constantine's breath caught in her throat. She held Nicole, terror gripping her insides as she gazed, unfocused, at the crystalline water, forcing her hands not to tremble.

CHAPTER 31

As Nicole ushered Constantine out the back door of the main house, she heard Valentin's noisy Jeep approaching.

"Go quick, *fille*." Nicole patted Constantine on the back. "To the cabin. There will be lunch soon—and maybe a snack of your fish crackers later."

Constantine nodded and raced to the cabin, jumping down the steps. When Nicole had pulled the back door of the main house shut, Constantine crept back up the stairs.

The old house had missing boards and falling sections, so she stayed low, crawling over the smooth, gray stone of the yard. Reaching the side of the crumbling house, Constantine got on her knees to peek in the window.

Nicole greeted Valentin and Muddy when they came in the front door. The kidnappers spoke to each other in French.

"The arrangements are now set," Valentin said. "Tomorrow, as soon as Hollings arrives with the old woman and the two Americans, we will get a call. Then, we take the little girl to a rendezvous point."

"Okay." Nicole swept a strand of hair from her eyes. "Do we know where?"

Muddy set a large paper bag on the rickety old table.

"They will tell us on the call." Valentin paced back and forth. "But we are to begin the surgeries tomorrow morning. The adverse effects of the plane flight should have dissipated by then."

Muddy faced Valentin, frowning. "Dr. Solaine . . . he is too ill to operate on Constantine."

"Muddy is right," Nicole said. "That shell of a man is not able to perform surgery. What if—"

"Why do you think we can debate this?" Valentin threw his hands in the air. "It is decided! Mr. Twa insists on having stem cells and bone marrow harvested from the girl before he sells her to Hollings, so that is what we will do. He probably plans to propagate the blood line in a laboratory somewhere." Scowling, he folded his arms. "Regardless, it is not our concern."

"It's not right," Muddy said. "She's just a little girl."

"And you are just a big, stupid man." Valentin slammed his hand on the table. "Now, do as you are told." He shoved the bag at Muddy. "Take them their lunch. Make sure the girl eats and sleeps today. Plenty of water and antibiotics."

As Muddy picked up the bag, Constantine crawled away from the house and ran back to the cabin. She was barely inside when the back door of the main house banged shut.

"You are playing a dangerous game." Dr. Solaine stepped out from the shadows.

Constantine gasped.

Did he see me spying on them?

"Here come lunch food!" Muddy walked across the stone yard, swinging the bag.

Solaine walked toward her. "What do you think you're doing, sneaking to the house like that? You risk getting us both killed."

Constantine narrowed her eyes. "Instead of just me?"

"Watch your tongue, child." The doctor sneered. "You may end up at the bottom of that cliff yet."

As Constantine opened her mouth to speak, a giant shadow fell over her.

"You not hurt her!" Muddy yelled. He raced to the feeble surgeon, seizing him by the collar with one hand and lifting him off the ground. "You never hurts her."

"Let go of me, you idiot!" Solaine grabbed Muddy's wrists, twisting in the big man's grasp. The surgeon's feet kicked in the air.

"If you hurt her, I hurt you." He dropped the doctor and reached inside the bag, pulling out a cloth napkin. Going to the bedside, he grabbed Solaine's coffee cup and poured the contents over the cloth. "Are you see?" Muddy shouted, stuffing the lunch bag under his arm. He grabbed the front of the doctor's shirt and dragged him outside.

Solaine kicked and flailed as Muddy pulled him over the gray stone.

"Cleo!" Constantine ran after Muddy.

"You not hurt her!" Muddy dropped the paper bag and hauled the doctor to the electric fence, lifted him up as he brandished the wet cloth. "You never hurts her!"

Solaine struggled against Muddy's grip. "Let me go!"

Constantine stood in the yard, her jaw agape. "Cleo!"

Muddy's face was red, his eyes wide. "You never hurts her!" He hurled the wet cloth napkin into the fence. It exploded in a shower of sparks. "Never! You never hurts her!"

Smoke poured from the napkin as it sizzled on the electrified wires. A small flame burst from its folds.

Muddy grabbed the doctor's collar with both hands, shaking him. "Never!"

"Muddy!" The back door banged open. Valentin ran across the stone yard with a gun in his hand. "What do you think you are doing?"

Muddy looked up, his eyes wide. "Not hurt Constantine!"

"Help me!" Solaine screamed. "This monster will kill me!"

"We need the doctor." Valentin pointed the gun at Muddy. "Put him down. Now."

"Not hurt her!"

"She doesn't belong to us!" Valentin cocked the weapon. "Put him down. I won't say it again."

Nicole burst forth from the house. "Everyone, stop! Stop this now!" Her hand on her lip, she gazed back and forth between the two men.

Muddy glared at Valentin. Narrowing his eyes, he let go of Doctor Solaine and walked forward.

"Cleo!" Constantine gasped. "Stop!"

"Muddy!" Nicole shouted. "No!"

Muddy kept walking.

"Cleo!"

As Muddy got closer, Valentin took a step backwards, kicking the brown bag.

The gun fired. Muddy flinched, a tuft of his shirt pocket popping like confetti. He stumbled sideways, his jaw dropping, then glared at Valentin and took another step forward.

"Keep away from me!" Valentin fired two more rounds.

The giant threw his hands out, blood splattering from his chest. He looked at Constantine. "He doesn't . . . hurt you."

The girl clasped both hands over her mouth.

Muddy's eyes rolled back in his head. He collapsed onto the rusty High Voltage sign, sending up an explosion of sparks. His massive body bounced forward, but the sign snagged his shirt, pulling him back. He slammed into the fence a second time, screaming as smoke burst forward from his shoulders. Reaching out, he clawed the air as his torso convulsed in spasms. He thrust forward again and again, straining and reaching, but the sign held him by his snagged shirt. Muddy grabbed for the buttons of his shirt, his hands thumping clumsily into his chest.

"Help him!" Constantine cried. "Someone, do something. Turn off the power!"

Nicole raced to the girl and swept her up, turning her face away, but Constantine twisted around.

As Nicole carried her to the cabin, Muddy dangled on the fence, his body on fire. His arms turned black, his tongue hanging out of his mouth as smoke billowed upward around him. The shirt ignited, sending flames dancing across his chest and face. He threw his head back, screaming and kicking, reaching again for the snagged shirt, unable to free himself from the fence.

Slumping forward, the shirt ripped, and Muddy fell face-first onto the ground. A small piece of charred, smoldering black cloth clung to the sign. Smoke rose from Muddy's unmoving body.

Standing in the gray stone yard, gun in hand, Valentin stared at the smoldering corpse. Next to him, the breeze pulled at the brown paper bag.

"He was only getting their lunch." Nicole gasped. "As you told him, Valentin." She cursed, spitting on the ground. "He let the doctor go. He was only trying to take the prisoners their lunch."

Valentin looked at the bag at his feet, the brown paper waving back and forth with the wind. "Take the girl into the cabin." Valentin walked toward Muddy's corpse and nodded to Solaine. "Old man, when the body has cooled, you will help me dispose of it."

"Yes," Solaine stammered. "Of course."

"I saved your life just now." Valentin glared at the frail, wreck of a man. "You could say thank you."

Backing away, Solaine nodded. "Thank you, sir."

Valentin bent down and picked up the bag, holding it out to the doctor. "Here is . . . your lunch."

With trembling fingers, Solaine took the bag and rushed back to the cabin.

Valentin stared at Muddy for a few more minutes, then turned and walked to the back door. Putting Constantine down, Nicole wiped the tears from her eyes and followed Valentin into the house.

When the door of the main house banged shut, the little girl stared at the old man. "I'm leaving here. Tonight."

"I already told you," Solaine said. "There is no escape. The fence is death. The cliff is death."

"I'll take the path on the ledge."

"Then you will finish what you started yesterday."

Constantine glared at him. "I'm as good as dead anyway. You said so yourself. My Keeper always watched out for me. She taught me how to be aware and how to assess people. I—"

"You are a foolish child, with a child's foolish optimism." The surgeon retreated to his corner, stepping into the shadows by his bed. "You will die on the ledge path. It is slippery. It crumbles. I have seen the bodies floating in the surf. And if you get to the bottom safely, you drown in the water. The other island is miles away."

"I'm an excellent swimmer." Constantine puffed out her chest. "The best in my class. I could hold my breath for almost three minutes."

"Then it will take you three minutes longer to drown!" Solaine coughed, wiping his lip with a finger. It came away with blood on it. "If you survive the waves and the currents, you will die of exposure on the other island. It is a desert. The closest people are all the way on the other side."

"Then I shall have a long walk as well!"

"Until you are captured again, or you die. No one is going to come for you. No one ever comes." He leaned on the wall, sliding to the floor. "Do you know how many children have cried all night, wishing and hoping for their mother and father to come get them? And no one ever did."

Constantine looked down. "Hamilton will come. I know it. He said he would."

"And you think people do what they say in this world?" Solaine scoffed.

She gazed at the frail old man. "I think if you believe strongly in people, they will work very hard to not disappoint you."

Shoulders slumping, the doctor's head sagged onto his bony chest. "What makes you think I won't walk right out of this wretched cabin and tell Valentin what you have planned?"

"I think you're ashamed of the things you've done—the things that landed you here." Constantine lowered her voice. "That's why you do things to help you forget. But you don't want to see me die. If you did, you wouldn't have gone out onto that dangerous, wet, slippery ledge and stopped me from falling."

The old man turned away. "Don't count on me doing it again."

CHAPTER 32

The pilot appeared at Hollings' door. "What's going on back here? You can't shoot a gun in an aircraft!"

"Apparently I can," Hollings scoffed. "Now, you've got flying to do. Get back to the cockpit."

The pilot frowned. "Keep that weapon holstered. If you put a hole in the fuselage, the plane could depressurize. Remember that."

"And you remember." Hollings held up his pistol. "I've got a gun. The second this plane touches down, have it ready to get airborne again, understood? There won't be much time."

The pilot pointed at Hollings. "We're preparing to land right now. Keep your people in line." Turning, he headed back to the cockpit.

Hollings looked out the window. The airfield at Honolulu stretched along the island shoreline. Seaplanes and sailboats dotted the inner harbors and marinas.

"Ah, I'm practically tingling inside. We're about to close the biggest deal of our lives and get rid of our biggest rival at the same time."

Miss Franklin took the seat next to him. "What about Helena?"

"We'll show Twa's people the body and tell them that she suffered a stroke during the flight." He shrugged. "She's old, couldn't be helped, we did our best—that sort of thing. He might trim a little off the purchase price, but Keeper 27 was never what he wanted anyway."

The captain's voice came over the overhead speakers. "We will be landing in a few minutes. All passengers, fasten your seat belts and secure any loose items. Flight crew, prepare for landing."

The plane engines throttled back as the aircraft descended toward the airport.

"All right, miss. That's your cue." Hollings faced Miss Franklin. "Have this airplane land like it's a flying fortress. I want guns ready and aimed in all directions the second we land. When Twa's people appear, you and I will take a small band of armed guards with us to go out to make the trade. As soon as we verify that Constantine is present, your soldiers start unloading the money . . . then they attack and kill everyone in sight. We take the girl, load the money back up, and we go."

"He'll be expecting an ambush."

Hollings shook his head. "He'll be expecting a dozen guns, tops. Not the arsenal we brought. And if there's shooting, stick close to the little girl. Twa's people will have been told not to shoot anywhere near her, so that will be the safest place on this island." He exhaled, shaking his hands out like they had water on them. "I'm like a boxer before a prize fight. Can't wait to get this deal done and get to Jakarta. Got friends there who'll get us safe passage to Cambodia, and from there I can go anywhere on the planet that I want."

* * * * *

Trinn put a hand to her bruised throat. "I feel like my neck and shoulders were in a car crash."

DeShear knelt next to her. "They're slowing the engines, so I need to move fast. Helena says Hollings plans to start a shooting spree on the runway, but that Constantine isn't here."

"They've been holding her on the far side of Maui." Helena stood at Trinn's feet, steadying herself in the jostling cargo bay by holding onto a crate. "It's a barren, remote area on the desert cliffs, with an abandoned house."

DeShear pounded his fist into his other hand. "Then as soon as this plane touches the runway and begins to slow down, I'm opening that loading platform and jumping out. I'm going to get Constantine."

"Okay." Trinn sat up. "I'm coming with you."

"Hey, whoa." DeShear shook his head. "I'm not sure you're in any kind of shape—"

"Hey, yourself," Trinn said. "I might look rough, but I *won* my wrestling match with The Bahamas Strangler. I can go—so let's stop debating and figure out how."

Taking a deep breath, DeShear rubbed his chin stubble. "This plane will still be moving pretty fast when the wheels hit the tarmac. We can't wait too long to jump or we'll be spotted—and in range of any guns Hollings has."

Helena clutched her hands to her waist. "Can you jump into the water when we get close?"

"We're going too fast." Trinn got to her feet. "Water doesn't compress. Hitting it at this speed would be like hitting concrete."

Helena put her hand to her lip. "Oh, dear."

"We don't need them to slow down very much if we can cushion the impact somehow." DeShear inspected the wooden crates. "Maybe . . ."

"What about Helena?" Trinn glanced at DeShear.

"Everyone on board thinks I'm dead." Helena picked up the corner of her blanket. "I imagine if I lay on the floor and pull the covers back over my face, they'll continue to think so. I wouldn't think anyone would look twice at someone they already believe is dead."

"Okay." DeShear kicked the side of a wooden crate, breaking it into several pieces. He held up one of the boards, walking to the section door and jamming it under the knob. "That won't hold long, but it'll buy some time. Now we just need to figure out how to get off without getting killed."

Helena leaned over and pulled the blanket off the large aluminum stretcher. "I thought perhaps this might come in handy."

* * * * *

In the private cabin, Miss Franklin peered out the window as the runway got closer. Green grass and palm trees rushed by, getting larger and larger until the plane bounced as the tires made impact.

The pilot came over the intercom. "I've got a warning light on our tail loading platform. One of your people has opened the tail gate!"

Hollings' jaw dropped. "One of your hired hands is trying to make off with the money!"

Franklin raised her pistol and jumped up from her seat. "I'm on it."

* * * * *

The door knob of the rear compartment rattled, but the wedge of broken crate held it shut. Winds swirled through the cargo bay like a tornado as the platform inched downward. Lying on the floor with the edges of the blanket tucked underneath of her, Helena laid still.

"Ready?" Trinn crouched, putting a hand on each side of the heavy stretcher's frame.

DeShear shook his head. "We're still going too fast."

Thumps came from the compartment door as it cracked and splintered. A hole appeared in the center of the thin barrier.

Trinn glanced at DeShear. "Looks like we'd better go anyway."

A woman's hand reached through the hole in the door, grabbing at the knob. The loading platform lowered to where it was horizontal, slowly continuing downward.

DeShear nodded. "Okay. Do it."

Trinn laid down on the stretcher. The speeding runway loomed around the descending platform, continuing to angle downward. "We probably won't stay upright very long, Hank. When this thing flips, cover your face and head as best you can, and roll."

DeShear swallowed hard, putting his hands on the sides of the stretcher. He shoved it onto the platform, the wind pulling at his shirt.

The hand in the compartment door retracted, and the barrel of a gun appeared.

"When the platform hits the runway," Trinn said, "Shove off, jump on—and keep low."

A gunshot bounced off the side of the platform, sending up sparks. DeShear flinched, glancing over his shoulder. The door broke open. A woman and three soldiers rushed toward him.

"Stop!" The woman pointed her gun at him. "Stop!"

DeShear shoved the stretcher. The platform jolted, sparks flying as it scraped the runway. He gave one final push with his legs, jumping onto the stretcher as it slid off the back of the tailgate.

The stretcher rumbled and screeched as it sped over the concrete tarmac, bouncing wildly. The wind threw Trinn's hair into DeShear's eyes as he pressed himself down on her, clinging to the aluminum frame.

"Hang on!" Trinn shouted.

The speeding stretcher angled sideways towards the grass median, bumping and bouncing higher and higher, until it flipped over, spilling its occupants out.

DeShear closed his eyes and covered his head, rolling and smacking the soil like he was being beaten with a dozen sandbags from head to foot. Dirt flew everywhere, dumping into his ears and nose, filling his mouth as he rolled over the grassy patch.

He slammed sideways into a small bush, stopping. A cloud of dust passed. Cut and bruised, he lifted his head, spitting dirt and pebbles.

The cargo plane continued down the runway, its tailgate streaming sparks.

As the dust from his collision settled, he saw Trinn sitting up nearby. "Hey," he said. "You still alive?"

"Barely." She smacked the dirt from her legs and torso. "You?"

He nodded, getting to his feet. "I guess we made it. Now we need to steal some transportation."

Trinn stood, pointing to the marina. A dozen seaplanes floated in the calm waters of the harbor. "What about one of those?"

CHAPTER 33

The choppy noise of a big engine drowned out every other sound in the cabin. Constantine looked out the door in time to see a red helicopter zoom past the cliff and hover over the old main house. Solaine peered over her shoulder as the helicopter descended into a cloud of dust, landing in the front yard.

"We've got a visitor," the doctor said. "That's Armen Twa."

"What's he doing here?" Constantine stepped away from the door.

The doctor glanced at Constantine. "Inspecting the goods, I suspect."

"Well, he shall have to inspect quickly." She grabbed her red windbreaker and put it on, marching to the back door.

"Child, don't." Solaine swallowed hard. "If they lose you, they . . . have no reason to keep me."

She nodded. "Then we shall have to leave together."

"No . . ." The doctor wrapped his arms around himself, quivering.

Constantine peered at the bathroom door. "Could you tell them I'm in the loo? That may give me a few minutes. Perhaps . . . when they come after me, an opportunity will present itself, and you can get away."

He stared at the main house, rubbing his arms.

Zipping up her windbreaker, Constantine eased open the rear door and raced across the stone yard to the crevice.

* * * * *

"Change of plans." Armen Twa took off his Panama hat as he entered the main house. "One of my people has seen something at the airport they didn't like. It's an ant mound of activity. Bring me the girl. We leave now."

"She is just in the cabin," Valentin said.

"Take the Jeep and ditch it, too." Twa paced back and forth, scowling. "Nicole, go with him. There are a hundred cliffs on this island that *don't* have rocks at the bottom. Find the closest one and drive the car off." He glanced at the sparce roof. "I'd say we should burn this old relic, but we can't afford for the smoke to be seen."

Valentin nodded. "And then?"

"And then I have a jet waiting on Kahului Airport, on the other side of this rock. We get out of here until things cool down, then we figure out our next move. Now, where is the girl?"

"This way." Nicole headed to the back door, but Valentin pushed his way in front of her and held the door open for Mr. Twa.

"Constantine!" Valentin walked quickly over the stone yard. "Constantine, come here." He went down the cabin steps and looked around. "Constantine!"

The cabin was empty.

CHAPTER 34

As the cargo plane slowed to a stop, swarms of marines came out of the surrounding buildings. The military troops pointed their rifles at the plane as loudspeakers blared, telling everybody on board to surrender.

As the criminals were marched off the plane with their hands up, Dr. Kittaleye walked toward the procession, trailed by Ari and Special Agent Matt Eicholtz of the FBI.

Kitt pointed at Hollings. "There he is, Agent. That's the man who kidnapped me."

The FBI agent pulled Hollings out of the line. "Sir, come with me. You're under arrest."

"What?" Hollings shouted. "I've not kidnapped anyone! I've never seen this bird before in my life."

"Oh, you're not under arrest for kidnapping—yet." Eicholtz snapped handcuff on Hollings' wrist. "But the minute you touched down on U.S. soil with all those guns, that was a little bit of a violation of Federal law. We watched the whole thing on a satellite feed, thanks to the doctor you say you never met. Transportation and possession of illegal firearms carries a stiff sentence."

Kitt smiled. "Judging by that armory they're unloading, I'd say you'll be spending quite a few years in prison, fat boy. But let the nice FBI agent read you your rights. You can remain silent—and I'd love it if you would."

Eicholtz held Hollings' other wrist behind his back and finished handcuffing him. "Funny thing. About an hour ago we arrested a group almost as big as this one. Bunch of Asian fellas with a bunch of guns, looking for some kind of a meeting. Don't suppose you know what that was about?"

"Bugger!" Hollings shouted. "It was Twa! That dirty, double crossing—I mean . . . silent! I wish to remain silent! And get me a lawyer!"

As Eicholtz loaded Hollings into a squad car, another FBI agent escorted Helena from the plane.

At the bottom of the stairs, the elderly woman threw her arms around Kitt. "Doctor! How good to see you!"

"Oh, I'm so glad you're okay." Kitt squeezed Helena tight. "But I do have a bone to pick with you. Call Jaden Trinn's boss and tell him 'Mau-oui'? Call the President? And tell him 'Maui'? They thought I was crazy."

"Well . . ." Helena smiled, the wind blowing her gray hair. "Somebody obviously figured it out."

"Yeah. This guy did." Kitt gestured to Ari. "Helena, this is—"

"Aristotle Hiles," Helena said. "Of Israeli intelligence. Dear, I've met Ari once before."

"There's less gunfire this time." Ari chuckled. "But looking at all these weapons, it was close."

"How . . ." Kitt frowned. "How do you two . . ."

"I shall explain later, doctor." She turned to Ari. "Right now, I must ask you for an urgent favor."

CHAPTER 35

"You must hold the wall at all time," Dr. Solaine shouted, inching his way along the cliff ledge. Constantine moved sideways on the narrow path in front of him. "One bad move and you will land on the rocks."

Hugging the stone face, Constantine slid her red sneaker a few inches out, then moved the other one.

"Yes, yes. That's it." The doctor took a half step and peered over his shoulder. The big blue waves crashed over the rocks below. He turned his face and closed his eyes, shuddering. "And whatever you do, don't look down. Around the corner, the ledge narrows but there are no rocks below. But it is crumbly. You must watch yourself."

Constantine breathed hard, clinging to the cliff face as she inched forward. She peeked down at the crystalline blue waves, her stomach jolting. "We're so far up!"

"Not for long if you don't watch your step. Keep moving, but always hold the wall."

The path narrowed as it curved around the side of the cliff. Bits of the ledge had broken away, leaving gaps she had to stretch across.

"Yes. Good." Solaine panted. "Hold the wall and reach with one foot. Test the ledge. If it holds, take the step and move on."

Constantine looked ahead. "The path is getting smaller!"

"It is plenty wide enough for a little girl and an old man. Keep moving."

She looked down again. The patch of rocks had passed. Now, the waves smashed directly into the cliff face below, sending up a fine sea mist that coated the path and made it shiny. She grimaced, stretching her foot out as she clutched the stone surface. The wind whipped her hair into her face.

"Lean into the cliff," Solaine shouted. "Push your weight into the wall."

Each step grew more slippery than the last. Constantine kept her eyes on the path, carefully placing each foot as she moved.

A hundred feet ahead, the ancient lava slide loomed over the waves. The hardened lava water slide cascaded downward into the water where it was much calmer. The waves splashed against it, but without the hard *boom* they produced when they hit the cliffs beneath the cabin.

In the distance, the other island rose from the sea. It was brown and bleak, a lifeless desert of empty volcanic rock, swept bare by the ever-present winds.

The calm water between the two islands glistened in the sunlight.

The roar of a helicopter soared overheard, swooping downward as it flew past. Constantine flinched, gripping the cliff. Armen Twa's red helicopter swung in a wide arc.

"Your coat!" Solaine shouted.

Constantine looked down at her red windbreaker.

It will stand out against the gray of the cliff.

"They'll see us," he said. "Quick! Take it off."

Constantine took her hand away from the stone wall and immediately put it back. "I can't. I'll have to let go of the cliff and I'll fall."

"Take it off!" the doctor shouted. "Hurry!"

* * * * *

In the co-pilot seat of the helicopter, Valentin stared out at the water. Armen Twa sat next to him, speaking over his headset.

"Do you see anything?"

Valentin shook his head, pressing his microphone close to his mouth. "It's impossible from this height. The ocean is so big, with so many waves . . . each reflection of the sunlight is a false alarm."

Twa nodded, steering the helicopter toward the cliff. "I can't get too close to the cliffs. There's a strong wind shear. It wreaks havoc with the helicopter blades. It could crash us."

Valentin scanned the water and the stony cliff face. "I don't see how they could be on the side of the cliff. Not this far away from the cabin. Try the grounds again. They have to be—"

"Look!" Nicole pointed to a red dot on the cliff wall. "It's Constantine."

"Where?" Twa gripped the control stick, keeping the helicopter in place. "I don't see anything."

"The red!" Nicole patted the back of Valentin's seat. "It is the windbreaker I gave her. Get closer!"

Twa shook his head. "I can't. The wind shear will push us straight into the cliff wall."

"She is there!" Nicole shouted. "And there is Solaine!"

"The old fool." Valentin took out his pistol.

"What are you doing?" Twa's eyes went wide. "I need that girl. She's worth a lot of money!"

"Not if she falls and drowns in the ocean." Valentin opened his ventilator window, pointing his weapon toward the cliff. "Maybe I can persuade her to return to the cabin."

* * * * *

"I think they've seen us," Solaine shouted. "The helicopter's not moving. I told you, get that jacket off."

"I can't!"

"Then be sure to take it off when you hit the water, or it will bind around you and pull you to the bottom. Now, keep moving."

A shot rang out. The cliff wall above them burst into a puff of gravel, falling down around them. Constantine shrieked.

"They're just trying to scare us." Solaine blinked dirt out of his eyes. "They won't hurt you— you're worth too much."

Constantine gazed at the path ahead. It narrowed for a few feet, then had a two or three foot gap. Sharp edges of broken stone glimmered in the light. "The path! It's broken off! What do we do?"

"Even your little legs can reach across that." Solaine took another step. "Hold the wall and stretch out."

* * * * *

Twa leaned down and pulled a small machine gun out from under his seat, handing it to Valentin. "Put away that pea shooter of yours and use this."

Valentin's jaw dropped. "Are you sure?"

"You wanted to scare them. This will do the job." Twa pointed at the cliff. "Shoot ahead of them, on the path. These ledges are like glass. They will shatter, leaving them no choice but to retreat."

Hefting the gun to his shoulder, Valentin closed one eye and took aim. The cliff bounced up and down in his sight. "Try to hold the helicopter steady, sir."

"It's impossible—the wind shear. Just don't hit the girl. We can always find another surgeon."

* * * * *

The rocks in front of Constantine exploded in a spray of bullets. She squeezed her eyes shut, clinging to the wall.

When she opened her eyes again, the gap in the ledge path was ten feet wide.

Another spray of bullets shattered the stone cliff over their heads. Rocks tumbled past them.

Solaine grabbed Constantine by the shoulder, tugging her windbreaker. "I told you, get that red jacket off!"

"Stop!" She screamed. "You'll make me fall!"

He jerked the windbreaker halfway down her arm. "Take it off!"

He pulled again. The stone wall drifted away from Constantine's face. She swung her hands out, clawing at the gray wall as it moved farther and farther away. Solaine tugged at her windbreaker again.

As she turned to scream, her feet went out from under her. She dropped a few feet, then jerked to a stop as the old man held her jacket by the collar. She swung out a few feet, then back, slamming into the cliff, then felt a hard tug and saw Solaine's feet go past her.

The windbreaker jerked again, yanking her into Solaine's downward path. Her stomach surged as she dropped away from the ledge and plummeted down toward the water.

* * * * *

"Fool!" Twa grabbed the machine gun back from Valentin. "What have you done?"

"Nothing! I didn't shoot them." Valentin pressed his face to the window. "They . . . they fell."

"All the same to my wallet." Twa scowled. "They could never survive a drop like that!"

"Wait, please," Nicole begged. "Let us watch. Maybe . . ."

The water pounded the bottom of the cliff, churning it into a white foam. Wave after wave rushed forward, crashing into the stone wall. Only the white foam was visible.

Nicole put her hands to the side of her face. "Oh, no."

"What?" Twa peered over the water. "What do you see?"

"Look." Nicole pointed, shaking her head. "There."

A thin man floated face-down in the water, shoeless as he drifted in the waves. His greasy hair floated outward from his frail old head like seaweed, his shirt torn halfway off his body.

The current dragged his corpse back toward the rocks.

The next blue wave picked him up and hurled him forward, rolling and raking him over the rough stone edges. His corpse flopped onto a flat section of rock, facing the sky, until the next wave pummeled forth. As the water receded, it dragged his limp, ragged body over the sharp rocks, where it was picked up by the next wave.

Solaine tumbled back and forth like a rag doll in the mouth of a bulldog, until the pieces were too small to recognize as human.

"See there." Nicole gasped. "It is her. Is Constantine."

The red windbreaker floated in the surf, drifting toward the rocks.

"She has drowned. Oh, the poor child."

Solaine's body had disappeared. Now, the red windbreaker drifted toward the rocks. The next wave picked it up and carried it over the sharp gray edges, ripping the jacket into pieces.

"They are gone." Valentin shook his head. "Killed by the fall and finished by the waves. No one could survive that."

"No!" Twa pounded the dashboard. "My money! The girl was worth a fortune!"

Valentin glanced over his shoulder. "We'd better get out of here. Your troubles at the airport may not be far behind."

"But my money!" Twa shouted.

"You can make more money!" Valentin grabbed his boss by the arm. "She's gone. They're both gone."

"You don't understand." Twa sagged over the control stick. "She was worth—"

A blue and yellow sea plane soared out from behind the far side of the cliff, flying fast and low.

Valentin looked up. "What's that?"

* * * * *

In the co-pilot's seat, DeShear gripped the sea plane's frame as Trinn pulled the aircraft into a wide curve. "That's them, Hank."

"Okay." DeShear glared at the red helicopter. "Can this thing land on one skid?"

"Probably, but it won't be pretty. Why?"

"Because I want you to drive the other one into Armen Twa's tail rudder."

Trinn winced. "What if Constantine is in there?"

"She's not," DeShear said. "If she was, he wouldn't be hanging around. Take him out."

Muzzle flashes burst from the red helicopter. Bullet holes appeared on the sea plane's windshield.

"Roger that. Hold on." She pulled the control stick back and sent the plane into a deep dive, swooping down toward the hovering helicopter.

The shooter fired again as the tail rotor loomed in the little plane's windshield.

"Hang on," Trinn shouted, ramming the throttle forward. "Haaaaang onnnn!"

DeShear gritted his teeth, bracing for impact.

The sea plane swiped the rear end of the helicopter, lurching its occupants forward. Alarm signals blared over the aircraft's cockpit. The plane swayed back and forth.

"Hold on." Trinn flipped switches and pulled hard on the stick. "This could get rough."

DeShear glanced out the window. The pontoon skid sailed downward to the water like a vertical torpedo. The helicopter stayed where it was, its splintered tail section dangling from the main chassis.

He pounded the side of the door. "It didn't work!"

"Easy," Trinn said. "Give it a second."

She eased the control stick to the left, turning the plane. The helicopter began to rotate.

"Without the rotor's counter force," Trinn said, "the helicopter body will spin—fast."

The red helicopter rotated faster and faster.

It drifted sideways, losing altitude, as it spun at a dizzying speed. Careening toward the water, the damaged helicopter was a red blur, a nauseating spinning top, hurling toward the rocky cliff.

It crashed into the gray stone wall and plummeted onto the rocks below—and the blue army of waves attacked. The first few swells dragged it over the jagged stone tips; the next dozen waves swallowed it into the sea.

Trinn circled her wobbly aircraft, watching the red wreckage submerge. A few more waves swept forward to the wall, then there was nothing left but bubbles.

She stared into the water. "Hank, we have a little fuel, but . . . I don't see anything else out here."

"There!" DeShear pointed. "I see something!"

A tiny blonde head bobbed in the water, swimming toward the next island.

"Put us down!" He shouted. "That's Constantine!"

DeShear yanked off his headset and unbuckled his seat belt, climbing between the seats toward the hatch.

Trinn jerked the control stick back and forth as the plane wobbled in flight. "Wait for me to land!"

She circled, easing the throttle back and coming in low. DeShear climbed out onto the skid, gripping the wing support, then dived in.

"Constantine!" He swam toward the little blonde head. "Constantine!"

Choking, Constantine lifted her head from the water and looked around. "Hamilton!" She coughed, lowering her head and swimming hard. The water turned white with splashes.

He swam to her, pulling her up into his arms. "Constantine! I'm so glad you're safe."

The little girl panted hard, burying her head in his shoulder. "I held my breath under the water and swam away. I think the doctor helped pull my coat off, for a decoy."

"It must've worked." DeShear closed his eyes, blinking back a tear. I'm sorry they took you. I just . . . I couldn't—"

"Don't worry. I wasn't scared." She sniffled, a tear rolling down her cheek. "I knew you'd come for me. You said you would."

He exhaled sharply, her words putting a lump in his throat. Closing his eyes, he held the little girl, rocking back and forth.

The sea plane hobbled toward them, nearly sideways in the water. Trinn cut the engine as she approached, sticking her head out the window. "I had the choice of letting you two drown or landing and probably not getting this thing going again, so . . . I guess we'll radio for the coast guard."

As DeShear grabbed the pontoon, Trinn crawled out of the lopsided aircraft, holding the wing support. She smiled at DeShear as he hugged Constantine, and two little arms wrapped around his neck as if they would never let go.

A dark triangle splashed in the water to her right.

"Hey, check it out." Trinn pointed to the ripples in the water. "Dolphins!"

Constantine lifted her head. "Where?"

Grinning, DeShear grabbed the leg of the pontoon and hoisted her on top of the float. With a quick thrust of his feet, he hauled himself up and sat next to her. "Where are they?"

"Right there," Trinn said, pointing. "Look toward the sunset."

Sea water dripping from his forehead, DeShear squinted in the bright light. Thirty feet away, a dolphin broke the surface, spinning on its tail and landing with a splash.

Constantine squealed, slipping her tiny hand into DeShear's. He looked at her, smiling as she peered out over the waves. Shaking his head, he sighed and put his arm around her, pulling her close as he turned to watch the dolphins frolic.

The dolphins disappeared as the hum of an engine approached. Another sea plane, cruising low over the waves, eased its pontoons into the water. As it throttled back and motored toward them, Helena, Ari and Kitt waved from the windows.

"I think I know those people," Constantine said.

DeShear grinned, waving at the approaching plane. "Think we can hitch a ride?"

CHAPTER 36

DeShear clung to the side of the four-seater all-terrain vehicle as it bounced over the chilly Virginia countryside.

"What do you think?" President Brantley stopped the vehicle, gazing at a cluster of horses grazing in a nearby meadow, their breath blowing steam as they ate. Massive oak trees dotted the perimeter of the estate. "It's big, it's safe, and my place is right next door. And let's face it, if they can secure a property like this for me, they can secure one for you."

Shoving her hands into her coat pockets, Trinn leaned forward from the back seat. "Well? What do we think?"

"I don't know." DeShear tugged at the collar of his jacket. "Something like this has to be pretty pricey, Mr. President."

"Geez, Hank." Trinn slapped his arm. "You have three billion dollars."

"I don't. Constantine does."

"Then let's ask her." Jumping from the vehicle, Trinn walked to the large stables. Constantine sat in the doorway of a far stall, wearing a thin sweater and surrounded by Helena and Kitt. "Ladies, Mr. DeShear has a question for Constantine. He'd like to know if—"

"Miss Jaden! Look!" Constantine held up a tiny white rabbit with tiny black spots on its rear end.

Inside the stall, Taylor, the President's young niece, sat next to a pile of hay and several other small bunnies.

Constantine stroked the rabbit, cradling it like a baby, its ears lowered close to its head and its prominent nose sticking up. "They're practically babies, and Taylor said I could have one."

The bunny looked at Trinn and wiggled its nose.

"Well, that little guy is adorable." Trinn put her hands on her hips. "What do you think, Hank?"

Constantine nuzzled the bunny's cheek. "I've named him Cleo, after a friend I met." She gazed up at DeShear. "Can I keep him, Hamilton? Please?"

DeShear winced. "A rabbit . . . sounds like a lot of work."

"I would brush him every day and feed him plenty of healthy greens—they don't really like carrots, you know. Just the tops. And—"

"Yeah, but . . ." DeShear shifted on his feet. "See, the thing is, if we get a rabbit, we'd need a place to keep him. Now, President Brantley said we could stay next door at his ranch for a few weeks while we decide what we're going to do, but after that . . ."

"The President also said this property is for sale, Constantine." Trinn folded her arms and smiled. "We could buy it and live here—if you wanted to."

Constantine gasped. "Like a proper family?"

"Something like that." DeShear squatted next to Constantine, rubbing Cleo's belly. "We'd need to have a room for me and Miss Jaden, and you—plus a room for Helena, and maybe one for Miss Kitt, if she's going to stay on and help out."

"Oh." Constantine's face fell. "Then I suppose we shouldn't buy the house unless it's got lots of space for everyone. How many bedrooms does it have?"

"Oh, about twenty, if you include the guest house." DeShear grinned.

"Twenty! Then Cleo could have his own room!"

"I guess he could, yeah."

She wrapped an arm around him, holding her bunny with one arm and squeezing DeShear with the other. "Can we buy this house, then? Please?"

"Okay." DeShear stood. "I'll tell the real estate agent to write it up."

Constantine squealed, setting Cleo down and hugging DeShear again. Cleo hopped out of the stall, making his way to the stable door.

"Constantine," Helena said. "Your bunny's escaping."

"Oh, no!"

The girls chased the rabbit toward the door. Cleo made a sharp turn and shot to a nearby hibiscus bush as the other rabbits stuck their noses out. One by one, they made their escape into the yard.

DeShear faced President Brantley. "Do we need to worry about that? Like, are there hawks outside?"

"There are," Brantley said, "but when we want to round them up, we just shake the treat can." He handed a plastic tumbler of food pellets to DeShear. "That brings them back pretty quick." The President turned to his aide. "Belinda, we probably should get going. I shouldn't keep the Prime Minister waiting."

Trinn walked with the President. "Which country?"

"Bahamas. He allegedly wants to apologize for allowing a plane full of guns to fly to Hawaii. But his real reason is, he's apparently got some local Magistrate climbing the walls, thinking he's about to be assassinated because we took Mr. Hollings into custody. I'm sure we'll work something out." He hugged Trinn. "You did good work again, Jaden. And Helena's new friend Kitt is sharp. Either of you can call me any time. I told Ari Hiles the same thing. You're friends of the President—well, for a few more months, anyway, until my term expires. But you've earned the right to have my direct number, so don't hesitate to use it. As far as I'm concerned, I still owe you."

"Thank you, Mr. President."

Brantley shook hands with DeShear and departed for his teleconference.

Hank took Trinn's hand and strolled to the stable door, leaning on the frame. In the yard, Constantine lay on her belly in the grass, nose to nose with Cleo, petting his tiny white head. Helena and Kitt looked on.

"So," Trinn said. "Kitt is a doctor of psychology? It was nice of you to hire her."

DeShear nodded. "Dr. Kittaleye needs a job, and she minored in parapsychology. Helena thinks that could be very useful for Constantine. So, Kitt will stay in the guest house and we'll see how it goes."

Trinn lifted DeShear's arm and put it around her waist, snuggling close. "Helena says it might be good, huh? What do you think?"

"I think it might not be a bad idea to have a psychologist around. The kid's been through a lot. Helena, too."

She put her hand on his chest. "I can't help but get the feeling you're nervous about something. Wanna tell me what it is?"

DeShear snorted. "I just agreed to buy a thirty million dollar Virginia estate. What would I be nervous about?"

"Hey." She looked at him. "It's me. What's up?"

"Okay . . ." DeShear shifted his weight. "Maybe I'm a little nervous. I just . . . this is great and all—the house, the area . . . And Brantley's right, the security professionals can make this place as safe as his next door, just like they do for important senators and dignitaries . . ." He glanced around. "She'll attend a super secure school where Presidents' kids go when they're small. They'll make sure she gets back and forth to school every day . . ."

Trinn nodded. "But . . ."

"But will she ever *really* be safe?"

"She's safe right now." Trinn gazed toward the grassy courtyard. Constantine rolled in the grass with Cleo. "Look at her, playing the way a child should. She doesn't have a care in the world, and when she does, she has Helena and Kitt—and you and me. That's a start—a great start. She never had peace like that in the chateau."

DeShear stared at the tree line. "I let my guard down for a second on a fishing trip, and they took her. There could be others. Waiting out there somewhere."

"They took her—but you got her back. And the most powerful person in the world has lent you his ranch. Nobody's getting in there. With the money from the trust, you can make this place as secure as his. He just said so."

"I guess." DeShear took a deep breath and let it out slowly.

"But you're going to worry anyway, aren't you?"

"About Constantine? Yeah."

"Then you're officially a parent, I guess." She rested her head on his chest. "We'll figure our stuff out like everybody else figures out theirs—and we'll do it together." Standing upright, she took his hand and pulled him out the door. "Now, come with me. Your family's waiting for you."

DeShear grinned. "Our family."

"Yeah," she said. "So, come on."

THE END

Hamilton DeShear, Jaden Trinn, Constantine, and Helena

will return in

DARK HOUR

The Gamma Sequence, book 5

Order it now!

Note to Readers

If you have the time, I would deeply appreciate a review on Amazon or Goodreads. I learn a great deal from them, and I'm always grateful for any encouragement. Reviews are a very big deal and help authors like me to sell a few more books. Every review matters, even if it's only a few words.

Thanks,

Dan Alatorre

ABOUT THE AUTHOR

International bestselling author Dan Alatorre has published more than 40 titles and has been translated into over a dozen languages. His ability to surprise readers and make them laugh, cry, or hang onto the edge of their seats, has been enjoyed all around the world.

Dan's success is widespread and varied. In addition to being a bestselling author, he achieved President's Circle with two different Fortune 500 companies, and mentors grade school children through his Young Authors Club. Dan resides in the Tampa, Florida, area with his wife and daughter.

Join Dan's exclusive Reader's Club today at DanAlatorre.com and find out about new releases and special offers!

OTHER THRILLERS BY DAN ALATORRE

The Gamma Sequence, *a medical thriller*
Rogue Elements, *The Gamma Sequence Book 2*
Terminal Sequence, *The Gamma Sequence Book 3*
Double Blind, *an intense murder mystery*
Primary Target, *Double Blind Book 2*
A Place Of Shadows, *a paranormal thriller*
The Navigators, *a time travel thriller*

Made in the USA
Las Vegas, NV
12 June 2021